A professor  *gym...*
and walk *saw*

RUNAWAY FATE

Katherine wasn't looking for anything extraordinary in her life. She had a job she loved, a husband she adored, and a home in the beautiful seaside town of Moonstone Cove.

Okay yes, she worked too much and had fallen out of touch with all her friends, but that happened to everyone, right? And sure, she was feeling a little creaky in the mornings and couldn't drink coffee after noon, but that was just life at middle age.

Four minutes was all it took for fate to run away with anything that resembled normal.

Now Katherine is trying to fit mysterious psychic visions into her previously ordered life. She's playing referee between a displaced Southern mama and a sarcastic mechanic with a chip on her shoulder. And her quiet life has been upended by a mysterious rash of violent acts by students at her school.

Thankfully, her new friends have powers of their own, and together they just might discover who or what has it in for the quiet citizens of Moonstone Cove.

Runaway Fate is the first book in the hot new Paranormal Women's Fiction series, Moonstone Cove, by *USA Today* best-selling author Elizabeth Hunter. It's fiction for lovers of magic, mayhem, and a solid afternoon nap (when they can squeeze one in).

PRAISE FOR ELIZABETH HUNTER

Another PWF home run! For those that absolutely loved the Glimmer Lake series, get ready to dive into the perfect book for you. ...there are so many surprises waiting for you in Moonstone Cove that will keep you burning through the pages well past bedtime.

— THIS LITERARY LIFE

Elizabeth Hunter hits another home run with this first novel in Moonlight Cove series.

— BOOKNERD, BOOKSELLER, AND BIBLIOPHILE BLOG

You will find laughter, heartbreak, tears, heart-pounding moments and warmth in Hunter's latest novel, I cannot wait for readers to get their hands on it.

— DANIELLE, GOODREADS REVIEWER

RUNAWAY FATE

MOONSTONE COVE BOOK ONE

ELIZABETH HUNTER

Runaway Fate
Copyright © 2020
Elizabeth Hunter
ISBN: 978-1-941674-60-4

All rights reserved. Except as permitted under the US Copyright Act of
1976, no part of this publication may be reproduced, distributed, or
transmitted in any form or by any means, or stored in a database or retrieval
system, without the prior written permission of the author.

Cover: Damonza
Content Editor: Amy Cissell, Cissell Ink
Line Editor: Anne Victory
Proofreader: Linda, Victory Editing

If you're reading this book and did not purchase it or it was not purchased for
your use only, please delete it and purchase your own copy from an
authorized retailer. Thank you for respecting the hard work of this author.

Recurve Press LLC
PO Box 4034
Visalia, California 93278
USA

This book—and all Wine Wednesdays—
Are dedicated to the Sisterhood of the First Miracle.
I heart you all.

CHAPTER 1

*I*f Katherine Bassi could've predicted a time and place for her life to change irrevocably, it would not have been at the Blue Wave Gym on State Street at four forty-five on a Thursday afternoon.

Katherine attended the gym because she enjoyed the yoga class there. But that didn't start until five o'clock, so at four thirty, she hopped on one of the few available treadmills to warm her muscles up, walking on a machine going nowhere and staring at the bustling pedestrian traffic in downtown Moonstone Cove.

It was a little town nestled in the heart of the Central California coast with pebbled beaches and crumbling cliffs dotted by wind-twisted cypresses. Moonstone Cove was a town famous for three things: abundant vegetables, an annual wine festival, and a small but excellent state university specializing in marine-biology research, which was where Katherine worked.

As she increased the pace on her treadmill, Katherine focused on the steady stretch of her thighs and calves. Properly warmed muscles were a prerequisite to get the most out of her twice-weekly yoga class. The class was focused on flexibility and joint maintenance, two areas Katherine knew were vital for older women.

She was forty-seven and in reasonably good health, which meant her knees ached, her legs twitched at night whether she wanted them to or not, and she'd slowly moved farther and farther back to focus on her monitor at work.

Which was fine. As Katherine's mother often said: "Aging can be unpleasant until you consider the alternative."

Katherine wasn't really looking for change. She had a job she loved, and she'd been married for twenty years to a man she adored. She was the happy and indulgent aunt of four children her sister and in-laws were raising. She didn't have many friends in Moonstone Cove—even after fifteen years—but she still loved her home. She had a house that overlooked the ocean, and she fell asleep to the sound of the waves every night.

The only improvement she would make was her husband, Baxter's, feelings about acquiring a dog. Nothing too large. Something medium-sized and fluffy. Katherine had never owned a dog, but the longer she lived in Moonstone Cove—which was undoubtedly a dog-friendly place—the more certain she was that her life would be improved by one.

Baxter was unconvinced; she was working on him.

As she pushed the buttons to increase her treadmill pace, she glanced around the gym.

On her right was a young man wearing a Central Coast sweatshirt, his head down as he listened to music and jogged at a steady pace. On her left was a young woman in a Central Coast Volleyball T-shirt.

The Blue Wave Gym gave a discount to students, faculty, and staff at Central Coast State, so the number of blue-and-green sweatshirts and T-shirts around the aerobic-machine room was noticeable, but plenty of local people from town were mixed in as well.

In the row before her was a middle-aged blond woman in ruthlessly coordinated sportswear, sweating her heart out on an elliptical machine. There were professionals leaving work early and plenty of familiar faces even if Katherine didn't know their names.

Seeing people from outside the college was one of the reasons Katherine enjoyed coming to this gym. Since she and Baxter were both professors, it was nice to break out of her limited social circle.

"Hey!"

Katherine looked over her left shoulder.

"You dropped your towel." A freckled woman with a curly cap of short dark hair held a white towel out to her. Katherine had seen her before. She liked the rowing machines and regularly lifted weights.

"Thanks." Katherine reached back and grabbed it, then folded it in thirds and placed it on the small bar below the control panel on the treadmill, all the while never slowing her pace. "Are you waiting for this machine?"

The woman shrugged. "I'm good. I've got time." Her eyes seemed focused farther down the row of equipment.

Katherine glanced at the clock on the wall. "I'm just warming up before the five-o'clock yoga class. I'll be done in a few minutes." It was 4:40, and she would need at least ten minutes to walk to the yoga classroom and set up. Katherine hated being late for anything but especially classes. She slowed her treadmill to cool down.

"I can wait." The woman's eyes swept around the gym before coming back to rest again on whatever she had seen down the row. Her eyes narrowed, but she didn't move from her spot near the wall.

Katherine returned to the closed-captioned television that was broadcasting the local news. There was something about the classic-car show on Beach Street that weekend. The weather forecast jumped onto the screen. Seventy-five and sunny on Friday. Seventy-three. Seventy-six. Yep, pretty much perfect all week. When you lived on California's Central Coast, you didn't get to complain about the weather.

At 4:44, she stopped the treadmill and grabbed her towel. She dabbed her forehead and looked for the dark-haired woman to point out the machine, but she was already on a different treadmill.

Gymgoers were shuffling locations as some left for the day and others switched routines. Katherine saw the color-coordinated blond woman heading toward the hallway where the yoga classroom was located and wondered if she was a new attendee.

Katherine walked toward the aisle, passing another college-aged man running fast on a treadmill. Unlike the people around him, he was running at full speed. A blue-and-green hoodie covered his head, and something familiar about him made Katherine pause at the back of his machine.

It came to her in a flash.

The world around her washed into shades of grey as Katherine saw the man stop and pull a black handgun from under his sweatshirt. It was black and had an odd bar sticking out from the handle. Everything around her moved in slow motion as the young man raised the gun and started firing across the gym.

The sound of screaming was sharp in her ears.

Once, twice, the gun fired again and again. He didn't stop. The world around her seemed watery and out of focus, but she heard people screaming. Glass shattered. More screaming.

She blinked and her ears popped. The world around her came back into focus and vivid color. No one was screaming. The gym was filled with the familiar sounds of treadmills and pumping workout music. The clock on the wall read four forty-five.

Katherine was frozen at the base of the young man's treadmill when she saw it start to happen.

He braced his feet on either side of the treadmill, unzipped his blue-and-green sweatshirt, and reached toward his waistband.

This isn't a daydream.

"Gun!" Katherine screamed and dived for the man, knocking him off-balance. He toppled back and fell on her. The spinning track shot them off the rear of the treadmill and into the next row of machines. "He has a gun!"

The world compressed around her. She was struggling with the man, but he was so much stronger. Where was the gun? She saw it in his hand and reached for it.

He elbowed Katherine in the temple and rolled away, trying to lift the firearm and take aim. She felt something cold and hard strike her temple.

"No!" The blond woman stood over them, her face red

and angry. She reached her hand out, and the gun jumped into her palm.

Katherine blinked.

Sounds of chaos filled the gym as people ran and yelled. Someone shouted, "Police!" Throughout the chaos, the sounds of loud electronic music filled the air.

The young man elbowed Katherine again, snapping her head to the side. She saw stars and rolled into the still-spinning treadmill as the man scrambled toward the blond woman who had his gun. He was on his knees when the compact, dark-haired woman leaped over two treadmills and jumped on the attacker, forcing him back to the ground with a thud and a solid punch to the jaw.

"Stay down!" She looked to be about a third of the size of the guy, but the woman grabbed his shoulders, forced him to the floor, and yelled into his face. "Calm down! Stay down!"

As if by magic, the man's body went limp and he relaxed completely.

The blond woman was holding the gun on him, but her hands weren't even shaking. She glanced at Katherine. "Ma'am, you doing all right?" She spoke with a pronounced Southern accent. "He hit you pretty hard. Think you might be bleeding on your forehead a little."

The dark-haired woman glanced at the woman with the gun. "You a cop?"

"No." The blond woman laughed a little. "Just grew up with a lot of good ol' boys. You doin' okay?"

"I'm good." The dark-haired woman didn't move off the man. "Please tell me someone is calling the police."

Katherine rolled up to sit and propped herself against the front of a stair-climbing machine. "I'm okay." She watched their attacker lying completely still under the small woman. "I think I'm okay."

Almost everyone in the gym had fled and most were milling around outside on State Street. Katherine could see them through the windows.

A man in a bright blue shirt ran over to them. "We called 911." His muscles bulged from beneath his shirt, and the word TRAINER was emblazoned on the front. "What can I do? Do you want me to hold him, Toni? How can I help?"

The blond woman didn't move an inch, and the dark-haired woman the man had called Toni didn't budge.

"I think we'll just stay exactly right where we are until the cops come." Toni kept her hands pushed into the man's shoulders, but the young man who'd wrestled so fiercely with Katherine had gone limp. He showed not a hint of resistance.

The trainer looked at the woman with the gun. "Uh... miss?"

"It's Megan, sweetie. Megan Carpenter. I'm good here," the blond woman said. "I'm new at the gym, but I'm fine with guns and I can wait with these nice ladies for the cops." She glanced down. "This is a real fancy extended magazine, young man. I don't think this model is legal in California."

The young trainer was running his hands through his curly brown hair. "Oh my God. Holy shit. Patrick and Jan are gonna kill me."

Katherine cleared her throat. "If you're talking about the owners, I doubt you're going to get in trouble. No one could have predicted this."

Except Katherine had.

She had seen the man pull the gun from his sweatshirt.

She'd seen him raise it and shoot people. She'd heard screams and glass shattering.

But it hadn't happened yet.

Katherine glanced at the clock. It was 4:49. In four minutes, everything about her life had changed.

She looked at the two women, Megan and Toni. All three of them were exchanging nervous glances and trying to pretend not to notice the others' scrutiny. Katherine had never seen either of the women before that day, but she could read the question on both their faces.

What on earth just happened?

CHAPTER 2

Baxter gave Katherine his best stern face. "Tea."

"Coffee."

"Darling, this is not the time for your typical morning brew. You've been through a shocking experience. The last thing you need is caffeine."

"Tea has caffeine."

She was being contrary. She knew her husband was right, but it was so rare for Professor Baxter Pang, tenured professor of mathematics and cochair of the department, to be bossy that Katherine was almost enjoying it.

Baxter lectured her in an elegant Hong Kong accent that had remained crisp through decades of living in the United States. "Darjeeling has approximately fifty milligrams of caffeine as opposed to the typical stew-like mixture you make in your french press, which easily contains three times as much." He crossed his arms over his chest. "Tea."

He would have looked more intimidating if his dark hair weren't in need of a trim and sticking up at odd angles at the crown.

But the accent... The accent still worked.

"Fine." She sighed. "Tea."

"Excellent."

One of the benefits of being married to the same man for twenty years was that he knew exactly how you took your tea even if it wasn't your drink of choice. As Baxter fussed over the kettle, Katherine tried to plan her day.

She'd arrived home to find an extremely distracted husband with a mobile phone stuck to his ear. The news of the shooting had been everywhere, even penetrating her husband's mental bubble.

Every teaching assistant Baxter'd ever had would tell their friends that though Professor Pang was unfailingly polite, he lived in a world of his own making, filled with theoretical mathematics and cross-continental chess games with his younger brother in London. He might smile and nod if you told him something related to current events or pop culture, but he likely had no idea what you were talking about. He enjoyed jogging along the boardwalk near their house and playing racquetball with a few of his colleagues once or twice a week.

It wasn't that Baxter set out to be uninformed, it was simply that current events were rarely more interesting to him than mathematics.

Katherine said, "I have to go to the police station today."

He glanced over. "Why? You spoke to the police yesterday."

"I don't know how much I told them was very useful. I hardly remember any of it, to be honest. This is the formal statement."

"Should you go with an attorney? We can call Kimi."

Kimi Nomura was their family attorney. She helped them write trusts and make wills and occasionally looked at a contract. She'd probably never even been to a police station.

"I don't think Kimi really deals with criminal stuff, Bax. I'll be fine."

"If you say so, darling."

Katherine tapped her fingers on the table and tried to sift through her thoughts. "Have you heard anything more about the... perpetrator? The man they arrested?"

"No." He frowned a little. "They made a point of not saying his name on the television, which I thought was odd."

"I think there's a theory that much of the motivation for these kinds of mass shootings is notoriety for the perpetrator. If that's the case, avoiding the man's name makes sense."

"It's an interesting theory." Baxter poured water over the loose tea leaves in the glass teapot. "Psychology."

Katherine said it before he could. "Soft science."

"They're just not as exact in their research." He brought a scarred wooden tray to the table in the breakfast nook that looked over the north edge of Moonstone Cove.

Katherine smiled. "Well, people are messy."

"Hmmm."

"Psychology is probably kind of useful in understanding criminal behavior though."

"I suppose you're right." Bax sat across from her and looked out over the ocean.

When they'd bought the house fifteen years ago, Moonstone Cove had been a sleepy college town and houses along the north end of the cove had been well within their budget as long as they were prepared to do some home repairs. They could never afford their little two-bedroom house if they were buying today.

It was a redwood-shingled craftsman bungalow with panoramic views of the ocean on the west, a wide deck that wrapped around the entire house, and more than enough room for two introverts. Katherine and Baxter liked North Beach because it was quiet and away from the pier. It didn't attract tourists or students except on the weekends, and the old wooden boardwalk passed through an extensive preserved area that was rich with birdlife.

The north end of the cove was also deserted, so when the weather was good, Katherine could run in the sand, which she enjoyed.

Also, no gunmen were likely to shoot up the beach because targets were too dispersed.

What a morbid thought.

Baxter poured the tea and Katherine watched him. His hair was silver at the temples and his eyes were creased in the corners, but he still had a lean build with excellent proportions. When she'd first met him in her midtwenties, she'd imagined that he attracted too much female attention to be interested in her.

Katherine thought she was a perfectly average-looking person with symmetrical features, medium brown hair, and nice greenish-grey eyes. She didn't focus much on her looks; it wasn't how she was raised.

She'd thought Baxter was startlingly handsome at thirty. He was even more handsome at fifty, and his eyes still lit up when he spotted her across the campus.

"Who is that dashing man pouring me tea?" she murmured.

The edge of his too-stern mouth lifted in a half smile. "I believe it's your husband."

She reached for the tea he handed her. "I must be brilliant."

"As a matter of fact" —he leaned down and placed a lingering kiss full on her lips— "we're both certified geniuses."

"You're *joking*."

"I'd never joke about that." He glanced down at her feet. "What are you wearing?"

He'd taken the day off from classes to fuss over her, which she appreciated even if she didn't need it.

"My feet are not cold."

"How could they *not* be?" He nudged her slippers toward her toes. "Put them on."

"Fuss, fuss, fuss," she whispered. "Do I need a hat too?" She slid on her slippers. "A sweater?"

"Are you going outside?"

"It's September, not January."

An edge of tension tinged his voice. "You were nearly shot yesterday."

"There is no reason to think—"

"You tackled a grown man carrying a gun and rode off the end of a treadmill. You shouldn't be going anywhere. You have bruises everywhere and a large cut on your head. You should be resting in bed and keeping your muscles and joints warm."

"And eating soup?"

A hint of humor filtered through Baxter's tense expression. "Soup might be in order."

"I feel fine." In fact, Katherine felt very sore. She had a

13

horrendous bruise on her hip, both her knees were aching, and the low-grade headache that had started sometime after the police had arrived the day before hadn't left her even for a minute.

She kept seeing the grey-tinged vision in her head. She didn't know what had happened, but her mind kept circling around to it. What had it been? Vivid imagination? Had she picked up tiny clues about what would happen that she wasn't recalling? If she had, it would be the first time she'd been that observant about anything outside a research study.

"What do you think about visions?"

"Visions? As in precognition?"

"Yes."

"Oh, I don't think that's possible."

Katherine's mind kept circling back to an unusual conversation she'd had months ago with a friend of a friend, a woman from Glimmer Lake in the Sierra Nevada mountains.

Katherine was a biophysicist who studied neural systems. From an academic standpoint, she'd always been intrigued by the concept of parapsychological phenomena.

Or, as some of her students would put it, "psychic stuff."

From a theoretical standpoint, Katherine was of the opinion that any number of cognitive processes that seemed supernatural could have perfectly reasonable scientific explanations that current cognitive science hadn't identified.

Had she ever had any reason to expect she'd experience those phenomena in anything but an academic way? Absolutely not.

But life seemed to be forcing the theoretical into the practical.

"I'm going to take the rest of the week off." Baxter lifted

his tea to his lips. "I'll speak to Margaret about it tomorrow. I don't think there's anything she needs me to do over the next few days. We already had our departmental meeting."

Katherine sipped her own tea. "It's Friday."

"Is it?" He adjusted his glasses. "Are you sure?"

"Yes. Very sure."

"I see." He picked up the newspaper, which had an article about Moonstone Cove's recent brush with violence. "Then I'll take next week off if you prefer."

"Don't be silly. I'll be fine tomorrow and back in the classroom by Monday." She glanced at the paper and felt a chill crawl down her back. She had to distract herself. She couldn't keep dwelling on the horrible vision and her brush with death. "Baxter?"

"Yes?"

"I have an idea."

"Oh?" Baxter paged through the newspaper.

"Yes, something to make me feel better."

He lowered the paper, frowning a little. "What's that, darling?"

"I would feel a lot better—more secure, I mean—if we had a dog."

His mouth went into a flat line. "Of all the times."

"Not a large dog." She managed to keep her face straight. "Just a small... a medium-sized dog. I hear animals are very good for mental health."

"You're only bringing this up because—"

"I can sense that you want to fuss over me, and you're more likely to give in when you've recently feared for my life?"

The amusement returned to his handsome brown eyes, and all was right with Katherine Bassi's world again.

Except that it wasn't.

Even if she hadn't been sporting physical bruises, her mind knew that something very bad had almost happened. While she slept the night before, the shooting had replayed in her head; bullets tore through metal, glass, and bodies. There was blood everywhere. In her mind, she hadn't stopped anything and dozens of people had paid the price.

What if you had ignored the vision?

She second-guessed herself in retrospect. Was it simply a vivid imagination? How could she have known? Nothing about the young man had tipped her off. The incident was a series of impossible events stacked one on top of another.

"What do you think about visions?"

"Visions? As in precognition?"

Katherine hadn't seen the gun before she'd tackled the man to the ground, but she'd known he would have it. She hadn't seen the woman named Megan take the gun from the attacker, but it had suddenly been in her hand. She hadn't heard the small woman named Toni negotiate with the unnamed student. She'd told him to be calm, and he was.

What on earth had happened?

And what was she going to tell the police when they asked her to give an account?

CHAPTER 3

*K*atherine had expected to sit alone in a small room, waiting for an officer to interview her under harsh lights. Apparently she'd been watching too much television.

That afternoon at the Moonstone Cove police station, she was led to what looked like an average employee break room with a coffee maker bubbling in the corner near a Formica table set. Several couches were placed along the edge of the room, and there was a small television tuned to a sports station high in one corner.

"Not what you were expecting, huh?"

Katherine turned and saw the dark-haired woman named Toni sitting in the corner. She was wearing a pair of jeans and a blue work shirt with Toni embroidered over the pocket.

"It's not." Katherine walked over and held out her hand. "We didn't properly meet yesterday. I'm Katherine Bassi. I'm a physics professor at Central Coast State."

"Fancy." Toni smiled a little. "Antonia Dusi. Toni to my

17

friends, family, and people I go through life-threatening situations with. Which is you."

Katherine smiled. "It's nice to meet you, Toni. I just go by Katherine."

"Not Kathy? Kat?"

"Katherine's only two syllables, so it seems a little useless to shorten it."

"Fair enough." Toni had curly cropped hair and a no-nonsense demeanor. "You ever been to the police department before?"

"Uh..." Katherine racked her brain. "Not here exactly. I've been to city hall next door. You can renew your passport there."

"Right." She nodded to the glass window that looked out over the police department office. "My cousin works here. And I've had to bail some of my employees out over the years. It's pretty low-key. I think Drew Bisset's going to be interviewing us. He's the detective handling the case."

"I see." Katherine cocked her head. "You've bailed out employees?"

"I have an auto shop here in town. Dusi Brothers? It's my dad and me. Over the years, we've hired some guys who don't always know their manners."

Now her boldness made sense. She worked in a male-dominated field and managed a business. Though her stature was small, she probably commanded a great deal of respect since she came across as very competent.

Katherine took a seat on one of the couches seconds before the third person in their unexpected rescue squad came through the door.

"Hey, y'all." Megan walked over and held her hand out to Toni. "Nice to see you again."

Toni gave her a bemused smile, shook her hand, then turned her eyes to the television in the corner.

Megan shifted her attention toward Katherine. "Hello. Your name is Katherine, isn't it?"

"Yes. And yours is Megan, and that's Toni in the corner. How are you doing?"

"I'm fine! Sure glad I've been taking that kickboxing class, you know?"

Her smile wasn't insincere, but it was a little forced. If Katherine had to guess, Megan was *not* fine.

Not that it had affected her fashion sense. She was just as color-coordinated as the day before, wearing a blue blouse that brought out the color of her eyes and a pair of wide-leg capris in summer yellow with a straw purse with blue and yellow trim.

Katherine motioned to the couch next to her. "Would you like to sit down? Apparently we're waiting for the detective on the case. I'm sure he's very busy."

"Thank you." Megan sat and clutched her purse. "It's just all over the news, isn't it? My kids were so shocked when they heard my name. My husband too."

Katherine smiled, trying to set the woman at ease. "How many children do you have?"

"Three. My oldest daughter is eighteen, my son is sixteen, and my youngest daughter is fourteen. We just moved here from Atlanta about a year ago."

"What brought you here?"

"My husband's work. He sells agricultural equipment."

In Moonstone Cove, the college might bring in young

people, but agriculture still paid the bills. The Central Coast had one of the finest climates in the world to grow vegetables, berries, and wine grapes.

Katherine asked, "How do you like the area?"

Megan put on a bright smile. "I love the weather! It's a little harder to get to know people here than back home."

Katherine could only imagine. She and Baxter had lived here for years and she still felt like an outsider sometimes; though they had a close-knit community at the university, their neighbors still considered them the "new couple" in North Beach after fifteen years.

"And what do you do?" Katherine asked.

"Right now just... being a mom." Megan flashed her "everything's just fine" smile again. "I had an events-planning business back in Atlanta, but..."

"It's hard to relocate things like that."

Megan laughed a little. "More like impossible. How about you? Do you have any kids?"

"No. My husband and I are both professors, so we're very involved at the college. We have four nieces and nephews though. Two in San Francisco and two in London."

"Oh." Megan's eyes went wide. "What do you teach?"

"I'm in the biophysics department, which is an interdisciplinary department that involves people with degrees in physics, like me, but also biology, biochemistry, physiology, computational biology... all sorts of people. It's very collaborative."

Megan's eyes were the size of saucers. Toni laughed in the corner.

"Damn, Professor, you're like a certified genius or something. I could have sworn you were a football coach with that tackle yesterday."

Megan's mouth hung open a little. "That is *really* impressive. *Wow*. I bet you meet the most interesting people in your work."

Interesting? That was one way to put it. "I'm on a research team right now, but I also teach. I really love teaching. I love students."

"Cool." Toni was engaged with the conversation again. "So did you know the kid from yesterday?"

"I didn't recognize him," Katherine said. "He was wearing a Central Coast sweatshirt though. Do either of you know his name?"

"Justin McCabe," Megan said softly. "My husband knows the chief of police from the golf club. He called him last night when the news didn't say anything about who the shooter was. He is a student at Central Coast. No criminal record at all though."

"I'll have to ask around at school." The confirmation that the attacker had been a student weighed on Katherine's heart. "I always worry that there are signs we miss as educators. I worry about the school becoming so large that we miss students who need help."

Had someone missed warning signs? Did the young man live in a dormitory? Did he have family close by? What kind of support system did he have? Or not have?

"Some people are just nuts," Toni said, her voice flat. "Or evil. That's no one's fault."

Katherine didn't agree, but she didn't want to start an argument with a woman she barely knew.

Megan looked between Katherine and Toni several times.

Katherine could sense her tension growing. Something was bothering her. Something had her nearly bursting.

"That gun just jumped into my hand, y'all." Megan finally spoke. "I didn't grab it. I didn't even reach for it. I just thought in my head 'someone needs to get that gun away from this kid,' and then it just flew into my hand all on its own, and I don't know what to think about that. I don't know what to think at all."

Katherine stared at Megan with wide eyes. Toni was staring too.

The door opened and someone said, "Professor Bassi, Detective Bisset can see you now."

"Professor Katherine Bassi."

The detective who said her name was younger than she was. His skin was a dark, unlined brown, and his closely cropped hair showed not a hint of grey or silver. Still, the expression in his eyes as he examined the yellow notepad on his desk told Katherine that he was not an inexperienced police officer.

He looked up and offered her a polite smile. "How are you feeling today?"

"Like a forty-seven-year-old woman who recently took up tackle football." Katherine settled into the upholstered chair across from the detective. "I don't recommend it."

Detective Bisset chuckled.

"But nothing is broken. No permanent damage. I'm craving potato chips, but I think that has something to do with seeing them in the break room."

"I can have an officer get you some if you'd like."

"No, I'm okay. But thanks."

"The manager of the club who witnessed your actions said you tackled the man from behind, disarmed him, and knocked him to the ground."

Katherine chose her words carefully. "I tackled him. I don't think I intentionally disarmed him, but I might have knocked the gun from his hand. I don't really remember."

"But you remember seeing his weapon."

She thought about what she could say. Had she seen the man pulling out his weapon? In her vision she had. Close enough. "Yes, I saw the weapon. It was a handgun. I couldn't tell you much more than that; I don't know much about guns. It was black and had a brown handle."

Detective Bisset frowned a little, tapping a pen on the notepad in front of him. "From behind?"

"What's that?"

"You saw the gun from behind the gunman?"

She kept her voice and expression even. This was far from the most intimidating interview she'd ever had. That belonged to her first doctoral dissertation panel. "I must have seen it at an angle. Why else would I tackle a complete stranger?"

"Good question." He looked up. "*Was* he a complete stranger?"

"He was wearing a CCSU sweatshirt, but I didn't recognize him. That said, it's very possible he's taken one of my general-ed classes. I sometimes have over a hundred students in those sections."

Detective Bisset nodded. "So you might have known him."

"*Known* him would be an overstatement. My teaching assistants—graduate students—would have been the ones interacting with him if he was taking a class from me, grading his papers or answering questions, things like that. I don't remember him ever visiting me during office hours, but honestly, like I said, it's possible. I see a lot of students in my general-ed classes."

"How many of those do you teach?"

"Usually I teach two general-ed classes per semester and two upper-level physics classes as well as supervising a number of graduate students in the department. And then I have a collaborative grant project I'm working on right now."

"Busy."

"Yes. But I enjoy my work."

"So you did not know Mr. McCabe." He flipped to another page in the folder. "And Mr. McCabe says he has no memory of this incident."

"Pardon me?"

Detective Bisset looked up. "He says he remembers you tackling him, but he doesn't remember having any intention of shooting anyone. He doesn't even remember taking a gun to the gym."

"That seems improbable."

"I agree." He closed the file. "It's a strange case, Professor Bassi. Very strange."

Katherine frowned. "Does he have a concealed weapon permit?"

Concealed carry permits were very hard to obtain in their county. She knew that because an old neighbor of hers was a survivor of domestic violence, and even with her ex-husband stalking her, Clara hadn't been able to obtain a concealed carry permit. She'd eventually moved out of state.

"He doesn't."

"So why would he bring a loaded firearm to a gym?"

"Perhaps he was fearful. It's possible he brought it for his own protection. At the end of the day, the only crime actually committed was Mr. McCabe having a concealed weapon."

"So that's it?" What was the detective getting at? Was Justin McCabe accusing her, Megan, or Toni of attacking him unprovoked? "He was going to kill people. I know it."

Detective Bisset frowned. "Understand, Professor Bassi, I have no doubt that you're telling the truth and Mr. McCabe was planning violence. I'm trying to collect as much information as possible because we need to give a solid case to the district attorney. What we have currently are three citizens who stopped a crime in progress. But we don't know what that crime was going to be. Mr. McCabe has no history of violence or radicalism. From all accounts, he's a pretty normal kid going to the local college." Detective Bisset tapped a pen against the manila folder. "Do you see my problem?"

"I don't know what you want me to say. Do you want me to apologize for stopping him before he shot anyone?" Katherine heard the edge in her voice. "I can't imagine you would. That would be absurd."

The detective narrowed his eyes. "I'm trying to get a clearer picture of what happened. Did he say anything? Threaten anyone?"

"No."

"Did he point the gun at anyone in particular?"

"Not that I saw."

"So you saw a gun, immediately surmised that he was going to shoot someone with it, and tackled him."

"Yes."

"It never occurred to you that the man might have had the gun for valid reasons? That he was a concealed carrier or carrying for his own protection?"

No, I had a vision that the man shot around the gym and killed a bunch of people. That's how I knew he was dangerous.

Except she couldn't tell that part to a savvy and obviously very perceptive police detective.

"Was he treated by medics at the scene?" Katherine asked.

"What?"

"Was Mr. McCabe treated by medics? Was he checked out?"

Detective Bisset closed the manila folder and leaned forward, his hands clasped on his desk. "Not at the scene, but later, yes."

"Did they find a bruise or a blister around his left waist from where he was carrying the gun?"

"I don't see what—"

"Are you a runner, Detective? I used to trail run. I've had to cut back to treadmills now, but I used to train a lot."

Detective Bisset shook his head. "I prefer swimming."

"That's a good choice. My mother-in-law is an avid swimmer and constantly tries to convince me to switch because it'd be easier on my knees. I'm trying out the elliptical machine, but I don't love it like I enjoy the treadmill."

"I'm not sure what exercise—?"

"That man was running when I tackled him. At quite a high speed. When we hit the treadmill, I flew off the back.

His sweatshirt was soaked—he'd been jogging for a while—and the shorts he was wearing didn't have an elastic waist. They were cargo shorts. He was running and carrying a weapon stuffed in a pair of cargo shorts where it would have rubbed against his skin. After that long at that intensity, the friction would have been painful."

Detective Bisset nodded slowly. "You're saying that if he were a concealed weapon carrier, he would have had a proper holster. He wouldn't have been running with a gun stuck in his waistband that would make him bleed."

"Did he have a blister or any cuts on his left hip?"

"I believe he did."

"If Justin McCabe had gone to the gym and just happened to bring his gun because he was going to the range later or even if he was afraid for his life for some reason, he would have had the correct equipment." Katherine sat back in her chair and folded her hands on her waist. "Did you have any other questions for me?"

The corner of Detective Bisset's mouth turned up. "Do you ever lose arguments, Professor Bassi?"

"All the time. I haven't been able to convince my husband that coffee is better than tea or that we should get a little fluffy dog. But I do think I have pretty good instincts about people."

Especially when I have visions about them.

"I think you do too." Detective Bisset rose and held out his hand. "My advice? Get the dog. Just pick one out and bring it home. If you make it a rescue, he won't be able to argue with you."

Katherine stood and shook his hand. "I feel like you're speaking from experience."

"I have a wife and two ten-year-old daughters. Guess how many dogs I have?"

"One?"

"Four." He shook his head. "When your wife looks up at you with big brown eyes while holding a little fluffy animal, you know you're not going to win that argument."

Katherine smiled. "I may take your advice."

"Take this advice too: please don't tackle any more gunmen. I really hate the thought of you and your friends out there" —he nodded to the break room— "getting hurt because you're making citizens' arrests. Leave that to the professionals."

"They're not my friends. We don't even know each other from the gym."

"That's surprising."

"Why?"

He shrugged. "According to witnesses, you three ladies make one hell of a team."

CHAPTER 4

Katherine spoke to a junior officer to finish her official statement, which was routine and mostly consisted of handing over all her personal information to the police and being informed that in the event of a criminal trial, she could be called upon to testify.

Since Justin McCabe didn't seem like someone with mob connections, Katherine assured them that she'd be available.

As she walked toward the exit, she spotted her fellow crime thwarters still sitting in the glass-walled break room.

"That gun just jumped into my hand, y'all. I didn't grab it. I didn't even reach for it. I just thought in my head 'someone needs to get that gun away from this kid,' and then it just flew into my hand all on its own, and I don't know what to think about that. I don't know what to think at all."

It didn't feel right to walk away without saying goodbye. After all, they might occupy wildly different spaces in the world, but they'd been through something together. It wasn't easily explained, but it was... something.

Katherine veered toward the break room just as Detective Bisset was approaching it.

"Professor Bassi, did you forget something?"

"I was just going to say goodbye to Toni and Megan." She kind of wished the detective wasn't going to accompany her, but what could she say? *Please leave me to my own awkward social interactions, Detective. I don't want an audience.*

That would probably seem suspicious.

She walked into the break room ahead of the detective and gave a small wave to Toni and Megan. "I just wanted to thank both of you for being there yesterday when everything happened." She heard the detective behind her. "I'm finished, so I'll be heading—"

"Oh my God!" Megan exclaimed with a broad smile. "You're Black!"

Katherine blinked. "I beg your pardon?"

Toni muttered, "What the fuck?" Her eyes darted between Detective Bisset and Megan.

Katherine looked over her shoulder.

Detective Bisset's expression was blank. "Yes, I am, Mrs. Carpenter."

"Sorry." Megan's cheeks went flaming red. "I am so sorry. That probably sounded strange. It's just that I'm from Atlanta, and there are like... no Black people around here compared to back home. It's really strange." She stood quickly and held out her hand; her cheeks were still flaming. "It's nice to meet you, Detective."

The mood in the room had shifted quickly from tense to amused.

Detective Bisset took Megan's hand. "Nice to meet you too. And you're right. There aren't many Black residents in the Cove. My family and I are some of the few. I'm originally from Chicago, so I know what you mean. Love the accent, by the way; my mother's people are from Georgia."

"Thank you," Megan said. "I think most people around here think I'm dumb."

Toni rolled her eyes. "Whatever."

Megan's smile was strained. "Like her."

Katherine felt the twin urges to walk away quickly and to pacify the situation. After a second of internal debate, she forced herself to go with the latter impulse.

"You know, when people are working from different cultural frameworks, it's easy for misunderstanding to take hold," she said. "Kind of like... right now."

All eyes in the room turned toward Katherine. It reminded her a little of being in a classroom, which set her at ease.

She motioned toward Toni, who was sitting in the corner, glaring at Megan. "For instance, some people might assume that a person working in skilled trades like Toni didn't excel in traditional education."

"They wouldn't be wrong," Toni said. "I hated school."

"But your line of work requires you to constantly update your skill set as technology develops, so practically speaking, you're probably more educated than the majority of college graduates."

"Maybe," Toni muttered. "Thanks, I guess?"

"And others" —Katherine looked at Toni, then at Megan — "might assume that someone with a Southern accent conforms to the negative stereotypes about Southerners promoted by mainstream American culture without recognizing that really, all people have accents that are mostly an accident of geography."

All three of them were staring at her, so Katherine just kept speaking. "In fact, people have multiple accents they use in different situations, all of which have nothing to do with intelligence. I imagine Detective Bisset's voice sounds very different when he's interrogating a suspect versus when he's speaking to his daughter."

"Depends on how clean her room is," he muttered.

"I hadn't thought about that 'cause it's what we're used to hearing on the television and in movies," Megan said. "But y'all have California accents. They're kind of... flat. Sorry if that sounds rude."

"No offense taken," Katherine said. "My husband has a very unique accent since he was born and raised in Hong Kong but educated in England. He also speaks four languages, so that's changed his accent over time." She smiled a little. "I was born and raised in San Francisco, so I think my accent is—like you said—very flat."

Megan was staring at her intently. "You are such an interesting person. I think I could listen to you talk about anything."

Katherine smiled. "You'd probably disagree if you took one of my classes."

"I don't think so," Megan continued. "I'm not sure I'd understand all of it, but I bet it would be interesting."

Detective Bisset cleared his throat. "Ladies, I hate to interrupt, but we really need to continue with the interviews. Toni, I know you've been here a while, but do you mind—"

"I'm cool, Drew." Toni had already turned her attention back to the television. "I told the guys I'd be busy today."

Katherine held her hand out to Megan. "Good luck, Megan. I hope you feel more welcome in Moonstone Cove soon. After all, you're a local hero now."

Megan shook her hand vigorously. "It was so nice meeting you. And... um." She glanced at the detective. "You've got a great tackle."

"Thanks."

Katherine suspected that Megan wanted to talk more about the odd statement she'd blurted out about the gun leaping into her hand, but not in front of a police detective.

"It was very nice to meet you both." Katherine nodded at Toni, smiled at Megan, then walked toward the door. "Maybe I'll see you around town."

Toni nodded. "Nice to meet you too."

"Same." Megan obviously wanted to say more. "Hopefully I'll see you."

Katherine walked away from the break room with a more settled feeling in her stomach. The detective had obviously believed her, and as for Megan and Toni?

Whatever strange event they'd shared, it was more than likely she'd never see them again. After all, Moonstone Cove wasn't *that* small.

CHAPTER 5

*K*atherine ran through the events of the day before while she sat on her front porch and watched the sunset.

A gun that jumped into a person's hand.

A man who had to have an extreme amount of adrenaline coursing through his system suddenly going limp at the sound of a small woman's voice.

Telekinesis, telepathy, even ghosts. All of them could exist in theory. She knew science didn't have an answer yet, but she strongly believed that at some point, a logical explanation would be found for all those traits, likely as evolutionary relics of the nervous system that modern humanity had little use for.

Megan could be a telekinetic whose skill was triggered by an extreme fear for her life.

Toni could be an empath, though Katherine suspected the woman would dislike even the idea of influencing anyone with her emotions.

But emotions were chemical reactions in the brain.

Telekinesis was the manipulation of energy and magnetic fields. All those things could theoretically be accounted for by science.

Nothing could account for the screams she'd heard in her mind. The blood she'd seen. The scent of gunpowder in the air.

"What do you think about visions?"

"Visions? As in precognition?"

"Yes."

"Oh, I don't think that's possible."

As Megan so eloquently put it, Katherine didn't know what to think about that. And not knowing how to classify something put her on edge.

Precognition? There was no scientific theory for that. There couldn't be. Which meant that science couldn't explain something in her life. Which had never happened before in all her forty-seven years.

It was not a comfortable feeling.

It was Friday night and Katherine was on her third glass of wine. Baxter was in his study, playing evening/morning chess with his brother in London while she was quietly examining her sanity on the front deck with a bottle of rosé.

She stared at the phone number she'd written down months ago. What instinct had urged her to save it? It had been such a random call.

Monica Velasquez was a friend of an old college friend, a woman who was by reputation an intelligent, practical small-business owner and mother. She had no history of mystical thought or questionable mental acuity. She was, as her old friend Mark put it, "solid as a rock."

But Monica had called—clearly for herself, though she

used the "asking for a friend" excuse—and asked Katherine her scientific opinion on predicting the future.

"Oh, I don't think that's possible."

Clearly she'd be eating crow on that statement.

She took a deep breath, another swallow of wine, and called the phone number.

The phone rang long enough that Katherine expected it to go to voice mail.

"This is Monica."

Katherine had been mentally preparing to leave a message and was taken off-guard. "Mrs. Velasquez?" Was that her voice? She needed to calm down. "Is this Monica Velasquez?"

"Yes. Are you okay?"

Well, *that* was a loaded question. "I just... I'm not sure how to ask this. I don't even know if you remember me."

"Does this have something to do with Russell House? If there's a guest emergency, I'm not on-site, so you'll have to call—"

"What's Russell House? I'm sorry." Katherine stopped. Took a breath. She was calling a woman she'd only spoken to once months before. She needed to explain.

What was she supposed to say about any of this?

"I do apologize; I'm not making any sense. My name is Professor Katherine Bassi, and I believe I spoke to you around seven months ago about—"

"Precognition." The voice on the phone switched from confused to surprised. "Yes. Yes, I do remember you. Are you okay?"

"I'm fine. I'm..." *What was she?* "...unsettled. But I'm fine."

"Okay."

Katherine refilled her wineglass. *Just be honest, Katherine. This woman was honest with you and put herself out there even when you dismissed her. Just be honest.*

"I'm calling because something happened very recently, and I don't understand it, but I remembered our conversation from months ago." Katherine took a drink and cleared her throat when she drank too fast. "And I am so *sorry* if I seemed dismissive at the time. I admit, hearing about your... friend's experiences seemed so out of the realm of scientific possibility that I was probably patronizing. I apologize for that."

Hopefully that came across better than it sounded in her head.

Monica's voice was cautious. "Professor Bassi, what happened?"

"Are you the friend, Mrs. Velasquez?" Katherine suspected, but she needed to know. She needed to know if Monica Velasquez could give her answers. "I need to know if you were using a common distancing tactic to—"

"Yes, I'm the friend I was talking about. I experience precognition through dreams."

Relief. Immediate, unequivocal relief. "Then I need your help. Someone tried to commit a violent crime yesterday. A shooting. It could have been very bad, but it wasn't. Because... I saw it happen before it happened. And I helped stop it."

Even as she said the words, the images filled her mind again. Gunshots. Broken glass. Blood sprayed on walls...

"Okay. Katherine, I'm going to get your number and call you back in about five minutes with some friends of mine.

Everything is going to be okay, but I have a feeling you're going to want to talk to all of us."

What? Why?

Relax. You've interrupted the woman's night. Give her a few minutes. "Thank you. I don't know what's happening, but... thanks."

"Trust me. You are not alone."

Something tight in Katherine's chest—something she hadn't even been aware of—loosened and relaxed.

She wasn't alone.

SHE WALKED into the kitchen to grab something to eat. She'd had a big lunch, but she'd forgotten to eat dinner. She briefly thought about ordering something in; then she spotted Baxter through the office doorway, gesturing dramatically and speaking quickly in Cantonese with his brother on a screen.

She quickly put together a fruit tray and some cheese and brought them into the office.

"Katherine!" Her brother-in-law, Oliver, waved from the other side of the world. "I told Baxter I thought it was Valentine's Day in the States and he couldn't remember. I think it is."

"Is it?" She looked at Baxter with a frown. "What's the date?"

"The fourteenth, I think." His eyes lit up. "Oh! I suppose it is."

"Happy Valentine's Day." She set down the plate of pears and manchego. "I got some pears at the farmers' market. Is this enough for dinner? I have a call in a few minutes."

"This is lovely, darling." He squeezed her hand. "We always forget, don't we?"

"I know, but then we don't have to go to crowded restaurants." She waved at Oliver. "We should set up a family chat this week. I miss the boys."

"I'll tell Lily to message you." Oliver waved back. "Marco and Louis are in ten different directions these days. I have no idea what their social calendar is like."

"I think that's normal with teenagers. My sister says the same thing about hers." Katherine leaned down and kissed Baxter's cheek just as she felt her phone begin to buzz in her pocket. "Call's coming through. Enjoy your game."

She walked back to the kitchen as they continued their conversation. Once there, she grabbed the phone from her pocket and answered it. "Hello?"

"Katherine?"

It was Monica Velasquez again. "Hello. I'm getting something to eat. Do you mind the sound of chewing?" She'd had enough wine that she was feeling a little loopy. "If you do, it's called misophonia and it's completely valid, and I don't want to dismiss it, but also I've had too much wine and not enough food today."

"You're fine. I put you on speakerphone with my two best friends, Robin and Valerie."

"Just Val," said one voice. "I'm psychometric."

Katherine nearly tripped over her own feet. "You mean there's more than one of you?"

"Three to be exact. We all have different abilities,"

Monica said. "Precognition for me, obviously, which we've talked about."

"And I'm Robin," a third voice said. "I hope you're doing okay. Get your food, okay? Make sure you eat something."

"I'm getting some." Katherine hurriedly put together a plate of cheese, crackers, and pears. "I tend to forget to eat."

"My mother is the same way. My father constantly has to remind her."

"I have to remind my husband. He's even more absent-minded than me."

"I cannot imagine a house where people forget to eat," Val said. "I think my boys eat six times a day. Maybe more."

"They sound like teenagers." Katherine took her plate to the deck and sat down.

"They are, and they're hungry. Constantly. How about you? Any kids?"

"Just my students," she said. "There are more than a few of those. And I have two gorgeous nephews in London and a niece and a nephew in San Francisco."

"It sounds like you have a wonderful family," Monica said. "Have you told your husband about any of this yet?"

"Oh no." Baxter would immediately take her to a neurologist. "Absolutely not."

"Does anyone know?"

"Um... you three know." And it was possible that Megan and Toni suspected something, but that was a whole other problem she didn't know how to deal with. "I think that's all I can handle right now."

"Why don't you tell us about it?" Monica said. "Start from the beginning and describe what happened to you exactly."

Katherine spent the next few minutes giving Monica, Val, and Robin an accounting of the incident the day before. She tried to include everything she could think of, including what Megan had said at the police station and her suspicions about Toni's empathy.

"That's a lot," Robin said after she'd finished the story. "No wonder you're feeling frazzled."

"Frazzled?" She wouldn't have used that word, but it was a pretty good description. "Yes. I'm frazzled. I don't know what to do with any of this."

"Now, other than human understanding, I don't know how much we'll be able to help you. I'm a medium—"

"A medium?" Katherine blinked. "As in... ghosts? Spirits?"

"Ghosts, I guess you'd say. I haven't met any spirits that haven't belonged to a dead person. Not that I'm aware of anyway."

Katherine was extremely glad she didn't see ghosts. "And Val said she's psychometric." She glanced at her neighbors' deck, glad that they were rarely home. "So she reads memories and emotions from objects?"

"You got it," Val said. "Have you studied this or something?"

"Not formally. It's a bit of a side interest. I haven't really looked into it in years. I've been really busy with other things."

"So between you, the gun-moving gal, and the lady who calmed the guy down, I think you and I have the most similar talent," Monica said. "And my visions sound very different than yours."

"Yours was interesting." Val was speaking. "It was so

immediate. It seems like it would be really easy to doubt yourself."

"I had the same thought," Katherine said. "It would have been so easy to imagine that I was suffering from anxiety or had an overactive imagination."

"Why didn't you think that?" Robin asked.

She tried to recall the moments in the gym before everything had broken loose. "I just... knew. I could hear the screams. I smelled the gunpowder, and it was almost as if I could feel glass shards cutting me. In the moment, I knew absolutely that it would happen if I did nothing."

"So you tackled him," Val said. "Fucking badass, Katherine."

"Cover your ears, Monica." Robin continued, "I have to agree. Fucking badass."

Katherine stuffed some cheese in her mouth and swallowed. "Okay, but what do I do? This is not normal. Is it going to happen again? Is it a onetime thing?"

"There's no way of knowing," Val said. "You just have to wait and see. Maybe you'll get lucky and it'll only happen once."

"I'm not sure there's much you can do," Monica said. "All our abilities were triggered by the same incident. It's been three years and they haven't gone away yet."

"What incident?"

"Robin's car went into the lake," Val said. "We almost drowned."

"RIP faithful Subaru," Robin said. "I still miss you."

"So you had a near-death experience," she said. "And three years later... still psychic?"

"Yep," Monica said. "I thought I'd just get hot flashes in my forties, not visions."

Did an averted mass shooting count as a near-death experience?

Probably. Probably it did.

This wasn't good.

"I wish I could tell you that the visions probably won't happen again," Monica said, "but I found them to come more regularly the longer I had the ability."

"Like... every day?"

"Oh, nothing close to that. I'm not like Val."

"I wear gloves," Val said. "All the time. And I take antianxiety medications. They dull my senses just enough that I don't usually have an immediate reaction to everything."

"I have social anxiety and I'm medicated," Katherine said. "Do you think that might stop more visions?"

"Were you taking your medication when you had the vision?"

Damn it. Of course she was. She never missed a dose. "Yes."

All three women seemed to hem and haw. Several comforting mutters were audible.

"I think you'll just have to wait and see," Monica said.

"What should I do about Megan and Toni?" Katherine asked. "Should I try to get in touch with them? Ask them if they've ever experienced this kind of thing before?"

"If it was the first time they genuinely ever feared for their life, it may be new for them too," Robin said. "I'd at least try to contact them and see if they'd be willing to talk to you. Then you wouldn't be alone."

"Do your families know?" Katherine tried to imagine telling Baxter. He would immediately suspect a brain tumor.

"My husband knows, but I didn't tell him right away," Robin said.

"My boyfriend knows," Val said. "He actually suspected before I told him. He's a sheriff, and he worked with a psychic when he was down in Southern California. The real kind."

"Right." She was having a hard time taking everything in, but it did feel good to talk about it. It made her feel a little less on edge. "Monica, how about you?"

"My husband passed before it happened, but I have a boyfriend now, and he knows." Monica laughed a little. "He didn't exactly react well at first, but he's come around now."

"How did you convince him?"

"I helped him stop a string of serial arsons."

"Oh right. That's good. Not the arson, but the... stopping the arson." Was that an empty wineglass in front of her? Not anymore, it wasn't. Katherine refilled her glass.

"You sound stressed," Robin said. "I think the important thing is to make some kind of connection with Megan and Toni. Even if you don't become friends, having someone who understands what you're going through is really important. Megan, at least, sounds like she'd be open to talking again."

Megan seemed like a social person who would text Katherine on her phone and want to meet for lunch or have brunch or go shopping for purses together. In short, all the social things that Katherine avoided.

Then again, Megan was also likely as confused as she was, only she didn't have three nice psychics in Glimmer Lake giving her advice.

"I'll call her," Katherine said. "I think she'll be willing to talk."

CHAPTER 6

Katherine got ready for work on Monday with her head full of questions and her body full of aches. She'd once taken a tumble down a steep hill on a ten-kilometer trail race when she was thirty-two.

Her body was definitely reminding her that was fifteen years ago.

"Are you sure you're ready for work?" Baxter frowned at her over his teacup. "You experienced something traumatic four days ago."

"What else am I going to do?" Katherine nibbled along the edge of her bagel, wishing she'd spread more cream cheese. "Sit around here and think about how much my knee hurts? Work is better. I can sit for my lecture today if I need to. I only have one class, and if I don't make my office hours today, I'll just have to make them up later."

Why had she been so skimpy with the cream cheese on her bagel? Life was too short for skimping on cream cheese. Tomorrow she'd lay it on.

Baxter reached for the french press and refilled her coffee cup. "What about the Fred lab?"

"I don't think they need me this week at all actually."

The Fred lab was the university's affectionate term for the research project Katherine was attached to, studying the neural pathways of cephalopods as a starting point for smart prosthetics in humans.

She hadn't planned on studying octopus neural networks with two biomedical engineers, a marine biologist, and a neuropsychologist, but a consult had led to a fascination and an inevitable affection for the project's mascot, Fred, a large Pacific red octopus that lived at the center.

Fred wasn't a research subject—they had four smaller octopi that were the test subjects—but he was the unofficial mascot of their odd group, and the five scientists and the dozen or so graduate students working there were constantly devising new games to keep Fred amused.

"Job and Britt are in the middle of fabricating a proto-type, so they won't need me until they get to the program-ming stage and they're not there yet."

"That's convenient."

"I may go and check on Fred though. I have a puzzle in mind, and I want to ask Maria if she thinks it's too difficult." Professor Maria Gatan was the marine biologist in their research group and Fred's main caretaker.

"There seem to be few puzzles that cephalopods can't solve." Baxter lifted his mug of tea and drained it. "Fasci-nating creatures."

"Poodles."

"Hmm?" He lowered the magazine he was skimming. "What?"

47

"Poodles are highly intelligent. And they don't shed. They have hair, not fur. So no dander."

Baxter frowned. "I'm not sure—"

"Not a large one, I don't think. Or a very small one. They have a medium-sized poodle that would be perfect."

He set down the magazine. "Who would pick up the... refuse?"

"Who cleans the bathrooms now?" Katherine asked. "You have many fine qualities, Professor Pang, but cleaning isn't one of them."

He pursed his lips. "What about London?"

"Do we have a trip scheduled?"

"No, but we go regularly. And we go to Hong Kong." He stood and walked to the kitchen to refill his tea. "We can't take a dog traveling with us."

"Then I'll ask a friend to watch the dog while we're gone," Katherine said. "Well-behaved, cute, fluffy dogs are usually not a hard favor to ask."

"Who would you ask to watch a dog for us?"

Katherine opened her mouth to answer, then shut it. Who *would* she ask? Her sister was in San Francisco. She could hardly ask one of her graduate students—that was probably unethical. "I'm sure I could think of someone."

This was a tad depressing. She flipped through her mental index of friends and associates, but she was having a hard time coming up with ideas. Feeding and walking a dog for a weekend wouldn't be a stretch for one of the neighbors they were friendly with, but actual dog sitting?

"I'm sure I know someone." She stood and poured her coffee into the travel mug Baxter had set out on the counter. "Or we could board it. I'm sure there are kennels in the area."

"Hmm." His mouth was set in a stern line.

Katherine couldn't help but kiss it.

Baxter softened and smiled at her. "You do seem to keep coming back to this idea."

"A small dog." She put her hand on his chest. "Medium-sized. Poodles are smart and not overly needy. I've done my research."

He poured the rest of his tea into the travel mug next to hers. "We'll talk about it later."

She glanced at his tea. "Are you sure you don't want some coffee? Your fancy water is looking a little thin."

"I enjoy having a functional stomach lining and not what-ever scar tissue has enveloped your gastric mucosa, thank you."

Katherine smiled. "You driving or am I?" They only owned one car, and Katherine liked it that way.

Baxter kissed her firmly. "You risked your life four days ago to stop a criminal. Let me drive please."

"Fine." Katherine grabbed her messenger bag and her travel mug as she followed Baxter out the door to their small garage. Her husband opened the car door for her and waited until she was inside to shut it carefully. It was a little chivalric gesture that she enjoyed even after twenty years of marriage.

As they drove the ten miles to the university, Katherine stared out the window, watching the familiar green-and-blue hoodies of the many students on bikes and skateboards that grew more frequent the closer they got to the college.

"Have you heard any more about the young man they arrested?" Katherine asked.

"No. They've mentioned the basics of the incident in the

newspaper, but nothing more than that. It seems the town doesn't want to dwell on a near miss."

"He was a student." She glanced at Baxter's profile. "Justin McCabe. Does the name sound familiar to you?"

"No. Was he local?" They were stopped in traffic as they approached the faculty parking lot where they parked their old Prius.

"I don't know."

Baxter raised an eyebrow. "But you're going to look."

She shrugged slightly. "Wouldn't you be curious?"

"I probably wouldn't be observant enough to tackle a would-be gunman in a fitness center, darling. So it's hard for me to imagine what curiosity that would entail." He turned his eyes back to the road as traffic started to move. "I can ask if anyone in the math department knows him."

"Sure."

"There might be rumors swirling anyway. It's not as if Moonstone Cove gets much excitement."

"I know." She waited until Baxter parked before she opened the door. "It's one of the reasons I like it."

―――――

KATHERINE'S OFFICE was tucked away in a corner of the physics department. Because she was often loaned out to other departments, she tended to float through the building without becoming embroiled in any of the politics typical of large institutions. As cochair of the mathematics department, Baxter was constantly dealing with this grievance or that annoyance. Katherine managed to avoid all that.

She opened her office and nearly tripped over a pile of mail that had been shoved under her door.

I have a mailbox for that.

She tried to remember the last time she'd checked her mailbox in the main office. She couldn't remember. Hmmm. That might be the reason the secretary had shoved things under her door. She kicked the mail into a messy pile to sort through later and managed to find her way to her desk.

Some professors were tidy; Katherine was not. Her brain just didn't work as well when things were organized, or at least that's what she told herself. If Baxter didn't organize their house, it would be complete chaos.

Scholarly journals were piled on one chair and mail on another. Papers that needed grades were stacked on the edge of her desk, and various *Star Wars* memorabilia was scattered around her crowded bookshelves.

She didn't care how many physical laws the movies had broken, she loved them. One of her grad students had 3D printed her a completely unique lightsaber based on those carried by the Jedi temple guard, and it was hanging on the wall next to her diplomas. People were usually far more interested in the lightsaber than the diplomas, and she didn't blame them.

She tucked her messenger bag under her desk and woke her desktop computer as she called into the Fred lab.

The phone rang three times before someone picked up. "CNMS lab. This is Kaylee."

The Fred lab was technically the Center of Neuroengineering and Marine Sciences, but no one called it that except for whoever was answering the phones that day.

"Hey, Kaylee, it's Professor Bassi. Is Job or Britt available?"

"Oh my God, Professor B! Everyone is talking about what happened last week! How are you? Are you okay? Did you really tackle that gunman? I mean, you were kind of my hero before this, but wow!"

Katherine was a little taken aback at Kaylee's enthusiasm. The young woman was usually friendly but very focused on her work. She was one of Professor Shaver's graduate students and a great asset to the lab. "I'm fine, Kaylee. Thanks for asking. Just a little sore."

"I bet." A door opened and closed. "Britt just walked in. Do you want to talk to him?"

"Please."

"Hey, Britt, Professor B is on the phone."

"Katherine!" The timbre of the call switched to speaker-phone. "Do you mind if you're on speaker? I haven't eaten yet."

The break room of the Fred lab was usually overtaken by various tanks of water, the occasional dead fish, and often elaborate puzzles for Fred. Those unfortunate enough to have to eat meals at the lab had only the front office to use.

"No problem. I'm in my office today. I have hours this afternoon and a lecture at ten. Are you and Job still working on the prototype?"

"Yeah, he's having trouble with some of the joints." There were crunching sounds on the speakerphone. "I don't think we'll be ready for you until next week at the earliest."

"That's fine. I'm trying to take it easy this week, so that's kind of a relief. Did Ansel get the last numbers back to you?"

"I think he maybe sent them to Maria, but I didn't see a copy."

"I'll email him." She'd need that before she started on programming for the prototype. "So I can be out this week with no problems?"

"Yeah." He was speaking with his mouth full. "We're good over here. How you feeling? I read about what happened. That's crazy shit."

Katherine logged into the university's internal server and immediately saw two dozen messages pop up. She clicked on the messages and found the usual business forwards and department memos but also a surprising number of concerned messages from colleagues.

That was unexpected. And nice.

"I'm feeling fine. I've taken more than my share of tumbles trail running, but it's been a while. It's a good reminder why I stick to treadmills these days."

Britt snorted. "I can't blame you. Strange about that kid though, right?"

"Have you heard anything about him? I know he was a student here."

She shot off reassuring replies to most of the emails. Yes, she did copy and paste a few, but she'd only had coffee with Professor Mehdi in the psychology department once. A copy-and-paste reply was sufficient.

"Justin McCabe," Britt said. "Kaylee and I were talking about him this morning. She didn't know him."

"I didn't." Kaylee chimed in. "But my roommate dated someone in his fraternity. She was friendly with him."

"Fraternity, huh?" Katherine had her issues with some of the fraternities on campus, but that wasn't a typical profile for a lone gunman. A young man in a fraternity would be socially connected and well known, part of an established group. "Has he ever had any problems in the past?"

"No. And it wasn't a real wild fraternity either. Professional-social. He was in the agricultural business school."

"That's very odd."

"Weird, right?" It was Britt again. "No record. No problems with the law or any of his classmates. Then he just goes off and tries to shoot up a gym."

A cold shiver ran down Katherine's spine.

"It's possible there was a mental illness that was undiagnosed." Undiagnosed neuropsychological conditions could account for erratic behavior, but Katherine hated mentioning them because it played into too many stereotypes. Those suffering from mental illness were far more likely to be the victims of crimes than the perpetrators.

Nothing about this added up.

"I'm just glad you're okay," Britt said. "That could have been really bad."

It would have been. Katherine flashed back to the vision she'd seen of the gym. Blood and broken glass and screams.

"Yes." A heavy feeling sat in the pit of her stomach. "It could have been very bad."

"I heard he had a bunch of guns," Kaylee said.

"No, just one." Katherine sorted through her memories. "But Megan, the woman who got the gun away from him, said it was an extended magazine, I think?"

"That's bad," Britt said. "We're fucking glad you're okay, Bassi. We couldn't finish this project without you."

It might have sounded self-interested, but Katherine

knew that for Britt, it was about as affectionate as she could expect.

She skimmed through the rest of the messages in her inbox and made a few notes on her calendar. Her lecture wasn't until ten o'clock.

"I wonder if anything else is going to happen," Kaylee said. "They say weird things come in threes, right?"

Katherine looked away from her computer and frowned at the phone. "Threes? What else happened?"

"Oh, nothing like what happened at the gym or anything." Kaylee began to stammer nervously. "I heard... I mean, I didn't hear directly, but I know the person they were talking about. Kind of. I'm not on the rodeo team, but this girl was and... It was really weird, but I don't know if what happened to her—"

"Kaylee," Britt said. "What are you talking about?"

"It was just so sad and strange. This girl... killed her horse."

Katherine's stomach turned. The silence over the phone was leaden.

"She *what*?" Britt's voice was horrified.

"It was awful," Kaylee said. "Same kind of thing, completely out of nowhere. She was on the rodeo team, and it was her own horse, and no one knew what to think. Some people said it was an accident and she just gave the wrong dosage to the horse when it was sick, but then other people on the team were like, no way that's even possible, she knew exactly what she was doing. She was completely wrecked. Her family is from Santa Cruz, and I heard she ended up moving back and quitting school completely."

The world around Katherine went grey and muffled

again. She saw herself reaching for a piece of paper and writing down a name. Saw herself tucking the paper under her keyboard when someone knocked on her door.

Her ears popped and Kaylee's voice became clear again. "I think her name was Sarah Jordan. She was studying marketing, but she came from a ranching family—that's why she was so into the rodeo stuff. It happened months ago."

"That's terrible," Britt said.

Katherine reached for the paper she'd seen in her vision, wrote down the name, and slid it under her keyboard just as the knock sounded at her door.

When she realized what had happened, her breath caught.

Vision number two, Professor Bassi.

Someone knocked again.

"Hey, guys." Katherine's finger hovered over the phone. "I need to go. I'll talk to you later."

"See ya later. Glad you're safe."

"Bye, Professor B."

As Katherine rose and walked to her door, she tried to dispel the heavy feeling in her stomach. There had been another vision. There had been another *crime*. Was it unrelated? Something buzzing in the back of her mind told her it wasn't.

She needed to call Megan and Toni. She needed to find out what they knew and if they were still having the same psychic powers she was. She needed to find out more about Sarah Jordan, Justin McCabe, and what they might have in common.

Something very strange was happening in Moonstone Cove.

CHAPTER 7

"*I* am so glad you called me." Megan sat across from Katherine at the small café on Beach Street. "I was thinking about calling you, but I didn't have your number and I wasn't sure if you were listed."

Megan was listed, much to Katherine's surprise. She'd left a message on an answering system, only to receive a call back less than two hours later.

"I'm just glad I was able to find you." Katherine tucked her purse under the table.

It was Tuesday afternoon and lunch traffic had died down, but there was still a steady trickle of customers going in and out of the restaurant.

Megan looked around. "This is cute. I've never been here before."

"It's within walking distance of my house, so I come here a lot." Should she have told a relative stranger that? What if she wanted to avoid Megan in the future?

Do you actually think the woman is going to stalk you?

"You live this close to the beach?" Megan's eyes lit up.

"Jealous!" She sighed a little. "Rodney and I looked at places near the beach, but he didn't want to spend the money."

"They're expensive now." Katherine sipped her green tea. "When we bought, North Beach was pretty cheap. So lots of our neighbors work at the college too."

Megan gave her a smile, but it looked a little forced. "You must know so many interesting people."

She could see the tension around the woman's eyes. "You don't like it here, do you?"

"The café?" Megan's eyes went wide. "No, it's nice. I—"

"California." Katherine had the urge to take Megan's hand. Which was strange as she wasn't an affectionate person. "You don't like Moonstone Cove."

Megan's mouth fell open. Then shut. The cheerful facade slipped, and her smile fell. "No. I kind of hate it here. My kids love it. My husband loves it. And I hate it. It leaves me absolutely cold."

"I don't think you're talking about the weather."

"That too." A bitter smile curved Megan's lips. "Women here are not the friendliest. Back in Atlanta, I had so many friends. College friends. Mom friends. Work friends. Here, I don't know anyone and they all think I'm stupid and shallow because I guess if you like pink and have a Southern accent, that's what you are."

Katherine sipped her coffee. "I don't think you're stupid. Or shallow."

Megan narrowed her eyes. "But I have a feeling if we hadn't experienced what we did on Thursday, you wouldn't have said hello at the gym. Am I right?"

"I don't say hello to anyone I don't know." Katherine

clutched her mug. "Unless it's in a professional setting. I'm not outgoing."

"At least you're honest about it. Women here..." Megan shook her head. "There have been a few work events for my husband that wives were invited to, but most of the women there were phony as a five-dollar Rolex. And so much plastic surgery! Dear Lord, is it that common around here? Every single one of those girls had the same nose and teeth." Megan's eyes went wide. "It was unnerving."

"I have no idea." Katherine thought about the women she knew from work. "Not as much plastic surgery among college professors probably."

"So most of your friends." Megan paused to taste her coffee. "Did you get to know them through work?"

"Friends?" Did she consider her colleagues friends? "Um... no. I mean, I'm friendly with a lot of the people I work with, but I wouldn't consider them friends."

"So..." Megan frowned. "Who do you hang out with? Outside of work?"

"My husband." She thought a little bit. "And I want a dog."

"Don't get me wrong, dogs are great, but what about girl-friends?" Megan set her coffee down. "Who do you talk to about your husband? Or that annoying thing your mother is doing? Or... hell, hot flashes and all that crap."

Katherine blinked. "I... don't."

Megan cocked her head. "You don't what? You don't talk to anyone about that stuff?"

Baxter's question from the day before popped into her head. *Who would you ask to watch a dog for us?*

Oh. This was why she had a hard time answering that question.

"I guess I don't have many friends." Katherine frowned. "I never have. I talk to my sister in San Francisco, and I really like my sister-in-law, but she lives in London. Most of my friends from college have very different lives than me. And... my husband is wonderful. He's a great person to talk to." When she could actually get him to pay attention. Baxter could be a little... distracted at times.

"Katherine, no offense, but you need some friends. I can at least video chat with my girls from Atlanta and have a drink. You need to get some girls."

Katherine's previous life experience with groups of women was far from positive.

She'd tried to join a quilting club once because she was so impressed by the precision of the craft, but she wasn't coordinated enough with needles and she felt awkward asking for help. Her neighbor had invited her to a pottery class, but she'd only gone once. She didn't attend a church or temple. Her department was dominated by men.

She frowned at Megan, with her perfectly coordinated outfit and effortless, charming manners. "I don't think I fit into most women's social circles."

Megan's blue eyes were kind and more than a little amused. "Well cheers." She lifted her coffee cup. "I don't fit in with any of the women here either, so I'm officially volunteering to be your girlfriend. Want to form a book club where we don't actually read anything and drink wine instead?"

A short laugh burst out of Katherine. "Are you serious?"

"As a heart attack."

The grey feeling fell over her in a flash, and she saw

Megan fumble her coffee cup and spill caffe latte all over her pristine white pants. She jumped up and jostled the table, causing even more coffee to spill everywhere.

Katherine blinked and the grey feeling cleared. Her ears popped and sounds were crisp again; the smell of ground coffee was pungent in her nose.

Megan was sitting across from her, coffee cup in hand. "You know, I was thinking when you called—"

Katherine reached across the table and grabbed Megan's cup before it could tip over.

Megan blinked. "If you wanted some coffee—"

"You were about to spill."

"How—?"

"I saw you spill."

Megan sat, silent and staring.

Okay, Katherine, here you go. "The back of your right hand was going to hit the edge of your coffee cup and you would have spilled on your pants. Then you were going to jump up and the coffee would spill on your purse." Katherine folded her hands in her lap, wondering if that admission was the end of Megan wanting anything to do with her.

She'd been kind of into the book club idea.

"You saw him." Megan's voice was barely over a whisper. "That's how you knew. He barely had the gun out when it jumped into my hand. You saw what he was going to do."

She forced the words past the lump in her throat. "It was just a flash, but I saw... I have no explanation for any of it. Not my vision, not what happened to you and the gun. I have no idea what is happening any more than you do."

Megan looked around the mostly deserted café. "Has anything like this ever happened to you before?"

"Never." She leaned forward. "I have studied—in my spare time—parapsychological phenomena—"

"English, Katherine."

"Psychic stuff." She gripped her coffee cup with both hands. "I've studied some psychic stuff because I think that some things—like your telekinesis—might be evolutionary relics. Things that our ancestors did that we no longer control but our brains theoretically have the capacity for."

"You think my brain knows how to make objects move without me touching them?" Megan shook her head. "I've never had anything like this happen before. I tried to do it again, and I haven't been able to. Not even a wiggle."

"You probably reacted out of survival instinct, so you don't have control of it yet. I don't have any control over my visions. But think for a minute. Think hard. Have you ever feared for your life? I'm talking *real* and potent fear like you had on Thursday."

Megan took a deep breath and closed her eyes. "No." She opened her eyes again and looked at Katherine. "Not with that sudden adrenaline rush, nothing like that. I was pumped up for hours on Thursday night. I couldn't fall asleep until like three in the morning. That never happens to me. I love my sleep."

"That rush of hormones that your brain created could have triggered something you were always capable of but didn't need," Katherine said. "Not until that exact moment."

"What about Toni?" Megan asked. "You think she did something weird too?"

"I think it's pretty strange that Justin McCabe fought me so hard that I cracked my head and got really ugly bruises, but the minute she jumped on him and held him down, he went limp as a rag, don't you?"

Megan nodded slowly. "Yeah, that is weird now that you mention it."

"I think she may have an extremely potent form of empathy."

Megan sat up straight. "I'm gonna say that woman and the word *empathy* are not the best of friends. I tried talking to her, and—"

"I'm talking about a supernatural form of empathy. Something akin to mental influence where she experiences other people's emotions and in some cases can make them feel what she wants them to."

Megan pursed her lips. "Would extreme empathy fit with someone who is—excuse my language—an utter asshole? Because I tried talking to her, and she was—pardon my French—a complete bitch to me. Now, I am not someone who thinks everyone has to be my friend, but that woman was just rude. Just being in the same room with her made me angrier than— Oooooh, that's what you're talking about, isn't it?" Her eyes were round as saucers. "Good Lord."

Katherine watched Megan's body language. "Why do you do that?"

"Do what?"

"Your body language is defensive right now, and you kept couching your use of mildly offensive words when you spoke about Toni. I'm forty-seven. I've heard the words *bitch* and *asshole* before. I'm not offended."

Megan frowned and the arms crossed over her chest relaxed. "I don't know why I do that. I guess because my mama did."

"That makes sense."

"You didn't answer my question about Toni though. Does empathy fit with her being as asshole?"

"She probably doesn't realize what effect she has on people. She was likely angry she had to come into the station on Friday, and her anger affected you. She might not have any idea."

Megan muttered, "Not sure we want her in the book club."

"We have to talk to her," Katherine said. "She's probably as confused as we are. And with the way that her emotions could be influencing other people—"

"She's probably on the verge of causing another mass shooting." Megan sighed. "Okay, I'm up for finding her, but you better do the talking."

KATHERINE AND MEGAN walked through the clattering noises of Dusi Brothers Automotive Repair, following the pointed finger of a man who claimed to know where Antonia Dusi was.

It was Thursday morning and Katherine had taken the morning off work. She didn't have classes to attend and her office hours for the week were limited. With no need for her at the Fred lab, she had some freedom to meet Megan and seek out Toni.

"Do you see her?" Megan hung behind Katherine.

"No. Do you think that man was misdirecting us?"

Megan stood on her tiptoes and looked over the garage.

"Nah. I think I see her. She's in the second-to-last bay underneath that sweet little MG coupe."

Katherine looked over her shoulder. "Do you know much about cars?"

"Old ones like this? Sure. My daddy loves old cars. Don't ask me about new ones though."

"Toni!" someone yelled at her. "I think you got company."

"What?" Toni rolled out from under the dark green car, and her eyes swept the garage, landing on Megan and Katherine. "What are you two doing here?"

Megan gave her a little wave. "Hey."

Katherine shouted over the sound of an air compressor. "We were hoping you had a minute to talk! We had a question."

"Yeah no." Toni started to roll back under the car. "Busy."

"We could always just ask you here," Megan shouted. "In front of all your employees. It's kinda personal, but I'm sure y'all are really close friends and you wouldn't mind them knowing all your personal business and all."

Toni shot out from under the car and glared at Megan. "Listen, Atlanta—"

"We really do need a moment of your time." Katherine interrupted the impending argument. "I think you're going to want to speak to us. It's about last week."

Toni's glare moved from Megan to Katherine for a moment before her eyes narrowed. She wiped a bead of sweat from her forehead and pointed back toward the office where they'd entered. "Fine. If you're willing to wait for fifteen, I can give you ten minutes."

"Oh, can you?" Megan's voice was saccharine sweet. "That's just so—"

"Fine. That's fine." Katherine put a hand on Megan's arm. "We can wait."

Without another word, Katherine herded Megan back toward the garage office.

"The nerve of that woman," Megan said through gritted teeth. "Acting as if she's too good for—"

"We're here interrupting her day," Katherine said. "At her work. Just calm down and hopefully we can figure out exactly what is going on with Toni Dusi."

Megan offered up a harsh laugh. "Doc, first rule of wine and book club: telling a woman to calm down is a surefire way to drive her crazy."

"That makes zero sense."

"Give me a little time to research and I'm sure I can find an academic translation you can understand."

CHAPTER 8

*T*wenty minutes later, Toni Dusi walked into the back office where Katherine and Megan were waiting. She came in, wiping her hands on a red rag and glaring at the two women in her office.

"I don't know why you two are here, but if you think we need some kind of bonding—"

"How did you calm the man down last week?" Katherine didn't wait for Toni to finish. She'd found throwing a student off-balance with an unexpected question to be an effective way to break through recalcitrance. She was hoping it would work on Toni too.

Toni paused halfway to her desk and stared at Katherine. "What?"

Katherine raised her arm and showed Toni one of the greenish-purple bruises on her bicep. "I have another, equally colorful one on my side. Another one on my hip from where he knocked me over. And the leftovers of a mild concussion."

Toni looked confused as she finished walking behind her desk and sat down. "Sorry. That sucks."

"I'm a forty-seven-year-old college professor who tackled a man to the ground and fell off the back of a treadmill," she said. "My injuries don't surprise me. Justin McCabe was a young, strong man. What I do find surprising is that the minute you jumped on him and pushed his shoulders to the ground, he went limp. How did you do it?"

Toni was silent for a long time. "He lost his gun."

"He could have grabbed me," Megan said. "I'm not any stronger than Katherine. Probably less. He could have tackled me and gotten it back. He just gave up."

"He must have realized that his plan was useless," Toni said. "Maybe he had remorse."

"Or maybe you told him to calm down and he did."

Two bright red spots flamed on Toni's cheekbones. "If you're implying that I knew that kid or was involved in what he was planning—"

"I'm not." Katherine quickly stopped her. "That's not what I'm saying. That's not why we're here."

"I told you before," Megan said. "At the police station. The gun jumped into my hand. I didn't grab it—I just thought someone needed to grab it, and then it was in my hand."

Toni smirked. "Like magic?"

Megan lifted her chin. "Yeah. Like magic."

Toni rolled her eyes. "Oh my God. Professor, I know you can't be in on the woo-woo stuff, right?"

"I don't believe in magic. But I do believe there are things we don't understand yet," Katherine said. "Parapsychological phenomena—"

"Are you kidding me?" Toni leaned forward and propped her elbows on the messy metal desk decorated with parts catalogs and bumper stickers for Saint Simon's Elementary School. "I expect this shit from someone like New Age Southern Barbie—"

"If you expect me to sink to the level of your insults, you will be very disappointed," Megan said.

Toni never took her eyes off Katherine. "Didn't you say you were some kind of scientist?"

Katherine nodded. "Yes. I'm a biophysicist at the university. I'm currently collaborating on cephalopod neural research."

"You're what?"

"Octopus brains," Megan said. "She's studying how octopus brains work."

"Okay." Toni blinked. "You're studying octopus brains, but you think we have magic powers?"

"I don't know," Katherine said. "Do you?"

Toni's stare didn't waver. "Do you?"

Katherine looked over her shoulder, but no one was in the outer office. She turned back to Toni, glancing at Megan, who gave her a confident nod. *Okay, Katherine, time to lay all the cards on the table.*

"Yes," she said. "I'm seeing what I would describe as microvisions a few seconds prior to events. That's how I knew that young man was carrying a gun and was going to shoot up the gym."

Toni and Megan were both silent.

"I saw him take out that weapon and shoot across the room. He hit three people and broke the front mirrors." As she recounted her vision, she felt the room around her pressing in. Her hearing muffled. Her senses narrowed into the memory. "There were shards of glass flying everywhere and people screaming. Blood. Someone near me was hit in the neck, and the arterial blood spray—"

"That's enough." Toni's voice was sharp. "You've got a sick imagination, Professor."

"It's not imagination. It's what would have happened if I hadn't tackled him."

There was something she wasn't remembering. Something important about that day.

Megan said, "All three of us were close to him. She might have saved our lives."

Toni had been nearby, but she was distracted. Her attention was on something farther down the line of... *Oh.*

Katherine blinked. "You knew it was coming too."

Toni snorted. "Don't be ridiculous."

"You felt him. Or you felt something. His... anger maybe? His rage? I tried to talk to you..." Katherine reconstructed the final moments before the shooting in her mind.

"Are you waiting for this machine?"

"I'm good. I've got time."

"You were waiting at the end of the row. You had your eye on him," Katherine said. "You felt something."

Megan crossed her arms over her chest. "Listen, do you think it's easy for me to admit something weird like this happened to me? I don't know you, and you clearly don't like me for some reason. I barely know Katherine, but I can tell she's not a liar, and I bet you can too. Why would we lie about this? Why would we make this up? You know something strange happened in that gym. This is not in our heads."

"I saw what Justin McCabe was going to do a few seconds before he did it, and I was able to react," Katherine said. "Megan saw the gun, knew she needed to get it away from him, and she did. And you felt something from him, and you were able to calm him down with a single command."

Toni's face was frozen.

"I'm not saying you have to trust us completely, but at least tell us what you felt from him. How did you know he was dangerous? What was his state of mind?"

After a few long moments of silence, Toni asked, "Are you done?"

Katherine sat back, feeling defeated. Toni Dusi didn't look any more receptive to them than she had when they walked into the garage. If anything, she looked even less friendly now.

"Yes. I'm done."

Toni stood, grabbed the rag, and started toward the door. "Have a great day. Good luck in life. I'm sure you can figure out how to get out of here."

MEGAN DROVE them back to the Beach Street Café. Katherine stared out the window, feeling defeated. She felt like she'd let her friends in Glimmer Lake down, but she also felt like she'd let Megan down. Why? She had no idea.

Katherine had spent most of her life feeling like she was letting someone down. No matter what she did as a child, her exacting father didn't find it good enough. Her sister, a brilliant mathematician, had satisfied him. Her mother wasn't subject to his eagle-eyed inspections.

How ridiculous can you be? She berated herself silently. *Forty-seven and you're friendless, still trying to live up to the standards of a man who's been dead for fifteen years.*

She'd just reached a level of success in her career when her father had died of a massive heart attack. Her sister, who'd been a working mathematician at a national foundation for five years, had always been his favorite child. Katherine had been an afterthought.

Visions, Katherine? Really?

Every doubtful voice in her mind sounded like Dr. Edward Bassi.

Why does it matter now? What does it matter? You're trying to please ghosts.

"I don't know what's goin' on in your mind" —Megan's voice broke into her thoughts— "but try giving yourself a break, hon."

"Excuse me?"

"You're scowling at the dashboard like it slapped your mama." Megan raised an eyebrow. "You knew she was gonna be a hard sell. You're giving yourself a hard time because you half believe she's right."

"I know she isn't," Katherine said. "That's what's so frustrating."

"But if you hadn't had that vision," Megan said, "and I told you that boy's gun jumped into my hand, you'd be thinking I was a head case, wouldn't you?"

"Probably."

Megan shrugged. "Of all the weird things that happened to us, hers is the most normal-like. She's bound to be skeptical."

"You were way more judgmental than me about Toni. Why are you so relaxed about her now?"

"See, here's a difference between you and me." Megan smiled as she turned off State Street and headed for the ocean. "You're a supersmart college professor who's always been the smartest gal in the room. You're used to people listening to you and thinking, 'Man, that lady knows what she's talking about.' Me, on the other hand" —she shot a look at Katherine from the corner of her eye— "I'm used to people underestimating me. Comes with being blond and blue-eyed. Men trip over themselves to hold the door for me, but most of 'em think I'm dumb as rocks."

"I think you're very perceptive."

"Thanks. I am. Part of what made me so good at sales. I know what people want too."

"You're ahead of me on that," Katherine said. "I usually have no idea."

"Toni Dusi, she's hard as nails. She's probably had to be. She works in a boy's club. Did you see a single other woman in that place? Nope. And she works for her daddy, so she's got all that family stuff to deal with too."

Katherine could relate to the former problem, but the latter only existed in her nightmares. "Dusi Brothers. Maybe her father and her uncle?"

"And she's running the place now, which means she's like three times as good as any of her brothers or cousins."

"What does that have to do with—"

"You think she wants to talk about her emotions?" Megan shook her head. "Not in a million years. You telling her she's a supernatural feelings wizard is probably her worst kind of nightmare."

Katherine just decided to sit with the phrase "supernatural feelings wizard" in her head for a few moments.

"Wouldn't it be witch?" she asked. "A supernatural feelings witch?"

"No, in fact." Megan pulled into the near-empty parking lot of Beach Street Café. "I've been doing some research and — Where's your car?"

"I walked here." Katherine gathered her purse and unbuckled her seat belt.

"Oh, that's right. I keep forgetting you're a walker. You want me to drive you home? I can tell you're sore."

Katherine *was* sore. She was also wary of letting Megan know where she lived. Why?

"You don't think I'm going to stalk you, do you? I already told you all about me. I don't have anything to hide."

It wasn't fear—it was instinctive privacy and habit.

You're a forty-seven-year-old woman with no friends, Katherine.

She took a deep breath and turned to Megan. "Would you like to come over to my house and have a glass of wine on the deck?"

Megan's eyes lit up. "I'd love to!"

"Excellent." She rebuckled her seat belt. "Just go north on Beach Street for a few blocks. I'll point out the house."

"Holy shit, you actually live right on the beach, don't you?"

"The boardwalk runs right in front our house, and the back deck overlooks the ocean."

"I am so insanely jealous right now." She turned left and headed up North Beach Avenue.

"Why wouldn't you call Toni a witch?" Katherine said. "Isn't that how it works? Men are wizards and women are witches?"

Megan smiled. "I thought you didn't think it was magic."

"That doesn't mean I don't read fantasy. I've been a card-carrying nerd for forty years, Megan. Of *course* I read fantasy."

She laughed. "Well, I've been doing a lot of research online and witches—male and female—are practitioners of Wicca, which is a form of modern paganism. Wizards are just kind of general magic users."

"So do you think we're wizards?" Katherine was definitely not putting that on her business card.

The corner of Megan's mouth turned up. "I know you think it's all part of science we just can't explain yet, but I think something else might be at work, Doc. All three of us experienced something extraordinary at the same time. Three is a tricky number, you know. It means something."

"Mathematically elegant," Katherine murmured, watching the cottages and bungalows of her neighbors creep by.

"What's that?"

"Three." She turned to Megan. "Three is a very mathematically elegant number."

"I'll go ahead and take your word on that."

"Here." Katherine pointed to the redwood-shingled bungalow tucked between two Monterey cypress trees.

"Oh!" Katherine's mouth formed a nearly perfect O. "It's perfect."

"Well, my husband and our handyman would argue that point, but we love it." It felt nice that Megan—who obviously had a great sense of style—liked her house. "It's not big."

"It doesn't need to be." Megan opened her car door. "Look at that view!" She swiveled to the pebbled stretch of North Beach extending in front of them. "See, when I imagined living in California, this was what I pictured. Not some weird modern Mediterranean mansion in the hills with rooms we'll never use. What is a bonus room anyway? Right now it's just where we keep the boxes we haven't unpacked."

Katherine got out and shut her door. "I'm guessing your husband picked out your house."

"I didn't even see it before we moved." She frowned a little, still staring at the ocean. "It's fine. It's very large and luxurious. But it doesn't have any personality. Our house in Atlanta had character." She turned to Katherine's house. "This has loads of charm. Ours is just kind of... blah."

Katherine nodded to the stairs that led up to the broad front deck. "Come on in and let's get some wine. You can tell me all about it."

"Wine and ocean views? That's what I call magic."

CHAPTER 9

*K*atherine made her way to the Fred lab the following Monday. Physically, she felt much better than the week before, but mentally, she might have gotten worse. She'd experienced three more "microvisions" over the weekend. Two of them were mundane, but the third was a car accident she saw happen on the highway just seconds before a small sedan flipped on its side after being sideswiped by a pickup truck.

It was a stark reminder that while she might have been feeling better, life was still very much out of her control.

She walked across the campus, conscious of every student who sped past on a skateboard or bike. She saw a young man jogging in a university sweatshirt and felt an immediate increase in her heart rate.

By the time she reached the lab, she was a bundle of nerves.

"Professor B!" Kaylee looked up from behind her laptop with a giant smile. The young woman was in her midtwenties, but she still looked barely out of high school.

Appreciate it while you can.

Katherine had dealt with the frustration of a young face until her thirties. Then she seemed to go from "Are you a student here?" to "You look tired, Professor B" almost immediately. She knew she shouldn't complain about aging, but she wished she'd had a slightly longer time to enjoy looking old enough to drink legally before she had to deal with wrinkles.

"How are things, Kaylee?"

The young woman jumped up and walked around the desk. "Can I help you with anything? You look like you're limping a little."

Katherine rubbed her knee. "I have one leg that's still a little sore, but I'm so much better than I was last week. The walk felt good."

"If you're sure."

"I am." A thought tickled the back of her mind. "Kaylee, remember the girl you were talking about? The one who had the strange incident with the horse before Justin McCabe?"

"Yes." Caution filled Kaylee's eyes.

"I was wondering if you might have her phone number or know where I could get it."

"I absolutely do not." Kaylee shook her head. "I'm not even sure if I had her name right."

Katherine narrowed her eyes. Kaylee was acting strange, and she was pretty obviously lying. She'd freely offered the name of the student the previous week—it was Sarah Jordan—and she'd spoken openly about the rodeo incident, which had been written up in the student paper six months before. Katherine had been able to find the article with a quick internet search.

What was going on now?

"Okay. I was just wondering if I'd had her as a student. The name sounds familiar." The name didn't sound familiar, but Katherine couldn't figure out why Kaylee was suddenly so cagey. "I'll ask around. I was wondering if she and Justin McCabe might have had a connection."

"Did you have Justin McCabe as a student?"

"I did." Katherine hardly thought Kaylee was a gossip. She was mainly interested in human neurons. "I had Mr. McCabe in an Elements of Cosmology class." It was the most common general-education class she taught. "But he wasn't in my department."

"He was an ag business major."

"Correct."

Kaylee bit her lip and frowned. "You should ask Professor Shaver about Justin. I think he might have known him."

"You think I should ask Ansel about Justin McCabe?" Ansel Shaver was a psychologist with a specialty in cognitive science who was assisting in the Fred lab, primarily on the sensor readings for their cephalopod test subjects.

He didn't particularly like working with the animals, and the animals knew it. They regularly squirted him with water.

"Yeah." Kaylee's face told Katherine that something else was going on. Something significant. "But you don't need to tell him I told you that, okay?" Kaylee's eyes were trying to send Katherine a message she was woefully obtuse on.

"Okay. I'll ask. And I'll leave you out of it completely."

Kaylee let out a breath and smiled. "Awesome."

Katherine didn't care for Ansel Shaver much more than the four octopi did. Maybe it was her own experiences with psychologists when she was younger, but something about the man seemed cold. Her own counselor had been a warm and practical woman who guided Katherine through understanding her social anxiety. Ansel didn't have warmth.

How would he have known an agricultural business student? Why would he ever come in contact with him unless—?

Oh.

Ohhhhh. No wonder Kaylee wanted her name left out of it.

The only reason Katherine could think of for Professor Ansel Shaver to have interacted with Justin McCabe was because of his student study the year before. It was entirely confidential, but Katherine had been generally aware of a large study Ansel had directed the previous academic year. He'd teamed up with four other behavioral sciences professors to administer it if she remembered correctly. If Justin McCabe had been a participant in the study, Ansel might know him. Or he might have been one of a hundred numbers in a computer. It really depended on the study.

Which led to so many other questions.

What was the study about?

Could something involved in it have been the catalyst for Justin McCabe's attempted violence?

Unfortunately for her insatiable curiosity, there was no way for Katherine to access the information. The university was a vault when it came to the privacy of students who participated in clinical research.

Of course, this *was* Central Coast State. Officially, the participants wouldn't even use their names. Unofficially... it was a pretty small school. Inevitably, some students would know the professors or graduate students involved.

Katherine wandered back to her closet of an office at the Fred lab and looked at the stack of papers on her desk. They could all wait. Everyone could wait. She felt a sense of urgency come over her. Instinct? Magic? Something else entirely?

Something about Kaylee's urgency prodded her to find out more.

If Justin McCabe had been part of that study, what had been the objective?

Ansel Shaver was a psychologist. Had there been a pharmaceutical component? Central Coast didn't have a med school. Who else would have been involved?

Could something about a psychological experiment conducted the year before have had an effect on his behavior months later?

At least the pharmaceutical question could be easily answered. She looked through her bag, found the detective's business card, and picked up the phone to call the Moonstone Cove Police Department.

"Hello?"

"Hello, this is Professor Katherine Bassi at Central Coast State. I'd like to speak to Detective Drew Bisset."

"Let me see if he's available. I'm going to put you on hold a minute."

"That's fine." She waited on the line a few minutes before the phone clicked and Detective Bisset's voice came over the line.

"Professor Bassi," he said. "This is Drew Bisset. How can I help you? How are you feeling?"

"I'm feeling pretty well. That's kind of you to ask. A little sore, but no permanent damage."

"That's good news."

"I had a question about Justin McCabe."

"I'm not sure how much I can answer, but okay."

"Did he have any drugs in his system when he committed the crime?" Katherine asked. "I'm specifically thinking about prescribed medications, not illegal drugs. I promise I am asking for a nonfrivolous reason."

"Be that as it may," Detective Bisset said, "I can't tell you that."

"I'm asking because it's possible that Mr. McCabe—"

"Ma'am, I really can't tell you anything about the case."

She tried not to mutter the words she was thinking. Katherine had a voracious appetite for knowledge. Learning she didn't know something was not a surprise. Being told she wasn't *allowed* to know something was an entirely different level of frustration. Her bullheaded side had been roused.

"Can I have his family's contact information?"

"No."

"How about his lawyer's name?"

"Absolutely not. It's not a good idea for you to be asking anything about—"

"What about the name Sarah Jordan?" she asked. "Do you know anything about—?"

"Did you say Sarah Jordan?" Detective Bisset's voice had a sharp edge.

"Yes. She was another student at Central Coast, and five months ago she killed her horse. No warning. Everyone was shocked by the act. They said it was very out of character, just like they're saying about Justin McCabe and—"

"Professor Bassi." Detective Bisset cut her off. "I need to go."

Katherine felt a bit deflated but mostly annoyed. She wasn't accustomed to being dismissed so quickly. "Obviously I'm not a police detective, but if you could just tell me if the police conducted any investigation into—"

"I really do need to go." His voice was brusque. "I'm very glad you're feeling better after your ordeal, and if there's any information I need from the university, I'll be sure to let you know. Thank you so much for your offer of help."

Had she offered to help? The detective hung up the phone before she could ask.

"Irritating man." She set her phone down on her desk and glanced at the calendar blotter that was more doodles than appointments.

Let's meet this same time next week.

The week before, Katherine and Megan had poured two glasses of local pinot noir into aluminum travel mugs and walked along the beach for over an hour. Megan chattered about her house, her three children, and when they were well away from any onlookers, she tried moving some rocks on the shore with little success. They shifted a bit, but nothing as dramatic and powerful as the gun.

After that lovely afternoon, Megan had nailed Katherine down to meeting regularly for a glass of wine on Wednesdays. Now it was two days away and Katherine was looking forward to it.

She smiled as she jotted down a note for Wednesday afternoon on the calendar.

Drinks with Megan.

She could tell Megan about Sarah and Justin and her suspicions about the study and see what the other woman thought. Her mind was nimble, and she had a keen understanding of human nature; she might make connections that Katherine didn't see.

She glanced at the schedule for the week and noted that Ansel Shaver would be in by two o'clock that afternoon to take routine sensor readings for their four cephalopod test subjects.

Excellent. She could talk to him then.

———

SHE WALKED to the student center at one o'clock that afternoon to find something to eat. She settled on a chicken salad, the blandest of all midweek lunches but better than the dry-looking sandwiches.

She picked up the salad and stared at the clear plastic shell.

"We have a culinary school at this university." A voice sounded beside her.

She looked up. The young man speaking to her looked familiar, but she couldn't remember his name. "I know. We have an entire food science program too. It's baffling that we can't get better options."

The man also took a boring chicken salad. "At least the dressing is okay."

"I'd still be willing to be a test subject for the culinary school," Katherine said. "As long as flavor was part of the study."

"Agreed." He put the chicken salad on his plastic tray and held out his hand. "You forgot my name, didn't you? It's Greg Hammond."

"Yes!" He, like Kaylee, was another of Ansel Shaver's

grad students, but not one she usually saw at the Fred lab. "I knew you looked familiar, but I'm horrible with names."

"If I had to see as many students as you do every day, I doubt I'd remember anyone."

She waved a hand. "I don't do well with my lecture classes, but there's no excuse for not remembering someone who works so closely with Professor Shaver. I knew I'd seen you at the Fred lab. Is Professor Shaver your thesis advisor?"

"Yes. I fill in over at Fred occasionally, but I work at the behavioral science lab mainly. Though I'm also consulting with Alice Kraft in computer sciences on some things since my thesis has a tech focus, so I hang out over there too."

"You're a busy young man. Psychology and technology?"

"I want to focus on how data from wearable devices could potentially transform how mental health professionals evaluate patients."

"That's very interesting."

"Yeah. I mean..." He shrugged. "Everyone lies, right? But our bodies don't."

"That's definitely one perspective." A cynical one. "Good luck with that."

"Thanks. I'll probably... see you around the Fred lab."

"I'm sure you will." She knew Ansel depended heavily on his grad students.

In fact...

If Ansel was running a clinical study, Greg could very well have been the one inputting names into the computer, especially if he was active at the behavioral science lab.

She couldn't ask.

Could she?

Not directly, but...

Greg smiled and lifted a hand in a wave as he walked away. "Have a good day, Professor Bassi."

"You too." Should she? It was worth a try. "Greg?"

"Yes?" He turned back toward her.

"I was wondering if you'd heard about Justin McCabe."

His eyes flickered for just a second; then the young man's face settled into a careful mask. "I think everyone's heard about him."

"Did you know that I was actually at the gym that day?"

His eyes went wide. "I hadn't heard that part."

You're lying. Why would he lie? To avoid the appearance of listening to gossip? That was a definite possibility.

"Yes, it was a strange experience."

Whatever Greg had been thinking, the blank expression fled, and warmth filled his face. "I'm so glad you and everyone involved are okay."

"Me too." Greg had recognized the name, and she didn't think it was because of what happened at the gym. "But you didn't know him personally?"

"Who?"

You know who. "The young man who had the gun. Justin McCabe."

"Not at all." He held his tray in front of him. "I really need to get going, but I'm glad you're okay, Professor Bassi."

"Thank you."

Greg hurried toward the register without looking back.

Interesting.

By the time she got back to the Fred lab, Katherine's knee was aching, but she was looking forward to eating lunch at the front desk and listening to Kaylee and Denise, Maria Gatan's grad student, chatter about their lives.

She sometimes wondered if she'd been wrong to skip the experience of motherhood. She enjoyed mentoring her students and had a keen appreciation for young people.

That said, she'd only really started enjoying her nieces and nephews when they got into double digits. That left a lot of diapers, drool, and unintelligible screaming to deal with until offspring became interesting.

Yes, better she'd skipped all that.

"Hey, Professor Bassi." Denise and Kaylee both waved. "Did you have a meeting planned or something?"

She frowned. "Not that I know of. Did I forget something?"

"Oh." Kaylee and Denise exchanged a look. "I hope we didn't mess up."

"What did you do?" All Katherine wanted to do was sit down. It was over a half-mile walk round trip to the student center for lunch; her knee was starting to swell.

"There was a lady here—"

"She said she was a friend," Denise said. "So we told her she could wait in your office."

Would Megan have stopped by the lab? That seemed improbable. "Was she tall and very blond?"

"No. Short with dark curly hair."

Short with dark curly...?

Really?

"Huh." Her mind flashed into a grey-tinged vision that appeared and disappeared just as quickly. Toni Dusi was sitting in the chair across her desk, cursing at the soda she'd just spilled on her pants. "Okay, thanks."

Why did so many of her visions have to do with someone spilling a liquid? Was it that common?

The two young women were staring at Katherine with wide eyes.

"Did we mess up?" Kaylee asked. "I'm sorry. We should have called you."

"Yes. Call me next time. But you're fine. She is a friend of mine." She was just throwing that word around willy-nilly, wasn't she? "Please don't worry."

Kaylee and Denise's expressions both relaxed.

Katherine walked back toward her office—apparently she wouldn't be enjoying her eavesdropping today—and spotted a pair of legs in worn blue jeans parked across from her desk. Toni was muttering and wiping at her pants. "Stupid over-inflated—"

"Spill something?" Katherine walked into her office and immediately handed Toni a wad of tissues. "Looks like it went everywhere."

"Yeah." Toni set her lunch on the edge of Katherine's desk—it looked far more appetizing than Katherine's salad—while she cleaned up the soda spill. "I've been thinking about you and your friend."

"It's nice to see you too." Katherine should have been more friendly, but she was irrationally angry at her boring chicken salad after seeing the delicious-looking sub Toni was about to eat, and she didn't know why the woman was there after she'd dismissed them so quickly the week before. "Why were you thinking about me and Megan?"

Toni used her foot to kick the door closed as soon as Katherine got behind her desk. "You mean other than the obvious?"

"That we're all three experiencing parapsychological phenomena in conjunction with a near-death experience?"

Toni stared at her.

"We're all doing psychic stuff."

Toni wrinkled her nose. "Yeah. That."

"So you're admitting that you're experiencing things out of the normal range for you?"

Toni wadded the tissues up in her fist, braced an elbow on the arm of her chair, and leaned forward. "Tell me, Professor, do I seem like a crier to you?"

CHAPTER 10

"*N*o." Why did Katherine feel like she was being led into a trap? "You do not seem like a crier to me. Then again, biologically, *everyone* is a crier unless you have keratoconjunctivitis sicca, in which case you should be seeing a doctor."

Toni cocked her head. "You're a blast at parties, right?"

"I am, actually. I kill at trivia nights too."

That made Toni smile. "I can cry, and lately I've been crying a lot. Like a *lot,* Doc."

"I'd really prefer it if you call me Katherine."

"Fine, Katherine, not Kat or Katie, I've been crying way more than normal, and it's actually starting to become a problem." She reached for her sandwich. "Do you think I want to get pissed off while I'm tuning an engine and burst into tears? By the way, I'm going to eat because I only have so much time I can be away from the garage and traffic around this place is absolutely packed around lunchtime."

"Yes, I avoid driving anywhere near the college in the middle of the day."

"Seriously."

Toni claimed the corner of Katherine's desk and took a knife from her pocket to cut her sandwich in half. "Now, don't get me wrong. I come from a big-ass, emotional Italian family. Overreaction is not foreign to me. But the first time I got that super-overwhelmed feeling where I felt like I needed to cry or I would literally burst out of my skin—"

"You mean other than the extreme empathy during the incident at the gym?"

Toni paused and lifted her eyes to Katherine. "I don't know what that was. I don't know how I did it. I felt... wrong the minute I saw that guy."

"Something about him triggered your instincts."

She kept cutting her sandwich. "I have good instincts about people—it's hard to describe, but that's part of the reason my dad put me in charge of hiring guys for the garage when I was like twenty. I just had feelings about people, and I was a good judge of character. But when I walked past that kid the first time, my skin was literally crawling."

"Do you think you were sensing his feelings? The root of empathic power is understanding the feelings of other people."

"Maybe?" She frowned. "If I was sensing his feelings, then it was even weirder. Because I got nothing from him."

"Explain that. What do you remember?"

Toni paused cutting her food. "He was like... a void. A feelings black hole."

Even the idea of it caused her to shiver. "But you were watching him. Keeping close to him."

"I remember feeling drawn to him, which is weird when

you think about it because he gave me the creeps. But I couldn't not pay attention to him."

"Had you ever felt anything like that from a person before?"

"That emptiness?" She shook her head. "No. Nothing like it. And then I saw you tackle him, saw Megan holding that gun—I didn't even see him with the gun, I just saw it in her hand—I was so confused. At first I thought she was a cop or something. But then you were on the ground and that guy looked like he was about to murder you, and I just reacted."

"He knocked me off and you jumped on him."

"It wouldn't be the first time I took on someone way bigger than me because I'm an idiot." She pursed her lips. "I tackled him and pushed his shoulders down. Just sat on his chest. And the only thing I could think was this asshole needed to chill out. Whatever was happening, he needed to chill out." Toni looked away from Katherine, focusing on a spot over her shoulder. "I don't remember much else, just that massive adrenaline rush, that sensation where everything slows down a little, you know? And that feeling was so big inside me. He *had* to calm down. He had to, or people were going to die."

"And he did."

Toni nodded.

"Do you remember being surprised? Or feeling anything from him?"

"Not really. I remember thinking, 'That's right, asshole, you *better* stay down.' But that was probably supreme over-confidence. He could have flicked me off like a piece of lint. I have a big ass, but he was a bigger dude."

Katherine narrowed her eyes. "Do you remember touching his skin?"

Toni blinked. "Um... yes. My hand was kind of right where his neck and shoulder meet, and I remember because he was sweaty and superhot. Like way hotter than you would expect. The man felt like a furnace."

Katherine made a mental note to look up which drugs could cause a fever like that.

"I mean, I think he was definitely on something, right?" Toni sat back and took a bite of her sandwich. "There had to be some drugs happening there?"

"It's a possibility. I'm trying to find out more from the police, but they don't want to answer any of my questions."

"Hmm." She licked something off her thumb. "I can ask my cousin. He'll tell me."

"I don't think they're supposed to talk about ongoing investigations."

Toni looked at her like she was a gullible child. "Of course they're not *supposed* to. But he's my cousin. I'll find out if that guy was on anything."

"Okay." She wasn't going to argue. Katherine unboxed her salad and poured the thin dressing over it.

Toni paused with her sandwich halfway to her mouth. "Is that your lunch?"

"Unfortunately. There aren't many options at the student center, and I didn't have time to go to an actual restaurant." Her disappointment must have been clear on her face.

"That looks like a gas station salad."

Katherine looked at Toni's sandwich. "You didn't get that from a gas station."

"Would you believe my mom still makes my lunch for

me?" Toni smiled a little. "Not every day. But my dad still comes into the garage a few days a week to walk around and point at stuff. He's in his seventies, but it makes him happy. On days he comes in, my mom makes us both a lunch."

Katherine felt warm from the inside out. "That's lovely."

Toni's half smile turned into a full smile. "It is, isn't it? When I was younger, I was a little shit about it. 'Mom, you think I can't feed myself or what?' Now I'm just glad I still have both of them, you know? And my mom is a hell of a cook, so I can't complain." She reached across the desk and handed the other half a sandwich to Katherine. "Take this half. I eat all this and I'm going to be napping under a tree."

"Are you sure?"

"Yep." Toni leaned back, sandwich in hand. "You do that a lot."

"Do what?"

"Check with people. Check their reactions."

Katherine took a bite of the sandwich so she could think. "This is so good. Thank you. And yes, I do check people's reactions. I'm very good with numbers and theories, and I know how to interact with colleagues and students. But I think sometimes I come across as patronizing to other people when I don't mean to be."

"I don't see you that way. You're just smarter than about ninety-nine percent of the population, right?"

Katherine nodded. "That would be fairly accurate. I also went to college very early, so normal socialization was stunted. Most of the girls in my college classes didn't want to spend time with a fifteen-year-old, and I can't really blame them."

"Fifteen? That's brutal."

Katherine shrugged. "I didn't get along with anyone in my high school either. At least they mostly left me alone in college." High school? Not as much.

"I guess," Toni said. "Megan has you figured out. She doesn't think you're patronizing."

Katherine felt an immediate warmth. "I don't know why the two of you didn't get along, but she's very nice. She's an honest person. I appreciate that."

"She has, like, zero filter."

"Yes. I find it to be a huge relief."

"You can't just say everything that comes to your mind." Toni bit into her sandwich.

Katherine frowned and examined Toni's assertion more closely. "But you can. You might offend people, but you *can* actually say everything that comes to mind."

Toni shook her head. "Not if you want to remain living in my family."

"Good to know." Katherine made a mental note to avoid Toni's family. The thought made her stomach sad, because the sandwich was really delicious. "Megan has an excellent mind and she sees things in interesting ways. I like her perspective, and she's decided that she and I are going to be friends. We're having wine on Wednesday."

"Wine Wednesday? Is this like Taco Tuesday?"

"Maybe? It happens on my deck and we just started, so I don't really know all the rules. Just that there's wine on Wednesday and we're having it at my house because I have a great deck and an ocean view."

Toni's eyes lit up. "Hot damn. I should have been a professor."

"I very much doubt you make less than I do." Katherine

smiled. "We bought our place in North Beach about fifteen years ago."

"Oh, that's sweet. You got lucky to get in there before everything went crazy."

"Yes. Megan enjoyed the view. I think she lives in one of those new developments they built up the hill."

Toni made a face. "Careful—you have her over for too much Wednesday wine, you might not be able to get rid of her."

It bothered Katherine that Toni had such a negative reaction to Megan. She didn't understand the root of it, but she would find out.

"You probably have lots of friends," Katherine said. "You grew up here. You have a big family. Megan and I don't."

"Her? She's like Suzy Sunshine and Malibu Barbie rolled into one. The chicks who drive their Mercedes SUVs into my garage probably fell all over her when she moved here."

Katherine enjoyed the way that Toni painted mental pictures. It made understanding her intentions much easier. "You might think that, but I don't think it's true. She said she finds people here very cold. I think she's had a hard time making friends."

"Huh." Toni's eyebrows rose. "Well, maybe I'll join you for Wine Wednesday then."

"So you're admitting that the three of us are all exhibiting parapsychological phenomena and we have something in common?"

"Parapsychological—?"

"Psychic stuff." Better to stick with layman's terms. "We're all doing psychic stuff now."

"Yes. Fine." She rolled her eyes again. "Whatever. We're

doing psychic stuff and I don't understand it, but I'd like to figure out what to do with it. Can I come on Wednesday or what?"

Katherine smiled. "Of course."

KATHERINE DIDN'T WARN Megan that Toni was coming, so two days later when the silver-grey vintage Mustang convertible parked in front of Katherine's house on North Beach Drive, Megan's eyes went wide.

Toni stepped out of the car, holding a bottle of wine and wearing a grim expression, dark blue jeans, and a mustard-yellow T-shirt with SHIFT HAPPENS written on the front.

Megan stood and pointed at her. "I knew it!" She set down her wineglass. "I knew you knew it wasn't just in our heads!"

Toni looked around and waved her hand in a "sit down" motion. "Just chill, okay? I went in to see the professor—see *Katherine*—yesterday." She glared at Katherine. "I thought she was going to tell you."

Katherine sipped her wine. "Oh no, I was far too interested in observing this interaction."

Megan was all smiles, her previous irritation with Toni seeming to melt away at the woman's willing appearance on Katherine's deck. "See? Three of us now. There's something special about three."

"Don't get excited, Atlanta." Toni set down the bottle of red. "This is from my cousin's winery, but I didn't just bring it because I got it for free. It's actually good."

"Your cousin has a winery?" Megan's eyes lit up. "That's so cool."

"If you can think of a job on the Central Coast, from winemaker to electrician to marine biologist, I can almost promise I have a cousin doing it."

"Big family?"

"I have forty-two first cousins," Toni said. "And almost all of them have reproduced, so you can imagine."

"How about you?" Katherine said. "You don't have children?"

Toni shrugged. "I never found the right guy. Just didn't happen."

Megan said, "You don't need a man to be a mama. Not these days."

"Uh, you do in my family." Toni shook her head. "I would shrivel up and die from the lecture my mother would give me if I got pregnant without being married."

"Fair enough," Katherine said. "So now that we're all speaking to each other, what do we think happened two weeks ago? And what do you think we should do about all this... psychic stuff?"

"I don't have an answer for the first question," Megan said. "But check this out." She reached out her hand and her wineglass scooted an inch to the left. "I've been reading all this stuff about energy and channeling and—"

"Oh yeah." Toni reached into her pocket and brought out a corkscrew. "I'm definitely going to need alcohol for this conversation."

CHAPTER 11

"So the thing with Justin McCabe might not be isolated?" Megan asked. "How are you going to find out if this boy was in this study you're talking about?"

"I haven't figured that part out yet," Katherine said. "There's no way to do it that I can think of. Not legally anyway. I don't even know if they'd tell the police if they asked."

"I can't lie," Toni said. "What happened at the gym was awful and if that kid had something done to him, that's not right. But I'm more worried about my sudden, massive mood swings because I do not want to live with this the rest of my life. Tell me more about these women in Glimmer Lake."

"They were like us," Katherine said. "Three ordinary people who nearly died and something about that triggered psychic powers."

"But their powers are different than ours?" Megan asked.

"There are some similarities. Monica contacted me initially because she has visions and wanted to understand more about timelines from a scientific perspective. I couldn't really help her much. And her visions are completely different than mine."

"How long ago was it?" Toni said. "How long did they last?"

"Uh..." Katherine twisted the stem of her wineglass. "They had the accident over three years ago."

Toni's eyes went wide. "And they still have powers?"

"I'm afraid... Yes. They still have powers. This could be permanent."

Toni's face went pale. "Fuck."

"I thought wrinkles were going to be the biggest adjustment to middle age," Megan quipped. "At least I don't see ghosts." She visibly shuddered. "I would not be able to handle that."

"I second that shit," Toni said. "Feeling other people's emotions is bad enough." She leaned her elbows on the table. "There has to be a way to get rid of this."

Katherine decided it was time to pour another round of wine. The sun had started to creep below the horizon, but the fog hadn't come in, meaning the ocean and sky were layered in deep and vibrant blue, purple, and pink.

"The human mind is remarkably flexible," she said. "Even well into our later years. It can learn all sorts of new skills if it has to. Think about older people who have strokes and learn how to do complex tasks like speaking again. A sudden development of mental ability brought on by prospective trauma is hardly out of the scope of the possible."

"Just putting this out there," Toni said. "But I'm barely forty-one. I hardly think I qualify for a midlife crisis yet. All my grandmas are still living in their nineties. I'm not even halfway there."

Megan gave her a smile and clinked the edge of her wine-glass to Toni's. "Give your joints and chin hair three years and get back to us." She looked to Katherine. "So the girls up in the mountains are a medium, a seer, and a telekinetic?" She frowned. "Or maybe a psychometric. I need to look that up." She grabbed her phone and unlocked it.

"Seers? Psychometrics?" Toni shook her head. "Are we for real right now? This is like movie stuff. Book stuff. Not real life."

Megan looked up. "You mean you have psychic powers and you're still a skeptic?"

"I'd consider myself as skeptical as they come," Katherine said. "But I had no way of knowing that man would pull out a gun. I just saw it. If you have any reason to think I might have discovered his plot another way, I'd love to hear it."

Megan was still scrolling through her phone, worrying her lower lip red from her teeth.

Toni continued, "I'm just saying that sometimes we pick up on stuff that we don't even realize if we're observant. Call them vibes if you want, but they're normal human instincts, not magic. Maybe that's what you felt and your mind just made a leap."

Megan was still looking at her phone, but she piped up. "Doesn't explain how I could move stuff with my mind."

"Toni, for future reference," Katherine said, "you should know that I very often do *not* pick up on social cues at all. Even when they're very obvious. It took me four months to figure out my husband was trying to ask me out when I first met him."

Toni blinked. "Wow."

"Yeah. I can be very clueless. So the idea that I just

inferred this man's intentions from minute body language clues is wildly off base. Maybe it wouldn't be for someone else, but for me? Completely improbable."

Megan looked up from her phone. "What did you think he was doing?"

"Justin McCabe?

"No, your husband. You said it was four months before you realized he was asking you out."

"Oh that." Katherine took a long drink of wine. "I just thought he was being nice and offering to get food for me. I didn't realize he wanted me to go with him to the restaurants."

Toni smiled. "So did he?"

"What?"

"Get food for you?"

"He did!" Katherine laughed. "Wonderful man. For four full months he'd bring the most delicious takeout back to my office. I had no idea."

"What finally tipped you off?" Megan looked delighted.

"My officemate told me that I was ignoring that sexy math professor from London and if I wasn't interested in him, I should let Baxter know so she could ask him out."

Toni asked, "And he never said anything?"

"Oh no. Neither of us is very outspoken. We probably would have gone on like that for a year or more if that girl hadn't lost patience with me."

Megan and Toni both laughed, but Katherine could tell it was from amusement and not meanness.

"I think it would be great if we invited them here," Megan said. "Your three friends from Glimmer Lake, I mean.

We could probably learn a lot from them even though our powers aren't exactly the same."

Toni shrugged. "Maybe you and the telekinetic have something in common. And Katherine and this other lady who sees the future obviously could learn from each other. But empathy? Influencing someone with my emotions?" She shook her head. "I just don't see how any of them could teach me anything useful."

"If nothing else, those three women seem to have figured out a few mysteries in their own community," Katherine said. "And I'd dearly like to figure out why Justin McCabe tried to kill strangers at the gym." She turned to Toni. "Did your cousin tell you anything about Justin's toxicology report?"

"They did a regular drug panel when they arrested him," Toni said. "But my cousin said they didn't find anything except what his doctor had prescribed for him. And they thought they definitely would the way they took him into custody."

"How do you mean?" Megan asked.

"He was just kind of out of it," Toni said. "Like... drained. He didn't put up any fight. He seemed really confused. At least according to my cousin."

"So strange."

"Ordinary medications can still be dangerous if they're taken improperly," Katherine murmured. "Do you know what his prescription medication was?"

"Some kind of antianxiety medication, but I think it's the same one my mom takes," Toni said. "It's super-mild."

Megan turned to Toni. "How did you manage to get your mother on medication? My mother won't even talk about it."

"It was a knock-down, drag-out fight with her and my

older sister, but she finally gave in. She's a lot happier now and she doesn't freak out about flying."

"Good to know." Megan was concentrating on a wooden coaster on the table; her fingers were reaching for it. "I feel something," she said. "But it's like I don't know what kind of muscle to stretch."

Katherine couldn't even imagine *trying* to bring on a vision. Then again, telekinesis would be far handier in day-to-day life if you could control it. "What do you remember about what happened in the gym?"

"Me?" Megan looked up. "Not much. It all happened so fast."

"Same with me," Toni said. "I know you think I influenced this kid somehow, but I don't know how I did it. Is it really a psychic skill if I can't control it? Maybe it was a fluke. Maybe fate knew we just needed that one burst of psychicness to prevent this kid from killing people."

"That's possible," Megan said. "Like those mamas who manage to lift a car off their kid and stuff like that. It's not permanent."

"So why do I keep having visions?" Katherine asked. "Why is Toni crying at inconvenient times? Why can you make that coaster move—look, you're doing it right now when you're not paying attention."

The coaster had scooted halfway across the table while they weren't looking at it.

"Holy cow, look at that!" Megan was delighted.

Toni's eyes were glued to the coaster. "Okay, I agree, that's kind of magic-like."

"Kind of?"

"I think that's why we need to call the women from

Glimmer Lake," Katherine said. "If anyone knows what we're going through right now, it would be them."

"Fine." Toni took a long drink of wine. "But there is something weird going on. So far, we have two totally normal students who all of a sudden committed—or tried to commit —violent crimes. With no cause or reason anyone can find."

"There could be a connection," Megan said. "Could this girl Sarah and our guy at the gym have been in the same clinical study at the school?"

"That's a thought." Another one she couldn't confirm. Not legally. "It's possible. Her... incident happened after the study concluded, from what I heard."

Megan lowered her voice. "Do you think the professor running it—"

"Professors. Plural. There were four attached to this study; my colleague was the point person."

"Could he have done something to those kids on purpose? To their brains?"

Toni stared at Megan. "Kind of conspiracy theory, don't you think?"

"Do you have a better explanation?"

Katherine quickly jumped in. "Ansel Shaver is not the friendliest, but I hardly think he and his partners would be experimenting on student brains."

"Too ethical?" Megan asked.

"Too impossible." Katherine corrected her. "There are layers of protections built into maintaining student safety and confidentiality in university studies. Manipulating that system would get him nothing except a ruined career. He would never publish again. No one would be willing to work with him."

"Maybe he had another motive," Megan said. "Something not about university stuff."

"I want to point out," Katherine said, "that two is still a very small number. I don't know that it shows any kind of trend."

Megan and Toni stared at her with blank expressions.

"But..." She relented. "I'm also not a fan of coincidence."

Toni raised an eyebrow. "What about the government? Does this professor have anything to do with the military?"

Megan scoffed. "And you were accusing *me* of conspiracy theories."

"Unfortunately, considering the history of human study trials, it's a fair question," Katherine said. "But as far as I know, Ansel has no history of working on government studies. Funding from the government? Yes. But working directly with them? No."

Toni said, "And if the military were involved, they'd probably use soldiers for test subjects, not students."

Megan was staring at Toni, blinking with wide eyes. "They wouldn't."

"They have," Katherine said. "Frequently."

"So this study that these two kids were *maybe* involved in," Toni said, "do we know what the outcome was? Can we find out? Have they... I don't know, published anything yet?"

"No, it's way too soon for that. There would be follow-up..." Katherine pursed her lips and thought about just how many lines she wanted to cross. "For now, let me try to contact Sarah Jordan. Let me see what she's willing to share."

"And I'm going to spend some time at the library," Megan said. "Put my currently unemployed status to good use. I can look through papers and search the websites and message boards. So far, we know of two kids who had strange break-downs that led to violence." She shrugged. "Maybe there were more than two."

KATHERINE WAITED until she was on a break the next day to look up Sarah Jordan's emergency information at school. The system listed a number in Watsonville, California, along with an address, both of which Katherine wrote down. She also learned that officially, Sarah had taken a medical leave of absence but was still listed as enrolled with the university. As far as semipublic knowledge went, that was all she had.

Since Watsonville was a two-hour drive, she closed and locked her office door and decided to try a call from her personal phone.

Two rings later and a deep male voice picked up the line. "Jordan Ranch."

"Good morning. Is Sarah Jordan available?"

The man seemed to hesitate. "Who's this?"

Should she lie? Say Katherine, pretend she was a friend? She didn't have a "young" voice. She suspected she was the same age as the man on the other end of the line, which meant she was probably talking to a protective parent.

Lying was too complicated: she decided to go with the simple truth.

"My name is Professor Katherine..." She choked on her last name. "I was hoping to speak to Sarah."

"A professor?" There was a brief hesitation, but then he said, "I'll get her. Give it a couple of minutes; she's out in the barn."

"I'm happy to wait."

The line went silent, but Katherine could hear faint sounds of everyday life in the background. Someone was doing dishes. A door opened and shut. A dog barked.

Five minutes after the last voice had left the phone, another picked up.

"Hello?"

"Is this Sarah?"

"Yeah. My dad said you're a professor?"

"I am. I'm in the physics department at Central Coast State."

"I... don't think I ever took physics. What was your name?"

"Professor... Katherine."

"Okaaay. I'm confused." Sarah huffed out a breath. "I'm on leave from school. I haven't decided if I want to go back, to be honest. So if you're calling about next semester, I can't give you an answer yet."

"I'm not calling to find out your enrollment. In case no one told you, you're still listed as enrolled. And with medical leaves of absence, I think they only require documentation from your medical or psychological doctor three weeks before the end of each semester, so you have plenty of time to decide what you want to do."

"Oh. No one told me that. That's good to know." She sounded more relaxed. "So are you calling, like, to tell me about my school options or something?"

"I am not." She tapped her pencil and tried to think about what she could say. "I don't want to intrude—"

"Do you work with Professor Shaver or Professor Kraft?"

That she could answer. "I do work with Professor Shaver and some of his grad students, yes."

"Oh." Sarah's voice sounded more assured. "Give me a minute and let me call you back. This number okay?"

"Yes. You should know—"

"Okay, give me a minute."

The line went dead, and Katherine mentally rehearsed how she could tell Sarah who she really was.

I'm not a psychologist or part of the study; I'm just a new psychic trying to figure out who tried to kill me a couple of weeks ago.

I don't know anything about this study, but ask me about precognition!

Please don't report me to the ethics committee for contacting you.

Her phone rang with an unfamiliar number and she picked up. "Hello?"

"So you're doing follow-up about the gap, right?" Sarah Jordan was back on the phone. "I guess that's not surprising." She sighed deeply. "I know I didn't keep my diary for a while, but I'm back to reporting now. My sleep has still been really good. Uh... my doctor hasn't changed my Zoloft prescription at all, so that's still the same."

Alarm bells were going off in Katherine's mind. *Alert! Alert! Professional misconduct ahead!* "Um, Sarah—"

"And I've kept up on the visualizations and meditations too." Sarah Jordan continued without a breath. "I mean, eventually. You know what happened, right?"

Despite the alarm bells, Katherine was taking rapid notes as Sarah spoke. Unethical? So much. She was going to have to come clean to Baxter about this. And about the psychic powers.

Eventually.

"I don't know the details about what happened," Katherine said. "I know there was an incident with your horse, which sounds very tragic, and I'm so sorry."

Was this what they called a personal spiral? It felt like a spiral.

Despite the spiraling feeling, Sarah continued to speak.

"Thanks. I know..." The young lady took a deep breath. "I'm doing better. At first I stopped everything. My medication, the biofeedback exercises, everything. What happened at the stable was just too... weird. But about a week after I got home, I still wasn't sleeping, so I started up again, and I haven't had another incident since."

"That's great to hear." Katherine's pencil was flying across the page. "If you feel comfortable, from your perspective now, can you tell me what you think happened at the stable?"

"With Tucker? I mean... it was weird. I don't remember much."

"Whatever you remember is fine."

"We had a competition coming up for the rodeo team, so maybe that contributed?" Her voice became agitated. "If that's what it was, I will never forgive myself for putting Tucker at risk."

Katherine could hear that Sarah was looking for reassurance. "This wasn't your first competitive event with Tucker, was it?"

"Oh no. We'd done dozens of rodeos before that."

"Then I think there's no reason to conclude the competition had anything to do with what happened."

"Right." Sarah let out a breath. "Thanks for that. You're right. Like I said, it was weird. I went in the stables to find a quiet corner to do my visualization, you know? But all the things that were supposed to happen went opposite."

Katherine's pencil paused. "Can you elaborate on that?"

"It was as if someone broke into my head and started pushing me in the opposite direction of where I wanted to go."

A chill crept down Katherine's spine. "You felt like someone was *pushing* you?"

CHAPTER 12

"*Y*eah." Sarah spoke after a long moment of silence. "It felt like a push. Almost a physical one."

"Mm-hmm." Katherine kept taking notes and ignored the voices screaming in her head. *What are you doing? What are you doing?*

If anyone ever found out she was speaking to Sarah Jordan about a confidential clinical study, she would lose her job. She could lose her career. *Baxter* could lose his career.

But her curiosity wouldn't allow her to stop, and if she interrupted now, Sarah would know that something was very wrong.

Katherine wasn't even asking questions; Sarah Jordan wanted to talk.

"Everything started out normally," she said. "The same as it had been for months."

As Sarah elaborated on what had happened the afternoon she overdosed her horse and killed him, Katherine pieced together what Ansel Shaver's study was about. It sounded like Ansel and his fellow professors were combining biofeedback therapy with traditional drug treatment to measure the therapy's influence on anxiety and dependence on medication.

Sarah sounded like she'd told the story before. "You know we're supposed to do the visualizations at set times, right? But also if we start to feel a panic attack coming on. And I don't know what triggered it, but I was definitely feeling the signs of one, so I immediately visualized the outcome and then tried to walk backward in my mind to make it smaller and smaller."

Biofeedback therapy was a clinical process that focused on understanding and gaining control over involuntary stress responses like heartbeat, blood pressure, or breathing. By systematically learning the body's reactions to stress through multiple sensor readings, a patient could then use techniques like breathing exercises or guided visualizations to learn control over those reactions.

Sarah's voice began to waver. "But the visualization wasn't working. For some reason, instead of walking backward, I felt like someone was pushing me forward."

"I see."

Biofeedback had a proven track record in treating things like migraine headaches and chronic pain. It had a growing record in treating anxiety, which meant that Ansel and his team were likely building on existing research.

As a clinical study, it was working off a very solid foundation.

"Not pushing me physically," Sarah clarified. "But it's like we learned in the lab. I took a breath and a mental step. Then another and another. It's just that this time, the mental steps didn't go backward like we practiced."

"Right." To Katherine's mind, Sarah's backward visualization sounded like a nightmare.

What had happened in that barn?

"It got worse and worse. After a certain point, I don't remember what happened. People I talked to later said I wasn't talking or reacting to anyone. I don't remember any of it. I don't remember going to Tucker's stall. I don't remember... anything." She cleared her throat, but her voice was still hoarse as she continued. "It shouldn't have ever happened, and I don't know how it did. I did everything like we practiced at the lab. Tucker was... It probably sounds weird, but he was my best friend."

"I'm so sorry, Sarah. I wish I could tell you why any of this happened."

"I stopped everything for a while. I quit logging. I moved home. But then I started having trouble sleeping again, which is why I signed up in the first place. So I'm back on track now, and my sleep is way better again."

"I'm glad to hear that." Katherine's heart hurt. Whatever happened had traumatized this young woman. She was more determined than ever to find out if there was a tie between Sarah and Justin. "And I'm so sorry about Tucker."

"Thanks." Sarah spoke to someone in the background before she returned to Katherine. "I wasn't sure if I was still in the study since I'm not at school anymore. Does Professor Kraft want me to keep filling out my journal?"

"Professor Kraft?" Katherine had to be honest. This girl had bared her soul even if she'd done it unintentionally. Katherine wanted her to know she was trying to help. "Sarah, I need to be completely up front with you. I am not working with Professor Shaver on this particular study. I do work with him in a different department, but I contacted you because there was a different incident near school recently."

"You're not part of the biofeedback study?"

"I am not."

"How did you get my name? They said it was confidential."

"I'm looking into an incident that happened with Justin McCabe a couple of weeks ago, and someone mentioned what happened with you—"

"Something happened to Justin? Is he okay?" Sarah's voice was alarmed. "I'm friends with one of his fraternity brothers. Justin's the whole reason I was involved in the biofeedback study in the first place. He's the one who told me about it. I know that technically none of us were supposed to know each other, but I promise we didn't talk about it or anything. He volunteered to be part of it, and then he told me and... What happened to Justin?"

"He was involved in an attempted shooting at the Blue Wave Gym." Katherine decided she could share anything that was already public knowledge. "He was carrying a handgun with an extended magazine at the gym."

"What?"

"No one was hurt, but I believe he was arrested on attempted murder charges. The police are still investigating, and they didn't put his name in the paper—"

"That's not... You don't understand—that's not *possible*."

"I know it's shocking, but if you read about it in the papers, he was the student involved."

A sharp laugh sounded across the line. "Is this a sick joke?"

"I'm sorry, it's not. You're not the first person to say this was out of character, so I know it must be—"

"It's not shocking, it's *impossible*." Sarah's voice rose. "Do they even realize what happened to his little brother?"

"I don't know what you're talking about. I haven't heard—"

"Justin and his family moved to the Central Coast after his little brother was killed in a school shooting. It happened when Justin was like thirteen years old. To think he'd do anything like that is *absurd*. He was like the only guy in his fraternity who was super pro gun control because of what happened. Being involved in a mass shooting would be, like, his worst nightmare ever."

"I was there." Katherine could barely force out the words. "I saw it. He did have a gun, and he was going to shoot people."

"Then there's something else going on, because he would never ever do that, Professor Katherine." Sarah sounded like she was near tears. "Something is really, really not right with all this."

What had Katherine gotten involved in?

"Sarah, if I give you my number, can you ask Justin's family or friends to call me?" It was a risk, but Katherine felt like she needed Sarah on her side. "They might not want to talk to me because I was there that day and I gave a statement to the police, but I'm trying to figure out what was going on. I really want to help."

"Why?"

"Because I agree with you. What happened to you, what happened with Justin, something isn't right. Things are not adding up."

And I don't want to have any more violent visions of

death.

Sarah said, "I'll try to get their number, but I never met his family. I only knew him from my friend at the fraternity. They may not even talk to me."

"Whatever you can do will help." Katherine took a breath. "And for now, *please* keep our conversation confidential. I'm trying to help, but I could get into a lot of trouble just for speaking to you."

Sarah was quiet for a long time.

"Okay," Sarah finally said. "If you can help me and Justin figure out what happened, I won't say a word."

"You MEAN that boy had a little brother killed by a school shooter?" Megan was the first person Katherine called on her way home from work. "That poor family."

Katherine had the car to herself. Baxter had a late meeting with his department, and one of his colleagues would be giving him a ride home. It was four o'clock, and traffic downtown was stop and go as students and staff started leaving school for the day.

"It happened in Southern California when Justin was thirteen," Katherine said. "It sounded horrible. I looked up the news articles online after I got off the phone with Sarah. If they'd published Justin's name in the paper, I'm sure the media would have made the connection. The McCabes have been vocal in gun control debates."

"Do you think...? Could Justin have been trying to make some kind of political point threatening people?"

"If my vision was correct, he wasn't going to just threaten.

He was actually going to shoot."

"Do you think he...?" Megan let out a strangled sound. "I have no idea. It's like Sarah said—it just seems impossible to go through that and then do something like he did. And I can't imagine what that boy's mother is going through right now. I'm heartbroken for them."

"You know what would be worse?" Katherine made it past the clogged traffic on State Street and turned toward Valley Road to loop around the worst of the traffic. "If we hadn't been there and someone had actually gotten hurt. Think about that, okay? Right now Justin is in jail for *attempted* murder and not murder." And since Sarah had confirmed that Justin was involved in Ansel Shaver's study, Katherine was starting to think there had to be a connection. "Did you find anything else out today? Any other students that popped up in the news?"

"I didn't find anything," Megan said. "Other than the usual stuff. Parties that went a little wild. Drunk and disorderly stuff. Shouting matches. Nothing extreme like what happened with Justin or Sarah."

"But would something like what happened with Sarah have even made it into the news?" Katherine asked. "Unless something publicly criminal happened, people might try to keep it quiet."

"Especially when things seem so out of character," Megan said. "Toni called me earlier and said she asked around about what happened with Sarah. According to people she talked to—her cousin is a furrier I guess?"

Some of Katherine's neighbors in North Beach were horse people. "Do you mean a farrier? Someone who shoes horses?"

"Oh my God, that makes so much more sense than what I was imagining." Megan sounded relieved.

"Do I want to know?"

There was a long silence on the line. "Probably not."

"Okay, moving on."

"Toni called me earlier this afternoon after she talked to her cousin, 'cause she does the shoeing for the rodeo team since she used to be on it in college—you know, this really is a small town. I swear, y'all know each other like socks in a drawer."

"Okay?"

"Anyway, Sarah *loved* that horse. He was a big part of her life. Something happening to him might have been her biggest fear. And then you have a kid like Justin who lost a brother to a mass shooter—"

"A random shooting could have been Justin's biggest fear." Something tickled Katherine's brain. "What if part of this experiment was using that?"

"Using what?"

"The worst outcome. A subject's biggest fear." Katherine tried to relate it to something personal. "I have social anxiety, and my biggest fear is humiliating myself in front of a large group of people. It takes multiple forms in my head, but anytime I feel anxiety building, it's usually related to that."

"We need to find out who all was in that study."

"I have no idea how to do that. There's layer after layer of confidentiality papers to protect subjects in these studies. Just by speaking with Sarah, I've already put myself in a horrible ethical situation."

"Well, how about talking to Justin McCabe?"

"I might be able to justify that because of the personal

connection with the incident." Katherine sighed. "I'm hoping someone from his family will call me, but I don't know. I don't think I can just march up to the jail and ask to talk to him, you know?"

Or did people do that? Could you just put your name on a list?

"Hopefully they'll call," Megan said. "Also, for the record, I can't even imagine you humiliating yourself in front of people. You're so far from ridiculous that it's... ridiculous. I know, get a better vocabulary, Meg." She cleared her throat. "I just mean you're a very cool person and you're clearly very smart."

"Thank you." Katherine felt a surge of warmth. "But remember, it's anxiety. It's not logical. I can prepare for a lecture for weeks, but if my anxiety is flaring up, I might be convinced that the lecture will go horribly wrong no matter how many people reassure me."

"Do you take medication?"

"I do. I have for years. It helps a considerable amount." Katherine suddenly realized that she had nothing planned for dinner and Baxter would be late from work. "Damn. I need to figure out something to make for dinner." *Hmmmm. What meal would complement psychic revelations and admissions of academic impropriety, Katherine?*

She needed to tell Baxter what was going on. She dreaded it. Maybe not tonight.

"I love cooking, but I hate cooking dinner," Megan said. "Does that make any sense?"

"Completely. If I have a full day to plan and prepare something, I enjoy it. Baxter and I cook together on weekends."

"Same. Well, my husband doesn't help me cook, but if I can spend all day cooking something slow and drinking a glass of wine, maybe listening to music? So fun. Especially back home if it was a big family event or neighborhood dinner and I had a girlfriend over to cook with me and chat all day."

"I have no experience with anything like that, but it sounds wonderful."

"It is." Megan sighed. "But the act of making a meal every single night to shovel food into four ungrateful people just annoys the crap out of me."

Katherine frowned as she turned in to the parking lot for the local grocery store. "They shouldn't be ungrateful if you're making them a home-cooked dinner every night."

"Have you known teenagers in your life?"

She had a point. "I have, but I've never had to cook for them regularly."

"I swear, I want to throw their phones in the microwave and watch them explode when they get them out at the dinner table. But I'm stuck because their father does the exact same thing, so what am I supposed to say? It's infuriating."

Katherine realized that Megan rarely referred to her husband by name. "What's your husband's name again?"

"Rodney. And the kids are Trina—she's the oldest—Adam, and Cami is the baby. Of course, the baby is fourteen, but sometimes she forgets that and acts like she still likes me."

"I have a hard time imagining anyone finding you unlikeable." Katherine parked the car and grabbed the canvas bag she stored in the back seat pocket. "I think eventually you'll even win Toni over."

"Still crossing my fingers on that one. But as far as kids go, did you like your mother when you were fourteen?"

"Yes. She and my sister were the only ones who knew that I existed most days."

"What about your daddy?"

"He was closer to my sister. She's a brilliant mathematician, and she got her first PhD when she was twenty-one. She's an actual genius."

"Didn't you start college when you were like fifteen? That doesn't make you a genius?"

"According to my father, that made me slightly precocious." She walked into the grocery store and grabbed a cart. "Unfortunately, geniuses and slightly precocious physicists still have to cook dinner when their husbands are working late. Tell me what to buy. I never know what to make."

"Do you like Mexican food?"

"I'm a Californian. Of course I like Mexican food."

"Then Katherine, my friend, tacos are always the answer."

She turned her cart toward the butcher counter. "I can't argue with that and I wouldn't even want to."

"Tacos may be my favorite thing about California."

"I'm not sure our tacos completely make up for the outrageous property taxes, but they do help."

"Other than you, I mean. I like you more than tacos."

Katherine stopped and smiled in the produce department. "Thank you."

"Jury's still out on Toni though. She's not tacos, she's hot sauce. A little goes a real long way."

"Toni is hot sauce?" Katherine considered the comparison as she grabbed a few onions, a handful of serrano chilies, and some limes. "Okay, that's fair."

CHAPTER 13

*B*axter was devouring the tacos. "These are delicious, darling."

"Thanks. I was talking with Megan while I did the shopping and she suggested tacos. I don't know why I don't make them more often."

Baxter's smile was warm. "I'm so pleased that you're spending time with her. She seems like a very nice person."

"She is very nice." Katherine reached over and squeezed his hand. "Careful—it sounds like she and Toni want to make Wine Wednesday a weekly habit."

"I think that's wonderful." He took another bite, swallowed, and carefully blotted his mouth with his napkin. "Would you rather I find somewhere else to be on Wednesdays?"

"We're not kicking you out yet. When we get to the spooky menopause rituals, I'll let you know."

"You mean I'll be left out of the bonfires and naked dancing under the moon? I suppose it's understandable, but I can't say I'm not disappointed." He finished off the last of his tacos and reached for her empty plate. "Have I mentioned lately that I wish we had someone with your sense of humor in the department? It's nothing but humorless complaints from everyone right now."

"That doesn't sound like your clan." Usually the math department was a friendly bunch even if they were completely uninterested in anything else going on at the university. If Baxter was wishing for someone with her admittedly anemic sense of humor, things truly must be dire. "People still unhappy about the renovations?"

He shrugged dramatically. "I can't help that the building hasn't been renovated since 1932 and the school wants to update it. It's hardly a surprise. Margaret and I gave everyone two years of warning, but they're acting like we dropped a bomb on them at the beginning of the semester."

"What's the main complaint?"

"That they're going to have to move offices, of course. We're splitting up the family for two whole semesters. You know they don't like change."

Katherine was fairly sure that disliking change was a prerequisite to any college-faculty admission. "Where are they going?"

"Most of them will be going to Meyer Hall."

Katherine nearly laughed out loud. "Oh no. Not the social science building."

The horror. The utter and complete horror. Katherine already felt sorry for the sociologists and psychologists who would be subjected to the insular mathematicians in Baxter's department.

"I tried to convince them that it would be a learning opportunity, but I don't think they're buying it. A few of them have openly stated that they won't be able to continue their research if they can't collaborate in adjoining offices." He set the dishes in the sink and grabbed the half-empty bottle of wine on the counter to refill their glasses. "How was your day?"

"Much less dramatic than yours." She tried to mentally sort through her day. "Office hours. Uh, had a meeting with Keisha, my new grad student. She's a delight."

"Where's she coming from?"

"Arizona State."

"Ah." Baxter's eyebrows went up. "Interesting."

"Had an enjoyable discussion in my Applied Physics class. That was fun. Really bright group this semester."

"No troublemakers at all? How very boring. What's Fred doing?"

"Not being boring, that's for sure. He figured out how to destroy the lamp in his aquarium again. Apparently Job's puzzle ball wasn't challenging enough. He staged a protest."

Baxter topped off her wineglass. "I wonder if they'd build us an aquarium in the new lobby of the math building."

"I really don't recommend it." Katherine sipped her wine. "Unless you're getting actual fish and not cephalopods."

"Cuttlefish?"

"They might be less rebellious than Fred."

Baxter turned on a speaker and hit a button on his phone, filling their galley kitchen with jazz. "Colorful too. Cuttle-fish, I mean."

"I've heard that."

Baxter held out a hand and Katherine took it. He pulled her to standing in his arms, swaying with the music as the sun went down though the large glass panes of their front windows.

She put her arms around his waist. She had to remember to feed him more. He'd always been wiry, but he was getting downright thin as they got older. She laid her head on his shoulder and listened to him hum in her ear.

I did something really unethical and I might get in serious trouble. She nearly blurted it out. *I'm having visions of things that happen minutes after I see them even though premonition makes no scientific sense.*

Was it unethical though? She wasn't trying to manipulate data. She wasn't trying to take advantage of the students in the study. She was trying to figure out why two of those students had experienced seemingly out-of-character violent outbursts within a few months of each other.

What if she hadn't been in the gym that day? What if Justin had killed people—possibly his worst nightmare—and had no idea why? What if some disassociation was a side effect of Ansel's study? Wasn't it more ethical to continue trying to find answers at this point, to protect study participants and the innocent people around them?

"You're thinking quite loudly, darling."

She propped her chin on his shoulder. "My lovely and wise Professor Pang."

"Yes, Professor Bassi?"

"I have a conundrum."

"I would be happy to help in any way I can."

What to say?

"I have a suspicion that a study Ansel Shaver did last year might have had something to do with the shooting attempt at the gym."

Baxter pulled away and looked at her, a frown creasing his forehead. "Why do you think that?"

"I was made aware that another student had a similar strange, violent outburst. When I spoke to her, she mentioned being part of the study and also mentioned that Justin McCabe was a part of it as well."

Baxter's face was blank. "Did you ask—?"

"She offered the information. I know it's still a grey area ethically, but she clearly wanted to talk, and I was there."

Baxter's hand tightened on her waist. "If the university finds out that you even spoke to her—"

"I know. I know." She took a deep breath. "But what am I supposed to do, Bax? If these... incidents have anything to do with Ansel's study, more people could be affected. I didn't intend to violate anything, but this is too important to—"

"You have to report him to the IRB."

The Institutional Review Board at the university was set up to monitor any research conducted using human subjects, and the buck stopped with them. If a study was flagged by the IRB, it would go nowhere.

"I only have suspicions right now," Katherine said. "I don't have anything to report. I don't even know if Ansel knows about the incidents at this point."

Baxter frowned. "There's no way to check without exposing yourself. You could file an anonymous complaint."

"Over a theory?"

"Let me think." He stepped back and poured himself another glass of wine. "Don't do anything yet. Let me think about this."

"If Justin McCabe's family contacts me, I'm going to talk to them. The young man is still in jail. He's being held without bail because the judge determined he's a danger to the community."

"He is a danger, Katherine!" Baxter's voice rose. "He could have killed you. He could have killed dozens of people. What kind of sick person—?"

"Shhh." Katherine pressed a kiss to his lips. "I'm fine. I wasn't hurt. Bumps and bruises only."

He put his arms around her and squeezed tightly. "I will follow your lead on this, but know that I do not carry any misplaced sympathy for that man."

"I looked at his student record." She spoke into his shoulder. "He was an excellent student. Involved. Engaged in his classes. He volunteered with that moving company that works with the battered women's shelter. This act was completely out of character. I want to know what happened."

Baxter was quiet for a long time. "You see connections where other people can't. You have a gift for it. It's why your sense of systems is so intuitive. Why your mind is so damn beautiful. But if this is a large study, it could be coincidence. Not everything is related."

"On a theoretical level, I can't agree with you."

He laughed a little.

There was no way she could tell him about the visions, not in that moment.

Another night. Another dance.

Katherine lifted her face to Baxter's and placed a long and lingering kiss on his mouth. "I love you very much, Professor Pang."

"I love you too."

"I can't do it," Katherine said. "I can't tell Baxter I have visions."

Toni shrugged. "Okay."

They were sitting on the front deck, and Katherine was opening the second bottle of wine. She'd called an emergency meeting since Wednesday was too far away. Also, it was Friday and Baxter was introducing a lecturer from Sydney that evening, so they had the house to themselves.

Megan frowned. "Don't you think Baxter's going to figure it out? I mean, you two seem really close."

Toni asked Megan, "Are you going to tell your husband?"

"I don't think he'd care," Megan said. "It's different for Katherine. She and her husband actually get along."

Toni winced. "Damn, that's depressing."

Megan made a face. "I know. It is. I just don't know what I want to do about it yet. Rodney's a good husband mostly. He's pretty involved with the kids. Less now, but he says that's because I'm not working, so he has to work more."

"But he moved your family out here for his job," Toni said. "That's why you're not working."

"We had that discussion a couple of weeks ago," she said. "It went super well. And by that I mean he ended up sleeping on the couch."

Katherine shook her head. "I don't think Baxter and I would fight, but he'd definitely assume I had a neurological condition."

"Maybe you do," Toni said. "Maybe we all do. Maybe this is a shared delusion and we all need to get our heads—" She stopped speaking when white wine splashed in her face.

Megan glared at her, her hand held out. A wineglass was

hovering in front of Toni's face. "Sorry, what was that? My hand slipped."

"What. The. F—?"

"How are you doing that?" Katherine scooted closer. "You're holding it steady. Did you have a breakthrough?"

"Of a sort. It helps when I get mad." She lowered her hand, and the glass fell to the table and tipped over. "Still working on it though."

Toni narrowed her eyes and wiped her cheek with a napkin. "Nice trick."

"Still think we have brain tumors?"

"Maybe you don't, but I" —Toni pointed at her chest— "started a fight today between two of my best guys. At least I think I did. I was in a pissy mood, and I needed to talk to one of them. And he was perfectly happy when I walked up. I chewed him out over something super minor, okay? And the worst part was, I knew it was minor when I was chewing him out. I just couldn't seem to stop myself. It was like the worst case of PMS ever."

Megan asked, "Were you warm?"

"No. I mean, not more than normal. Why?"

She smiled. "No reason. Continue."

"So I'm chewing this guy out and he's getting more and more pissed, and at the same time I'm getting more and more relaxed. It's like I was pouring my anger into him." Toni sat back in her seat. "That's not okay! I know that's not okay, but I don't know how to stop it."

"So at the beginning," Katherine said, "he was happy and you were angry."

"Yeah."

"And by the end of the conversation, you were happy and he was angry."

"Yeah. And then he went and had an argument with another guy, and like, two hours were wasted on that bullshit."

Katherine thought about the gym. "Is that what happened with Justin?"

Toni seemed to think a minute before she shook her head. "No. There's no way that could have been because I was pumped when I jumped on him. If he'd drunk my emotions, then he'd have been even more frantic than he was, not calm."

"Okay. So what you were doing today was involuntary."

"Yes."

"But you know you can push emotions onto people too."

"Right." Toni nodded. "Right. Okay, so if I feel like I did today, I need to stop and push those emotions back to whomever I'm getting them from. Like with Frank, I should have pushed his happy back to him, not just made him eat my mood."

"I think so. It could be that just being aware of it is going to help. You know—more than me or Megan I think—that what you do is under your control."

That seemed to please her. Toni gave Katherine a small smile. "At least that's something."

"I do what I can. Especially since I have no control at all about my visions."

Megan was lifting a wineglass again, spinning it in place. The movement was start and go, but it was mostly go. "But you have that big awesome brain. That's like an extra super-power, you know?"

"Yeah," Toni said. "And I have something that should make you extra happy. Or maybe just extra curious."

"What's that?"

Toni waggled her eyebrows. "My cousin at the department. He says he can get you in to see Justin McCabe."

CHAPTER 14

*M*oonstone Cove didn't have its own jail, which meant that to meet with Justin McCabe the following Monday, Katherine and Megan had to drive an hour south and sit in traffic during four-o'clock traffic.

She turned to Megan. "Making you miss the city yet?"

Megan made a face. "I never miss traffic. Still, this isn't all that bad. Y'all are just spoiled in Moonstone Cove because it's so tiny."

"Is it feeling any more friendly?"

Megan shrugged. "I'm glad we got to be friends. Even if the reason sucked pretty bad."

"And Toni?"

"You know, I still catch her giving me side-eye when she thinks I'm not watching. Before, I think it was the blond-bimbo assumption." Megan reached into her purse and flipped down the visor to reapply lipstick. "Now I think she just doesn't like me."

"She thinks your study of the occult is misguided."

"My study of the occult?" Megan shook her head. "Please

don't ever call it that in front of my mama if she ever comes to visit. She'll have me flying back to Georgia and in a Baptist rehab before you can snap your fingers."

"A Baptist rehab?"

"Oh yeah, it's a thing. And all I'm doing is research. It makes sense, right? We have all these abilities, we should at least learn how to use them and read what other people have written about stuff."

"I don't think you're misguided. I just said Toni thinks you are."

"Well, Toni is a little narrow-minded." Megan pointed to a sign. "There it is."

At the intersection of San Juan and Walden Street, Katherine saw a green-and-white sign with Jail in all capital letters. It was pointing to the right, so Katherine moved over to the right lane.

"Did Toni say she was gonna meet us there?"

"I guess she had some kind of errand to run," Megan said. "She said she'd meet us at the entrance but to go inside and put our names on the list."

"This feels very strange," Katherine said. "Have you ever visited anyone in jail before?"

"No. Never."

"Toni didn't seem that concerned about us being able to speak to Justin. I would have thought his lawyer would forbid him from speaking to anyone."

Megan said, "Maybe they did and he's just ignoring them. Who knows what the boy's thinking?" She put her lipstick back in a sky-blue purse that matched the stripe on her blouse and carefully fastened the closure. "I don't know how I'm going to feel seeing him again."

Katherine glanced at her. "You look great."

"Is it weird that I want to look good? I don't know why, but I do."

She smiled as she maneuvered past a postal delivery van and into the county-center parking lot. "I think it's your armor."

Megan nodded nervously. "Maybe so."

"He tried to take your control away from you in a place where we usually allow ourselves to be vulnerable, so you're controlling what he sees now."

Megan let out a slow breath. "I've never thought about it that way before."

"If it makes you feel more in control or calmer, then it's a good thing." Katherine found a parking spot under a spreading fig tree near the back of the lot that served the jail, the courthouse, and most of the county offices.

Megan reached across and grabbed Katherine's hand, squeezing hard before she let it go. "I'm so glad you're my friend."

Katherine felt a swell of warmth in her chest. "Me too."

Megan turned to her and nodded. "Let's do this."

They got out of the car and started walking toward the signs that said JAIL. Halfway to the building, Katherine spotted Toni leaning against a lamppost. She was wearing black pants and a black leather jacket; under her arm was a silver motorcycle helmet, and just past the lamppost Katherine saw signs for motorcycle parking.

"Hey." Toni didn't remove her sunglasses.

"Armor," Megan muttered.

"Yep."

Toni pointed her chin toward the jail. "You two ready to do this thing?"

———

Justin McCabe seemed a lot smaller wearing an orange jumpsuit and sitting behind a clear acrylic panel than he had wrestling them in the gym. Katherine sat in the center and Megan leaned close to the phone so she could overhear what Justin was saying.

"My lawyer says I should absolutely not be talking to you ladies," Justin said, "because you'll be testifying against me at trial, but there's not going to be a trial, so I told him it didn't matter."

"You're not going to trial?"

He looked like an old man in a young man's body. His hazel eyes were sunken, and there were purple rings under his eyes. His skin was fair but sallow, and his chocolate-brown hair fell limply over his jumpsuit collar.

Justin shook his head. "I remember the trial when my brother was killed. It was really horrible. I thought my parents were going to get a divorce and I was going to lose them too. I can't put them through something like that again."

Katherine felt her heart breaking open. Nothing about this young man said evil killer. Nothing said unstable. "Why did you agree to meet with us?" she asked. "How did you know it was us?"

Toni tapped her shoulder and shook her head. "Don't ask."

Justin watched their interaction, but all he said was "I wanted to thank all three of you for stopping me." He blinked hard. "I don't remember what happened that day. My lawyer and my doctor are trying to figure out what that means for me legally, but I know that whatever was going on, I wasn't in my right mind. And the thought of me hurting anyone—" He cleared his throat loudly. "It really would have been my worst nightmare. So really, thanks. I'll never be able to repay you for keeping me from becoming a monster."

Katherine heard Megan sniffing.

"Sweetie," she said, "we don't know quite what happened either, but I am going to promise you this, okay?"

Katherine said, "Megan, don't—"

"Atlanta, you better not—"

"We are going to figure out what's going on," Megan said.

Katherine groaned internally. Toni groaned externally. It was a silent symphony of groaning.

Megan continued, "If I have go back to school and get a doctorate in psychology, we are going to figure out what happened. You tell your mama that, okay?"

Justin just nodded. "I'm going to plead guilty to whatever, you know? I'm trying to do the stuff my lawyer says, and I'm talking with my doctor, like, every day. But I'm not trying to get out of punishment for whatever happened. I mean, it's stupid, right? You guys were there. You saw what I was about to do."

"Can you tell me what happened? Anything about the *why* that you can remember?" Katherine asked. "From your perspective."

Justin frowned, but he nodded. "Okay, so I'm not sure if you know about this, but after my brother died, I had a really bad time with panic attacks. Like, I wasn't even in the same school as him, you know? I was already in middle school. But

I had a really hard time going into the school building. Any building really. And you know my parents were all freaked out too, which didn't help. Not that it's their fault or anything."

"I know what you mean," Katherine said. "Their trauma exacerbated your trauma. None of that was illogical, by the way. You survived a violent event even though the shooting didn't happen at your school. I suspect you had post-traumatic stress disorder."

"I was officially diagnosed when I was fifteen." He nodded and smiled a little. "Are you a psychologist too?"

"No, I'm a biophysicist. But that means I have an extraordinary respect for our biological systems and the intricate and interwoven measures our minds and nervous systems can take to protect us. What your body and mind were doing with the PTSD was trying to protect you, Justin. It took a wrong turn, so to speak, but your mind and body were trying to do the right thing."

The corner of his mouth turned up. "I never thought about it that way. Thanks. That's actually helpful. I started trying different medications right after I was diagnosed. My parents were reluctant at first, but then my psychologist warned them that a lot of kids who didn't get the right treatment for PTSD self-medicated with alcohol or drugs, and I think that kind of scared them. They were supportive after that. They just didn't get it."

Katherine nodded. "I understand."

"But the longer you're on a medication, the more you have to take, right? And I'm a pretty big guy. I was worried about the medication losing its effectiveness or having bad long-term health consequences, so..."

Katherine could see him searching for words, but she didn't want to ask about the study. If he offered it, that was one thing. Asking crossed a line.

Megan said, "Justin, we know about—"

Katherine kicked her leg. Hard.

"Ow!"

Toni leaned forward. "Shut it, Megan. Let him talk."

Justin frowned, but he didn't look conflicted. "I had the chance to be part of a biofeedback study that was supposed to supplement my medication. The goal wasn't to *not* medicate at all, I think it was just to see if, by using biofeedback therapy, we could keep from increasing the dosage on my medications. Kind of that idea. It seemed super weird at first—they hooked me up with all these electrodes and plugged them into a computer. There were flashing lights when certain triggers happened." He smiled a little. "I can't lie, it was strange. I felt like I was in a science fiction movie."

Katherine smiled. "You're not the first person I've heard that from."

"Right? It's totally weird. But... eventually it worked. I could definitely tell when I was having triggers, and a lot of the time it was stuff I'd completely brushed off before. I realized that none of my panic attacks came out of nowhere. I could always tell when they were coming. It was kind of amazing, and it made me feel so much better. Like I had a lot more control over my body."

"That's great," Katherine said. "That sounds really helpful."

As Justin spoke about the study, Katherine could see the young man he was before the attack. His face was brighter. He looked confident.

Megan squeezed Katherine's hand, and she knew her friend was seeing the same things.

"So after a few weeks being hooked up to the computer," Justin continued, "you practice these visualizations to kind of gain control over your body's responses, right?"

"I've heard that's one method of biofeedback therapy."

"So there were a variety of visualizations you could pick from, but I picked the one that felt like the most direct, you know?"

"What was it?" Megan asked.

"Imagine the worst thing that could happen." Justin looked straight at Megan. "Sounds horrible, right? But see... that's where my mind wanted to go anyway. That's where it was always building. Being in that place and being trapped. So like... we were supposed to just go there. Throw water on it, kinda. Jump ahead and then step by step, walk backward."

It was the exact same technique that Sarah had communicated to her.

"Take one step. Then another. You already know how you got there, right? So you know the way back."

It made a horrible kind of sense, but it still seemed like a very risky visualization to Katherine. She didn't express that to Justin, but she wondered who had written that part of the study.

"I'd snapped out of two panic attacks in the past six months using that technique," Justin said. "I'd convinced myself eventually I'd be in complete control over them. That maybe I wouldn't even have to medicate anymore."

"Tell me about that day at the gym." Katherine asked, "What's the last thing you remember?"

"Jogging." He frowned. "I felt my phone buzz with the

reminder for my visualization exercise. I was going to put it off, but I recognized some triggers—body temperature is one for me. Heart rate. So jogging is kind of risky, but I really love it and it wasn't the first time I'd run or anything, but I didn't want to push it, so I got off the treadmill and walked to the locker room to just do the exercises."

Toni asked, "He left the gym?"

"You left the machine room?" Katherine asked. "Do you remember why you went back?"

"No." He shook his head. "The last thing I remember is being in the locker room. There's a part that's around a corner and more private, and I went there to meditate—had my headphones in anyway, you know—and get my body calmed down. I started the exercises and..." His expression looked like he was in pain. "Something weird happened. It didn't go right."

Katherine felt Toni tense behind her. Megan had her hand in a death grip.

"I was there... in my head." Justin looked like he was on the verge of tears. "I was trying to walk backward, and I couldn't."

Let him speak. Don't jump to conclusions. Let him tell you what happened.

His voice fell to barely a whisper. "It seems crazy, but it felt like someone was pushing me forward. Pushing me into my fear."

There it was.

He leaned back in his seat. "That was the last thing I remember until you guys tackled me."

Katherine had one more question. "Why did you have the gun, Justin?"

"I didn't." He shook his head and his eyes cleared. His expression was firm. More firm and clear than he'd been their entire meeting. All hints of uncertainty were gone. "I have never owned a gun. Never shot one. Never owned one. Never wanted to. You can ask any of my fraternity brothers. It was not my gun. I have no idea where it came from, no idea how it ended up stuck in my waistband, but it was not mine."

CHAPTER 15

*T*hey went out for coffee after their visit with Justin McCabe, but all three of them were quiet.

Megan was solemn and fidgeting with a smooth stone she'd found on the beach the week before. It was one of the famous moonstones, worn smooth from the waves and rocks on the beach, its powdery white exterior rippling with striations as Megan flipped it between her fingers.

"I really wish you hadn't promised that we were going to find out what happened," Toni said. "Did you forget he tried to shoot us?"

Megan's mouth dropped open. "Did you hear the same words I did? He apologized. He doesn't remember what happened. Something is going on with that boy."

"I don't care how out of it you are, you don't do things without having that in your heart." Toni leaned forward. "Without having imagined it in some way. And I don't buy the thing about the gun at all."

"I'm really curious about the gun," Katherine said. "And I agree with you on one point."

"Katherine!" Megan looked betrayed. "That young man—"

"He did have it in his mind," she said. "Couldn't you see it? His greatest fear was being in the same situation that killed his brother. However it happened, that fear was recreated in the most horrible way."

"The thing he feared most became reality," Toni said. "Like... a living nightmare or something."

"Very much like that."

Toni pursed her lips. "Like losing her horse might have been to that Sarah girl."

Two students participating in the same clinical study that shouldn't have had such an extraordinary effect. Katherine had been reading up on similar studies done at other universities and research institutions. While Professor Shaver and his colleagues' research pushed a new direction in treating anxiety, none of it was experimental or risky. This was a very focused study that could potentially advance treatments, but it wasn't a new drug. It was an established therapy.

Was the study simply a coincidence like Baxter had mentioned?

Megan said, "Sarah killed a horse. It may have been heartbreaking and awful, but she's not in prison. Where does all this leave Justin? He's still in jail."

"And I don't think he's going to fight being there," Katherine said. "His guilt was palpable." She glanced at Toni, whose face still read skeptical. "I agree with Megan. Whatever happened that day, I don't believe Justin McCabe would have intentionally shot up a gym."

"So what do you think happened?" Toni asked.

"The most obvious is a dissociative episode, but I don't

think the meditation he'd done routinely would trigger that."

"Maybe he was possessed," Megan said. "It happened in the Bible."

"I don't think it happened here." Toni lowered her voice and looked around. "If he was possessed, don't you think fate or whatever gave us these powers would have made one of us capable of, like, driving out spirits or something?"

"I don't know how any of this works," Megan said. "Why do you think I'm doing so much research? Which you make fun of, I want to add. You think I'm an idiot. Don't think I don't see the eyes you give me."

"I'm not going to deny that I think your packing tarot cards and sage and moonstones in your purse is ridiculous." Toni nodded at Katherine. "The professor thinks it's ridiculous too; she's just more polite than me."

"I don't know that tarot is any more ridiculous than any other divination," Katherine said. "And since I'm currently divining the future, I'm probably not in a place to judge." She took a long drink of her iced coffee and looked at Toni. "Of the three of us, you're likely the most equipped to do traditional psychic readings."

Megan's smile was smug. "Want to start a little shop on the beach, Toni?"

"Screw you," she said. "I'm not a party trick." She narrowed her eyes at Megan and stared.

A few seconds later, Megan's mouth dropped open. "Are you trying to empath me?"

Toni broke eye contact and leaned back in her chair. "Been feeling kind of irritated by all this shit. Thought I'd share."

The corner of Megan's mouth turned up. "Honey, I have

three teenagers. If you think I'm not wise to multiple levels of manipulation, you got another think coming."

"Both of you need to calm down, and I need to think." Katherine rubbed her temple. "Toni, the spreading irritation didn't just hit Megan, and I have fewer natural shields. Please stop."

"Oh." Toni sat up. "Sorry, Katherine."

"And Megan, I don't think we can treat any of our... gifts as more powerful or important than the others. Toni has an extraordinary gift, but so do you. Telekinesis is arguably the most useful gift of the three."

Megan shrugged. "It just seems weird to me."

"How?"

"I mean..." She cocked her head. "I don't want this to come across the wrong way, but of the three of us, my emotional intelligence is probably on the higher end."

"Are you calling me unemotional?" Toni's voice rose. Then she sat back and crossed her arms. "No, that's probably fair."

"I just think it's strange." Megan continued without answering Toni. "Don't you think it's strange? Why does Toni have super empathy and I have telekinesis? I mean, of all the things to feel like a party trick—"

"Telekinesis is—at its core—a connection to energy," Katherine said. "That's extraordinary. Isn't that what you've been tapping into when you practice?"

Megan frowned. "I'm honestly not sure. It's mostly trial and error. I guess, yeah, I have to feel a connection to things if I want to move them." She ran a thumb over the moonstone. "Like this stone here? I bet I could make it fly across the room if I wanted to. It feels like another part of my hand now."

Toni still had her arms crossed, but she looked slightly envious. "That would be so damn useful when I'm working."

"Kinda complicated to explain to your guys though, right? Doesn't matter." Megan shrugged. "Like my mama said, you can wish in one hand and piss in the other and see which one fills up faster. Wishing doesn't change a thing."

Toni pursed her lips. "I feel like I'd like your mother."

"If you want to put up with the lecture she'd give you about dressing" —Megan pulled out her air quotes— "'like a man' because your hair is short, and not having any babies by forty, I'm sure you'd get along great."

"Wow. Really?"

Megan just shook her head and closed her eyes. "There's a lot going on with that one. She's an opinionated woman, that's for sure."

Katherine did not think she'd like Megan's mother. She had her own opinionated matriarch to deal with and she didn't need another. "Getting back to Justin, what do you think we could find out about the gun? Toni, do you think your cousin at the police department would know where it came from? They have numbers, right?"

"Guns?" The corner of Toni's mouth twitched. "Yes. They have registration numbers. It's a good question. I'll ask him."

"Do y'all think I need to be worried about my kids?" Megan asked. "I mean, we don't know if there are more students out there like Justin. There could be loaded guns all over Moonstone Cove. I've been having Trina drive her brother and sister all over town, thinking it's safe as houses, but if there could be random violence—"

"It's probably as safe as it's ever been." Katherine sipped

her coffee. "Random violence is, by definition, random. Not that random violence is truly random."

Toni and Megan exchanged a look.

"There's probably some math equation that explains it," Toni said. "Do we want to ask?"

"You know we probably won't understand it. I'm just going to tell my daughter to be extra careful." Megan turned back to Katherine. "You ready to go?"

"I'm socially awkward," Katherine said. "Not hearing impaired."

"Mmmm." Megan grabbed her purse and rose to her feet. "Sometimes it's a little of both."

"Pretty sure you completely tuned out that conversation we were having about football," Toni said.

Katherine nodded. "Okay, you have me there."

KATHERINE DROPPED Megan off at her house in Ferraro Hills before she made her way through the narrow, twisty streets of the village on her way to North Beach. Noticing the lack of lights in the entryway when she pulled into the driveway, she checked the time.

That was strange; Baxter should have been home hours ago.

The front door was unlocked when she tried it. "Baxter?"

She could hear the ocean through french doors. She saw Baxter sitting on the back deck, looking out over the sea. She set her purse down and walked out to the deck. "Baxter?"

He turned and held his hand to her. "Darling."

She'd known her husband for twenty-two years and could read every single expression. "What happened?"

He took a deep breath and waited for Katherine to sit next to him. "Do you remember Abigail Chung?"

"Your grad student from last year? Yes, of course." She and Baxter usually had at least one nice dinner a year and invited all their graduate students to the house to eat, drink wine, and relax. Abigail was a brilliant mathematician from the Seattle area who had stuck in Katherine's memory for her wonderful sense of humor and being a fellow *Star Wars* enthusiast. "What happened to Abby?"

Whatever it was, it wasn't good. She could tell by the weariness in Baxter's expression.

"She and Margaret's grad student Shauna were sharing an apartment until just a few months ago. Abby moved in with her boyfriend after that. Very nice young man; I met him months ago." Baxter rubbed his face and pinched the bridge of his nose. "Shauna called Margaret today to tell us that Abby is in the hospital and Mario is too. That Abby... attacked Mario with a knife."

Katherine felt her stomach drop. "No."

"He's alive, but he is quite injured. Apparently, after she attacked Mario, she turned the knife on herself."

No, no, no, no, no. Katherine shook her head. The girl she knew was funny and excited about geometric proofs and Jedi lore. She was a little shy until she got to know you; then she blossomed and had the most brilliant smile. "Baxter, there has to be a mistake."

He rubbed a hand over his eyes. "She called the police. She told Shauna that she woke up in her own blood and thought someone must have broken into their home and attacked them. But the police are saying that there are no signs of a break-in. That Abby's fingerprints are the only ones on the knife and that it's quite evident from the scene that she was the perpetrator. I suppose from the blood evidence or something like that?"

"What's Mario saying?"

"He's still unconscious."

"But it's Abby," Katherine said. "I can't imagine her even defending herself if someone was attacking her. There's no way—"

"No way she would hurt someone she loved." Baxter's voice was soft. He turned to Katherine and took her hands in his, pressing them between his palms. "And I'm sure Justin McCabe's family and friends would say there was no way he would shoot up a fitness center full of people."

"No way Sarah Jordan would overdose her horse on tranquilizers," she murmured. "You think Abby was participating in the study."

"I think it's very likely," Baxter said. "I don't know what's going on, but if there is any way that I can help, I will. I don't care about the ethics of the thing. You and me? We'll be fine. Right now an innocent man is in the hospital, unconscious and gravely injured. And a bright and brilliant young woman is also in the hospital and under suspicion of attempted murder." He shook his head deliberately. "Not her. Not Abigail. I know this girl."

Katherine nodded and put her cheek on Baxter's shoulder. "We're going to find out what's happening."

She felt absurdly guilty for not foreseeing Abby's breakdown. Why would she see Justin McCabe's crime, but not

Abby's? Was it just proximity? Could she only see things right in front of her?

Just so you know, Baxter, I'm just the tiniest bit clairvoyant. Nothing serious, merely a slight case of visions, but I thought you should know.

Nope. She still sounded like a delusional person in her head.

Baxter put his arm around her shoulders. His voice was low and grim. "If Ansel Shaver had anything to do with harming these children's minds—"

"Bax." She reached up and squeezed his hand. "There's no reason to think that. He's not the friendliest person, but I've never known him to be unethical or cruel. We need to find out who was in that study. There were probably dozens of students, and it seems like any of them could be at risk."

She hadn't known Sarah or Justin before their violence, but she'd known Abby. If something could make cheerful, funny Abigail Chung a violent person, anyone was at risk.

"I may have an idea on that," Baxter said. "I don't know Shaver very well, but I know Anita Mehdi, one of the other professors who worked on it with him. We chatted a bit about the data collection and methodology months ago along with Professor Kraft."

"Alice Kraft? Isn't she in computer sciences?"

"Yes, but she was working with them on the reporting, I think? We spoke in general terms only, but I'm certain it's the same study you were talking about."

"Do you think Professor Mehdi would be willing—?"

"Maybe." He turned toward her, and the planes of his face were shadowed in the moonlight. "For Abby—for all the other students—I'm willing to risk the ask."

CHAPTER 16

*W*hen Katherine answered the door on Wednesday, she was expecting to see Toni or Megan even though it was a bit early for their usual meeting.

What she wasn't expecting was a trio of women with nervous smiles. The one in front was vaguely familiar. How did Katherine know her? Was she a neighbor? Someone from work?

"Katherine!" The woman with sandy-brown hair spoke first. "I am so sorry."

"For?" How did she know her? Not work, she was... "You're Mark's wife!"

"Robin. Yes. I am so sorry for barging in on you like this." She genuinely looked apologetic. "I know we're probably interrupting you, but—"

Katherine looked at the two women behind her. "Which one of you is Monica?"

A curvaceous brunette with dimples and warm brown eyes waved. "Hi, Katherine."

"It is so nice to meet you." She opened the door widely

and nearly pulled Monica inside. "I cannot tell you how reassuring it was for me to speak to you about..." Katherine suddenly remembered Baxter was in the study. "You know, I should introduce you to my husband." She shook her head and mouthed, "does not know" as she pointed to her temple.

Monica's and Robin's eyes lit up immediately.

The other woman with them had pink-and-black hair. She looked confused. "Doesn't know what?"

Monica elbowed her and pulled her down to whisper in her ear.

"Oh right."

"Baxter?" She leaned over to Robin. "Why are you here?" she whispered.

"Girls' break. Staying at the beach." Robin was looking around her, surveying the house. "Your house is stunning. Lots of cool midcentury pieces here."

"Katherine?" Baxter poked his head out of the study and his eyes went wide. "Oh. Hello to lots of new people."

The pink-and-black-haired woman pointed directly at him. "You have a kick-ass accent and I love it. It's Chinese but also British and it's awesome."

Baxter smiled. "I'm from Hong Kong."

"That would explain it." She stuck out her hand. "I'm Val. I'm not the ringleader, but I'm probably the instigator."

Baxter laughed. "Nice to meet you, Val."

Katherine stepped to his side. "Do you remember my friend Mark?"

He frowned. "Vaguely from running, right? College friend?"

"Yes." Katherine held out her hand toward Robin. "This

is Robin, Mark's wife. She and her two friends are here for a quick getaway, and they were nice enough to stop by."

Monica stepped forward. "Your wonderful wife helped me with a research question last year, and I'm so pleased to meet her finally. I'm Monica."

"Monica, it's very nice to meet you." Baxter looked around his kitchen, which was filled with women. "Are Toni and Megan still coming over?"

"Are they?" Monica sounded excited. "Oh, that would be perfect."

"I think so." Katherine was very tempted to grab Baxter, run into the office, and lock the door behind her. Two extra people in her house felt crowded. Contemplating five...

"If they're coming over, we might be too much company," Robin said. "After all—"

"It's fine," Katherine blurted. "It might be a little crowded inside, but we usually sit on the deck."

Val stepped toward the door and put her hands on her hips. "And why wouldn't you? That's one incredible view."

"You have incredible views too." Katherine turned to Baxter. "They're from Glimmer Lake." *Deep breaths, Katherine. In. Out. There is plenty of air.*

"Oh, it's beautiful there. I love to go up in the winter right after it snows." He frowned. "How long is that drive?"

"About four hours," Robin said. "Not too bad."

"Little complicated when you only have two hours' notice," Val muttered. "But yeah, the drive is nice."

His eyebrows went up. "Two hours?"

Monica elbowed Val. "She's just complaining because we dragged her away from work."

"She's a workaholic." Robin put her arm around Val. "We all are."

Baxter chuckled. "You're in good company here." He glanced at Katherine.

She was trying her best not to look panicked.

It was fine. It would be fine.

They could go outside.

The crowded feeling would go away and she'd be able to breathe.

Baxter saw her. "Darling, why don't you all go out on the deck, and I'll bring a bottle of wine. No reason to stay in here where it's crowded."

She was a brilliant woman. Absolutely brilliant. Not because of the two PhDs, that had nothing to do with it. She was brilliant because she married Baxter Pang when she was twenty-seven. How could she have known he'd be so wonderful?

"Thanks." She forced the words out. "Robin, Monica..." Dammit. She'd forgotten the third name.

"Val." The woman was already walking to the door. "Deck or bust for me. I want that ocean view."

She turned to Baxter. "When Toni and Megan get here—"

"I'll send them back." He leaned over and kissed her forehead. "Look at you. You're the center of attention."

"Make it stop," she whispered.

"If they're here too long, I'll come out and start telling them about the ABC-conjecture controversy."

"Careful. That's such a compelling story they may never leave."

"I know you mean that sincerely." He walked over and

opened the wine cabinet in the kitchen. "Go entertain the guests. I'll bring some wine out shortly."

"You are a prince among men." She reached for wine-glasses and hooked four between her fingers. "Thank you, Bax."

"You're welcome." He smiled at the women on the deck. "It's quite lovely to see other people appreciating how delightful you are, you know? It makes me feel rather clever."

She felt her cheeks flush as she walked to the door. "I'm paying you back for that compliment later."

"I shall look forward to it."

Katherine stepped out onto the deck with the four wine-glasses, a polite smile, and a spiraling sense of confusion about what exactly came next.

Her life didn't exactly feel like her own anymore.

"So." Monica scooted forward and reached for a glass. "Why don't I start by telling you why we're here?"

"You saw all of us?" Toni asked. "Like, in your vision?"

Monica nodded. "You were holding a gun on someone. You looked... intent. That's the only word for it." She turned to Megan. "You were throwing someone into a tree."

Megan's eyes went wide. "For real?"

"Do you have superstrength or something?"

"No, but I'm telekinetic."

"That might explain the superstrength," Val said. "Combine natural strength with supernatural?"

"Maybe," Monica said. "And then Katherine was..." She frowned.

"What?" Katherine felt a sense of impossible dread. What was Monica seeing? She didn't look happy. "What was I doing in the vision?"

"It looked like you were playing chess, but I couldn't see with whom." Monica held up her hands. "Sometimes the visions aren't exact."

"Chess?" Katherine didn't even like chess. Chess was Baxter's game. "Okay. Chess." Weird. She'd have to think about that one.

"I saw the vision last night," Monica said. "But we've been meaning to make a trip over here for a while. We talked to you a couple of weeks ago and then we didn't hear anything back."

Robin said, "We were a little worried."

"You'd have reason to be," Megan said. "Since the thing at the gym, we found out there was another young lady who may or may not have a connection to the boy who tried to shoot up the gym, and she had a very strange outburst too."

Katherine said, "And then just a couple of days ago, Baxter found out one of his grad students stabbed her boyfriend."

"Oh my God, is he alive? Is she?"

"Yes and yes, but they're both in the hospital."

Val narrowed her eyes. "Any history of violence or abuse?"

"Nothing," Katherine said. "No domestic violence ever reported. Very loving. Both perfectly normal kids in their midtwenties. The young man is still in a coma, and Abby—she was Baxter's student—is at the hospital, but she's being held on suspicion of assault with a deadly weapon. She claims she doesn't remember what happened. She woke up and they were both bleeding. Baxter talked to her parents yesterday. She's terrified and very confused. She's still convinced that someone broke into their house and she doesn't remember anything."

Monica shook her head. "God, that's scary."

"She was bleeding too?" Val asked. "So the police are saying she stabbed him and then herself?"

"That's what it seems like."

Val set down her wineglass and pointed at Robin. "Ghost."

"We don't know that," Robin said. "I can look into that if you can get me close enough to visit with the girl, but there could be something else going on." Robin looked at Toni. "You're an empath, right?"

Toni nodded. "Whatever that means. I'm still not quite sure yet."

"I've been doing some research with a few sources I've found that I trust," Robin said. "Empaths and mediums don't have much crossover, but there is some. Both powers involve connection with human energy. Maybe I can help you find some focus. It could be that you'd be able to sense a spirit's emotional presence even if you can't communicate with them. I might be able to teach you more about reading emotional signatures, which could come in handy."

"Do spirits have emotional signatures?"

"Oh yes." Robin nodded. "Very definitely. Sometimes they're more emotion than anything else."

"Interesting." Toni nodded. "Okay, I'd be game for that."

Val raised her hand. "Okay, who's the telekinetic?"

Megan said, "That's me."

"Just so you know, I'm hella jealous. Telekinesis is so

much cooler than psychometry," Val said. "Can you imagine being able to, like, do the dishes while you make yourself a cup of coffee? It'd be like having an extra hand."

Monica gasped. "Val, you might even be able to... fold all your laundry."

"Stop judging my laundry sofa. It's clean. Who cares if it's folded or not? My two boys? I doubt it. If they want folded clothes, they can fold them."

Megan raised her hand. "For the record, I don't have anywhere near laundry-folding control yet, but I do agree that would be awesome. Folding laundry is the worst."

Val pointed at her. "Thank you!"

Monica shook her head. "How can you say that when ironing exists?"

"Who irons anything anymore?" Toni asked. "The only person I know who irons is my mother, and that's only my clothes for mass on Sunday."

Katherine watched the interplay of personalities, completely fascinated. The five women around her were all very different, but it was evident that the three women from Glimmer Lake were longtime friends. They spoke to each other more like Katherine spoke to her sister.

Yet she could already see Toni and Megan showing some solidarity with each other even though neither was likely to admit it.

And her?

Well, she still felt a little bit on the outside, but she also felt included. She had a tie with all these women now. They were an accidental sisterhood of supernatural abilities. In another age, they would have probably been called a coven and burned for witchcraft.

Moving on from that pleasant thought…

"I haven't had any more visions," she said. "Rather, I haven't had any *helpful* ones. I might get a flash of a dish or a cup falling, which isn't helpful. I saw a car accident once; that was awful. I was able to stop a little boy from falling and hitting his head very badly at the grocery store last week. He was in the aisle over and was trying to climb out while his father shopped. I was happy I was able to save him from a few stitches."

"That's great," Monica said. "And at the beginning, I had a lot of mundane visions too. Mostly in my dreams, but sometimes waking ones. More dreams though. So I had this vision about you, and we've all been thinking about you girls. My thought was, what if we all took a few days off to come over here to the coast and help you all get a handle on this? I mean, we can't teach you everything, and I'm sure you're all busy—"

"Not me." Megan's smile was bitter. "I moved out here and I have no job. No business. My husband is constantly gone. My kids are all doing their own thing. I'm thinking about getting a dog just so someone is excited when I come home at night."

Awkward silence fell over the group. Katherine glanced at Toni, only to find the woman staring back at her, looking as lost as Katherine felt.

"I want a dog," Katherine blurted out. "A fluffy one. Medium-sized. Maybe a poodle."

"You should get one," Toni said.

"Agreed," Monica said. "Definitely get the dog."

"I'm more of a cat person," Val said. "But whatever floats your boat. And Megan, the upside to your children and husband being sort of assholes right now is that you have me for the rest of the week. I can't teach you how to move stuff, but I do know quite a bit about the psychic energy of objects. And we can commiserate about teenagers."

Megan took a deep breath and forced a smile to her face. "Thanks. That would be great. I'll give you my number."

"And Toni and I can work on the empathy stuff," Robin said. "I've been doing some research too." She reached down and took a manila folder out of her enormous purse. "And I have some ideas." She noticed everyone looking at the folder. "I like research."

Katherine felt an immediate kinship with Robin. She probably liked spreadsheets and charts too. A kindred spirit.

"And you and I can talk about seeing the future," Monica told Katherine. "I know your visions are much more immediate and literal than mine, but maybe we can learn how to stretch things so that whatever you see, you have more time to react. I used to have no control of mine, but lately I've been able to control them a bit more."

Katherine nodded and felt a little bit of her unease settle. "Yes. I think I'd like that. Control would be good."

CHAPTER 17

"So." It was Thursday, and Monica met Katherine at North Beach Coffee Company. "How are you?"

Katherine had barely taken her seat. She'd finished office hours that afternoon after two classes in the morning—Thursdays were her busiest day—and then sent two of her graduate students over to the Fred lab to do preliminary work on the current prototype that Job and Britt had tweaked.

"I'm..."

Overwhelmed.

Worried.

Stressed.

Confused.

She hadn't had any time that week to dwell on Abby at the hospital or think about Justin and Sarah's cases. She hadn't had time to do much more than keep her head above water.

Katherine's silence must have clued Monica in.

"I'm... busy."

"I know how complicated this thing can be," Monica said.

"You're dealing with normal life, which is always busy, while also dealing with this new and very unexpected power that you didn't ask for. Personally, I can't tell you the number of times I've wished I could switch with Robin or Val." She lowered her voice. "I don't want to know the future. I wish I could avoid it completely."

"Yes. Especially when you feel like there's nothing you can do."

Monica nodded. "Exactly! Remember when I first called you?"

"I told you that, in theory, trying to prevent a specific outcome could lead to the exact result you were trying to avoid."

Monica smiled sadly. "And yet..."

"It's impossible to do nothing," Katherine said. "I see that now. If I hadn't interrupted Justin McCabe—"

"People would have died. But you did something, and they didn't." Monica scooted closer. "Which is great. Hold on to that feeling, because there will be other times when you can't do anything. Times when you can see what will happen but it doesn't matter. It's just impossible to change the outcome. And times when you could change the outcome, but you know that things have to happen exactly the way you foresee them."

"How can you tell the difference?" Katherine got out the notebook she'd tucked in her purse and took a pencil from her organizer. "Are some visions different in some way? Do you have a process for—"

"I wish I could give you a rule." Monica shook her head. "I can't. It's more a sense of intuition."

Katherine put her pencil down. "That could be a problem. You may not have realized this, but I'm not the best at reading into things."

"I did sense that," Monica said. "But I also know you're a good observer. You've already got a good handle on reading Megan and Toni."

"Do you think so?"

"Sure!" Monica smiled, and it lifted Katherine's mood. "It's really obvious that you're getting close. I think it's admirable how the three of you have bonded over this. It's important that the people closest to you know that something in your life is different."

"They're the only ones who know." Katherine sipped her decaf iced coffee. If she had anything stronger at this time of day, she'd be awake all night. "Just Toni and Megan."

"You haven't told your husband or any other friends?"

I don't have any other friends.

"I told you." Katherine nodded. "As for Baxter... I think it would be better if I didn't tell him. He'd probably insist on a full neural evaluation."

Monica's eyes went wide. "He'd think you were mentally ill?"

"No, I think his first thought would be that there was a physical reason for the delusion." Katherine nodded. "A tumor or mild stroke maybe?"

"Wow."

"Well..." She shrugged. "You remember what I thought before. I would be skeptical too. Even though my mind is very open about neurological abilities we don't understand, seeing into the future just seems..."

Monica smiled. "Magical?"

"Too magical." Katherine offered a strained laugh. "I

can't tell you how many times I've nearly convinced myself that I'm imagining all this. But strange things keep happening, and now whatever is going on with the students and this violence... I don't know what to think, but I can't ignore it. And I have to do something—anything I can—to prevent another tragedy."

Katherine's mind was full of the call Baxter had made to Abby's former roommate that morning. Whatever qualms he'd had about intruding on a colleague's experimental study were gone. He'd grilled Abby's former roommate about Abby's habits, her medications, and anything she knew about Abby's participation in the Shaver study, which wasn't much.

"My husband knows that something is wrong," Katherine said. "He knows something strange is going on with the students and he wants to help. I think that's enough for now, don't you think?"

"It's up to you." Monica sipped her iced tea. "But please know I completely sympathize. My boyfriend" —she broke into a smile— "I still feel weird calling him a boyfriend. Is he still a boyfriend when he's pushing fifty and you're forty-eight? Anyway, he was a skeptic until he saw evidence. So I get it."

Katherine smiled at the clear happiness on Monica's face. "You know, sometimes I still refer to Baxter as my boyfriend, so I don't know why not."

"All I'm going to tell you is that it's obvious you're a good judge of character, so at some point, you're going to have to trust your instincts. Don't doubt your read on people so much. I think you probably know more than you realize." She reached for her tea. "You're obviously well matched with Baxter; I don't know why you think he'd doubt you."

"He'd doubt me because he's like me." Katherine looked out the window at the passing cars. "We like facts. Observable data. And if we don't understand a thing, we're relentless in trying to make sense of it."

"Is that what you're really afraid of? Your husband digging in and trying to make sense of you?"

Oh.

Hmmm.

"Maybe," Katherine said softly. "I'm going to have to think about that. The last thing I want is to become a problem Baxter has to solve."

"He adores you," Monica said. "It's completely obvious just from the few minutes I saw you together."

"I know my husband loves me." She tried to put her tangled thoughts into words. "I also know that he thinks he knows me. And I think he would be bothered if there was something about me he didn't understand. Does that make sense?"

"Yes." Monica nodded. "But do you really think he understands you completely? Do we ever really understand every part of a person? Do we need to?"

"That's the most important question," Katherine said. "The one at the end. Do we need to?" She tapped her fingers on her glass. "I don't know. You're a widow; I heard Robin mention it."

"I am."

"How long were you married?"

"A little over twenty-five years."

"Wow." Katherine's heart hurt for her. "I don't even like thinking about it."

Monica's eyes got shiny. "Yeah, it's not great. I'm not

going to say I moved past it because you can't be married to someone for twenty-five years and get over losing them. But Gabe—my boyfriend—he gets that. What I feel for him? It's so different than what Gilbert and I had."

"Do you think you knew everything about Gilbert?"

"After twenty-five years?" She shook her head. "Not even a little. People are too complicated, and we're growing and changing all the time. That's the exciting part."

"So that didn't bother you?"

"That's the fun part, Katherine." Monica's smile was incandescent. "In love. In life. In friendship. The change is the exciting part."

———

CHANGE IS THE EXCITING PART.

Katherine tried to keep Monica's advice in mind when she returned to the university on Friday morning. She had hours at the Fred lab, and she was supposed to have a meeting with Ansel Shaver.

It would be her first meeting with Ansel since she'd become convinced his research study in biometrics—which she wasn't supposed to know anything about—was connected to the unexplained violence of three students at the college.

"Morning, Professor B!" Kaylee was sitting at the front desk. She looked like she was grading papers. Ansel's other grad student, Greg—the one she'd run into at the student center—was sitting next to her. He appeared to be inputting some kind of data into the computer.

"Good morning, Kaylee. Greg." Katherine nodded to both of them. "What are you two up to this morning?"

"Ugh. Essays for Intro to Critical Thinking," Kaylee grumbled. "Someone kill me now."

"Want to trade?" Greg scowled. "I have about three hundred more entries in this spreadsheet if you'd rather do this."

Kaylee glanced at Katherine before she asked, "Is that the biometrics study?"

"You mean the sea of numbers I'm swimming in? I don't know why he wanted me over here for entry," Greg said. "Something about looking for patterns, but who has to do all the grunt work? I'm supposed to be meeting with Alice Kraft, but instead I'm doing all this bullshit."

Katherine was surprised Greg was complaining in front of one of Ansel's colleagues. It was unusual for a grad student, but then again, Katherine wasn't a gossip, and Greg would never be defending a thesis to her. He was probably far more politic with those in his department.

"Kaylee, is Professor Shaver in his office?"

"Yep." She flipped over another blue book. "He was in there arguing with someone on the phone, but he's been quiet for a while, so he's probably done."

"Mehdi," Greg muttered. "I think she's the reason he wants to reorganize everything too."

"Anita Mehdi?"

"Yeah." Greg didn't look up, and his brow remained furrowed.

What a sulky little boy.

That one would never last long with her. Odd. He'd been pleasant the other day.

Anita Mehdi had been the professor that Baxter was

going to feel out about the study. And now Ansel was arguing with her?

Hmmm.

Kaylee caught her eye and gave Greg a massive eye roll. The corner of Katherine's mouth turned up.

"Do you want me to call him?" Kaylee asked.

"Don't worry about it. I'll just pop in. He knows we're supposed to have a meeting this morning." She headed toward her office but stopped when Kaylee called her.

"Professor B!"

She turned. "Yes?"

"I heard about that girl in the mathematics department. She was one of Professor Pang's grad students, right?"

Greg looked up, suddenly interested in the gossip.

"She was," Katherine said to Kaylee. "She's a really wonderful girl. I hope they can figure out what happened."

Greg said, "I heard the police were going to charge her with attempted murder. That it was some kind of domestic situation."

Katherine turned to him. "Do you know Abby?"

He opened his mouth. Closed it.

Katherine knew he couldn't admit knowing Abby if she was part of the study.

"I... can't say," Greg said. "I might have met her. It's not a big campus."

Katherine nodded, never breaking away from his eyes. "To those of us who know Abby, we understand how out of character this is. She is a very special, joyful person." Katherine couldn't say what instinct told her to keep eye contact with Greg, but she was following Monica's directions.

Trust your instincts.

Her instincts told her Greg knew something. He might just be a grad student, but grad students saw the nuts and bolts of how university research happened. Katherine would bet her new psychic powers that Greg knew more than a little about Ansel Shaver's study, and he also knew something wasn't right.

He looked away first, back to the computer where he was entering data. "Huh. Well, I guess the police will investigate it, right? None of my business."

Kaylee had watched the interchange with wide eyes. "I really hope Abby and her boyfriend get better soon, Professor B."

"Thank you, Kaylee. I'll pass that along when I see Professor Pang."

Katherine turned and continued down the hall. She walked into her office, shut the door, and stored her briefcase in her file drawer. Then she opened her laptop and took a deep breath.

She'd be meeting with Ansel Shaver in just a little while.

So what are you going to do?

CHAPTER 18

She scrolled through the data printouts Ansel had sent to her, drinking coffee in his office and trying not to shout, *"What did you do to Abby?"* at him.

Katherine had a feeling that approach wouldn't produce anything useful.

"So these are... exactly what we were expecting." She glanced up. "That's good news. Were there any anomalies you wanted to mention?"

"Tank One managed to get his electrode off in the third set—"

"That's the one Maria calls Primo, right?"

Ansel looked up from his tablet. "What?"

He wasn't a handsome man, but he was striking. Ansel Shaver was tall with greying blond hair and striking green eyes. His hawkish nose was prominent, and the wrinkle patterns on his face indicated a man who didn't smile often but enjoyed being outdoors.

"Maria gave all the test octopi names. Tank one is Primo, tank two is Segundo, three is Tertius, four is—"

"Quatro, or something equally ridiculous?" His face held a slight sneer.

Ansel had always rubbed her slightly the wrong way, but she could never put her finger on why. Now she knew: he had no sense of fun. No imagination.

"No," Katherine said. "That one she just calls Bob. She said she couldn't figure out a good 'four' name."

His expression didn't change. "As I was saying, Tank One managed to get his sensor off in the third round of recordings. You can see that on the fourth spreadsheet. But if we discard that set, everything else is as expected."

"Okay. So we have a baseline. Excellent." Katherine looked at the charts, but instead of rows and columns of numbers, she saw an intricate network of millions of neurons connecting nine brains, each arm of the octopus an entity unto itself connected to a greater whole. The neural network was unlike any other on earth and stretched the limits of Katherine's imagination.

"They are so marvelous." She scrolled through the numbers.

"What are?"

"The subjects." She looked up. "Don't you think they're remarkable?"

"From a purely scientific standpoint, they're an oddity. I don't know that I'd call them remarkable."

And that is why Segundo squirts you every time you walk into the tank room.

"Hmm." Katherine wouldn't let his demeanor dampen her admiration of the unusual and clever creatures. "From a systems standpoint, cephalopods are remarkable. We have a lot to learn from them."

"I can concur with that."

Her mind wandered from cephalopod research to the study again. Had Ansel been as callous with his students as he was with the four octopi he measured regularly?

Had he been callous with them at all? Or where they—like the spreadsheets Katherine was looking at—merely numbers on a page?

"Ansel?"

"Hmm?"

How to ask...?

In the space of a breath, the grey descended around her. She was in Ansel Shaver's office and he was speaking.

"...you need human subjects for that?"

Oh yes.

What were they talking about? She was in the middle of a vision and there was something she was supposed to do. What had Monica advised her?

Pull back. Be an observer, not a participant. Try to draw the experience out. Notice everything. Use all your senses even if they're muffled. Stretch.

Katherine felt like she was moving with a weighted blanket draped on her body, but she moved back, pulled away, and felt herself stretch as if her body was elastic that could snap back anytime. Her senses were still muddy, but the vision moved even more slowly than she did.

"Oh no. God no. You don't have to actually interact ... what grad students are for..."

"How many graduate students would I need..."

"Katherine?"

She blinked and her ears popped. "Pardon me?"

Ansel Shaver frowned, and Katherine couldn't help but

notice that while the vision had stretched, the time had too. Events hadn't happened yet. She'd given herself time.

If she stretched the vision, perhaps she had a greater amount of time before it came to fruition.

"I think you were going to ask me something."

"I was going to ask you..." She racked her brain. *How to ask...?* Of course! If she wanted to ask him about the study, she could ask for *advice*. If there was anything men in academia enjoyed, it was giving advice—solicited or unsolicited. Especially to female colleagues.

"I'm thinking about structuring a study, and since you've done far more human subject research, I had a couple of questions I was wondering if you'd be able to answer."

Ansel looked up. "Human subject research in physics?"

"In *bio*physics."

"On what?"

It was a fair question. Most of the research Katherine participated in was similar to what they were doing in the Fred lab and involved biosystems analysis and far more numbers than people.

How to completely confuse a psychologist?

Incomprehensible physics talk.

"I've been thinking about reexamining the thermodynamic negentropy, or rather the specific entropy deficits of dynamically ordered subsystems in relation to physical surroundings." Any of her actual colleagues would be laughing at her.

Ansel frowned. "And you need human subjects for that?"

There it was; they were in the timeline of the vision.

"Do I need human subjects?" *Not even a little bit.* "Oh yes."

He opened his mouth, closed it, then shrugged. "What do you want to know?"

Yep, he fell for it.

Katherine pursed her lips and put on her best "indifferent academic" voice. "I suppose I wondered how much interaction I'd be expected to have with the test subjects. If I'm writing the protocols, do I have to actually oversee each step of the research?"

How much did you know these students? How close were you? Did you know you were somehow screwing up their brains?

Ansel shook his head. "Very little. With my most recent study, after initial enrollment I never saw them. Not once." He waved at the tablet. "They're numbers on a screen to me."

All study subjects would be given a number when they joined the study to protect their privacy. That way, anyone looking through the information would have no idea which student was which.

"Good to know," Katherine said. "I'm still teaching general-ed classes, so I want to be careful to limit my interaction with students." They were skipping around in the future. She'd changed something along the way, though she couldn't figure out what it was, but their dialogue wasn't tracking what the vision had been.

"Oh no. God no," Ansel added. "You don't have to actually interact with them. That's what grad students are for."

"How many graduate students would I need to dedicate to a project like that?"

"Depends on how it's structured, but with my last one, we had roughly seventy subjects and ten grad students running the actual interviews and methodologies we were testing. Who will you be working with?"

On a completely fictional study that doesn't need to be run and doesn't need people to do it? "I'm still debating. I'd be lead of course, but anywhere from five to six. Was your study survey based? How many partners?"

"Five total. And we were testing..." He seemed to consider for a moment before pushing on. "We were testing what some would call an alternative anxiety treatment in conjunction with more standard medical treatments."

"Not as a replacement for medicine but a complement?"

"Exactly."

"Interesting." She looked back at her tablet so as not to seem too interested. "I'd think there would be a lot of journal interest in that."

The corner of his mouth turned up. "I don't think it'll sit on a shelf."

She kept her eyes down on her tablet, making her words sound like an afterthought. "So you had two of your own students running things? And then everyone else contributed two of theirs?" She pretended to consider. "Yes, I can see how that would work."

"The grad students took care of all the grunt work, so to speak." Ansel smiled. "The majority of the information was collected remotely. Very little interaction at all. If I passed a participant on campus, I'd probably never recognize them."

"Ideal." It also meant that Ansel might have no idea that three of his study participants had had adverse psychological events in the past six months. "So did you end up with any Primos?"

He frowned. "I beg your pardon?"

"Sensors thrown off?" She raised her tablet with the spreadsheets on it. "Like our Primo. Data that doesn't fit the pattern? In a group of seventy, I'm assuming some will drop out, that kind of thing."

"Oh." He curled his lip. "Naturally. All that is caught in the follow-up. Which again, that's mostly on the grad students. They collect, we interpret."

"Fantastic." She returned to their cephalopod research. "Nine neural control centers. Nine. Fantastic. That would be like if we had five brains, each one controlling a limb independently. Can you imagine having five brains, each one controlling a different appendage? Talk about coordination."

"No."

"You don't think they're coordinated?"

"No." He looked up, his face a complete blank. "I can't imagine having five brains."

God, he was boring. Too boring to be a bad guy?

That, like so much of her life at the moment, was up for debate. No matter, she'd learned an invaluable lesson, and in a small way, she'd even changed the future.

BAXTER SAT on the couch in his study, his feet kicked up on an ottoman, tapping his chin and staring out the window. "And he offered that information freely?"

"I framed the questions as a hypothetical for a study I was considering putting together."

The corner of Baxter's mouth turned up. "With human subjects? In physics? What was this hypothetical study?"

"I don't even remember what I told him. Something

about thermodynamic negentropy." She waved a hand. "As soon as I said *negentropy*, his eyes started glazing over."

Baxter threw his head back and laughed. "He wouldn't even question it. He abhors looking ignorant."

"Do you know what negentropy is?"

"Only vaguely, and I would always defer to my brilliant wife in anything Schrödinger posited."

She waggled her eyebrows at him. "You do know how to flirt with a physicist, don't you?"

"Indeed, I excel in it." His smile waned. "So he seemed to have no idea about Abigail? Or the other two students?"

"Nothing in his demeanor said he was hiding anything or thought he had anything to be worried about."

"He's egotistical. Maybe he thinks he can get away with ignoring adverse reactions in his subjects."

"I agree he's egotistical, but he's also very focused on publication. That much was obvious. With something like this that could potentially have so many real-world applications, he might even be looking for a book deal."

Baxter held out a hand. "And that's not all the more reason for him to obfuscate?"

"Hiding the truth won't help him with the IRB. And anything that's produced for publication—especially if it's for a more popular publishing audience—would be absolutely scrutinized."

Baxter worried his lower lip, which he only did when he was thinking particularly hard.

"One of the students in the Fred lab said she heard Shaver arguing with Mehdi today."

Baxter nodded slowly. "I spoke to Anita this morning. I told her it was highly confidential, but that I had good reason to believe that Abby—whom Anita knows—was part of the study last year and that she'd recently had an aberrant psychological episode. I gave her the details of the situation, and she sounded very disturbed. I also told her that I had reason to believe two other students had been affected and she needed to look into it."

"Did you tell her you were thinking of filing a report?"

He shook his head. "Not yet. If it comes from someone within the study, it's better for everyone."

"I understand what you're saying, but where does that leave all the other students in the meantime?"

"I don't know," Baxter said. "But we currently don't have any idea what's causing this, so I don't even know if warning them would be useful. We might send students into a panic when it's not necessary."

Katherine got up and rounded the ottoman to sit next to him. Baxter tucked her under his arm and squeezed.

"I don't know what the right thing is," Katherine said. "I hate being in the dark like this."

"I know." He pressed a kiss to her temple. "I spoke with Abby today."

"How is she feeling?"

"Confused. Heartbroken. Mario is doing much better, so that helps, but he's still got a long road of healing and she feels extraordinary guilt. Mario has been advised by the police and his attorney not to speak to Abby at all."

"And she still remembers nothing?"

He shook his head. "If she does, she's blocked it out."

"Did you ask her directly if she was part of the study?"

"I did and she told me she was, but she had no idea how any of the exercises she was doing—which she found very calming—could have contributed to this. Once we start talking about that, someone took her phone away."

Katherine took a deep breath. "The police aren't going to be able to ignore this. That's two students acting wildly out of character and committing crimes within weeks of each other."

"I suppose it depends on who is investigating."

"The detective we spoke to after the gym was named Drew Bisset."

Baxter tapped his fingers along Katherine's hip. "Is he investigating Abby's case too?"

"Probably. How many detectives can there be in Moonstone Cove?" She sat up straighter and reached for her phone. "I know someone who might have an idea."

She dialed Toni's phone number and waited for her to answer.

The line picked up, but she only heard whispering voices on the other end.

"Henry, I told you... No, it's not them." She cleared her throat. "Katherine? Everything okay?"

She smiled. "Who's Henry?"

"He's... it's nothing. He's a friend." There was a faint burst of laughter. "Is everything all right?"

"I spoke to Ansel Shaver this morning. He's the one who ran the study. He seemed to have no idea that any of this might be connected, but Baxter spoke to another of the study leaders, and she may be looking into things. I was wondering about the police though?"

"What about them?"

"Would Detective Bisset be working on Abby's case too? Do you think they've made a connection?"

"Oh yeah. Drew's got Abby's case too. He saw the connection immediately, but he doesn't know anything about the study. Or I don't think he does."

"Meeting," Baxter whispered. "You three should have another meeting."

"Wednesday is two days away."

"Right."

"What's that?" Toni asked. She sounded distracted. "A meeting?"

"Baxter was suggesting we meet, but I reminded him that—"

"We'll see each other on Wednesday," Toni said. "I already have the wine. I stole another couple of bottles from my cousin."

"Do you think you can find out anything more about what the police think of Abby's case before then?"

"I'll try. I can tell my cousin she's a friend of a friend. He'll get why I want to know."

"Okay. Have you talked to Megan lately?"

"No, why?"

"I was just curious if she'd managed to speak to Justin McCabe's family."

"Was she going to try?"

"I don't know. Something about the way she talked about his parents made me think she might."

"Well, you're the psychic, so you're probably right."

Katherine glanced at Baxter, but his attention had already been caught by the crossword puzzle on the back of the newspaper. He hadn't heard.

"Toni, I better go. I'll see you on Wednesday."

"See you."

She ended the call and tossed her phone toward the other end of the couch. She watched her husband, who was studying the puzzle as if it contained the secrets of the universe. For the hundredth time, she considered telling him about her visions. About Toni and Megan. About why they'd become so close so quickly.

"Is that what you're really afraid of? Your husband digging in and trying to make sense of you?"

How would her analytical man analyze the inexplicable? Would she become an aberration? Disparate data in his well-ordered life?

No.

Baxter was too essential to her. She needed him. Needed his regard and his respect as well as his love. He was the most secure anchor in her life.

She leaned her head on his shoulder. "Are you playing a game, Professor Pang?"

He turned and raised an eyebrow at her. "Yes. But nothing as interesting as you." He set the newspaper to the side and slid his arm around her waist. "Did you have something else in mind?"

"I have an in-person study proposal I'd like to go over with you."

"Is that so?"

"Yes. In the bedroom."

Baxter stood up so quickly he almost knocked her off the couch.

CHAPTER 19

*T*he next day was Tuesday, and Katherine didn't have student hours, but she crowded into her cramped office with Keisha and Sydney, two of her grad students who were grading Intro to Cosmology essays while she tweaked her notes for her lecture on Thursday.

She didn't *only* have female grad students, but since women were still an unfortunate rarity in their department, she tended to grab any random female postgrads if she saw them wandering in the halls and scoop them up for her own.

"Professor Bassi?" Keisha asked.

"Yes?"

"You're married to Professor Pang, right? The math chair?"

"He's a cochair, thank God, but yes. Why are you asking?"

Keisha and Sydney exchanged glances. "So he knew that girl who stabbed her boyfriend?"

Katherine's stomach dropped. She knew that in a small college like Central Coast, the rumors had to be rampant, but it hurt to have a bright young woman like Abby be the center of this kind of speculation.

"*I* know Abby," Katherine said. "She was Baxter's grad student, and she came to our house on more than one occasion for student dinners."

"Oh."

Sydney said, "I'm so sorry about what happened. It's just really weird. Everyone is talking about it."

"I'm sure they are." Katherine looked at Keisha. "And don't feel bad for asking. It's a very strange situation, and I'd prefer you speak to me rather than listening to rumors. But yes, Baxter and I both know Abby. She's a wonderful person and I'm not sure what's going on, but she's one of the least violent people I know. We're all hoping she and Mario make a full recovery."

"I heard he almost died."

"I don't know about that, but I know he's doing better now." She tried to turn her attention back to her lecture, but Sydney and Keisha were still talking.

"That's just so freaky, you know? Like, you're just hanging out and then your boyfriend or girlfriend flips out and tries to stab you?" Sydney said. "It's like... is anyone safe?"

"That's crazy." Keisha glanced at Katherine. "I mean, the situation is crazy. Not the girl. I don't know anything about her. I just mean it's a crazy situation."

Katherine offered her a polite smile. "I know what you were trying to say. Like I said, I hope they figure out what's going on with her soon."

Even if Abby was exonerated legally, she'd probably have to leave Moonstone Cove. The town was too small, and people remembered everything. Katherine was still occasionally reminded of a gaffe she'd made at a department dinner.

In 2008.

Small towns. They had their pluses and their minuses.

"Sydney, when you're finished with those essays..."

The vision hit her like the sudden onset of vertigo.

The grey descended, and Katherine was in a high place where the wind cut sharply into her face. Immediately, she tried to step back, pull away, and look at the vision from outside the experience.

Time.

Her instincts were screaming at her.

She needed time.

It wasn't her on the roof. Who was she seeing? Where was she? She looked over the Central Coast campus. The dunes were in the distance and the ocean beyond. To her right was the green pasture next to the animal science building.

The architecture building. The roof of the architecture building.

She heard shouts from below. She turned her head and saw the girl staring into the distance, the morning sun casting her face in darkness as she looked toward the sea.

A hiccuping cry. A sniff.

Who was it?

She knew this girl. Who was it?

Her ears popped painfully as the vision passed, leaving Katherine sick to her stomach and dizzy.

"Professor Bassi?" Keisha was standing next to her. "Are you feeling okay?"

Katherine bolted from her office chair and ran toward the door.

"Katherine?"

She didn't have time!

Katherine ran down the hall and out the double doors of the old physics building, into the quad that surrounded a large fountain and reflecting pool. She saw the heights of the architecture building in the distance, the modern portico dominating the face of the pure white marble building.

She had no idea how much time she had, so she ignored the crunch in her right knee and the strain in her ankle. She shifted her mind into the hyperfocus she'd once practiced during trail runs.

No trail. No track. No rules other than get from the quad to the architecture building as quickly as possible. She mentally mapped out a route in her mind as she ran across the quad. The route would take her over ten minutes at a fast walk.

She didn't have ten minutes.

She maybe—*maybe*—had five.

Katherine leaped over a corner of the fountain and dodged groups of students, running as fast as she possibly could. Her lungs were burning by the time she left the quad. Treadmills and walks on the beach were not nearly as strenuous as the conditioning she used to do.

As she ran, she replayed the vision in her mind. She thought about every detail. The angle of the sun and the wind that cut into her face. The shadowed woman in the vision wasn't clear, but Katherine was certain she knew her. There was something about her that felt familiar.

She ran past the library and the maintenance building behind it, up the steps and through the clear glass doors of the design school, down the backside, even as people shouted angry curses at her. As she beat her way through the oak grove past the design school, she heard a siren in the distance and saw a small group gathered at the foot of the marble steps.

Katherine reached the architecture building at a run; she didn't slow, she didn't stop to speak to anyone. She'd been on the roof before and knew how to get there. She ran up the steps and pulled the doors open, heading for the elevator and past the clutch of students who were exiting.

Two minutes. Did she have two minutes?

She hit the back wall of the elevator and turned, punching the button for the top floor. A group of clueless students tried to enter behind her.

"No!" Katherine shoved them out a moment before the doors closed.

"What the hell?"

"Are you kidding me?"

"Back off!" She panted and glared at the students, who waited with annoyed expressions.

The doors closed and Katherine pushed the button for the top floor again.

In her mind, a clock was ticking. Her heart was pounding, and her adrenaline raced. She felt a strange euphoria she hadn't felt in years.

The doors opened and she ran to the roof access door. She pulled it open and rushed up the clanging metal stairs, reaching the roof door before she'd formulated a plan in her mind.

She caught a glimpse of the woman as she stepped toward the edge of the building.

"Stop!" Katherine screamed and held out her hands. She skidded to a halt as the woman on the roof turned.

Her eyes were vacant, but her face was familiar.

"Kaylee?" Katherine walked over and reached for Kaylee's hand. "Come here."

She was still awfully close to the edge, far closer than Katherine would ever be comfortable with. She was also silent.

"Kaylee!" She dragged the woman back, and it wasn't easy. Her feet seemed glued to the roof. Katherine stumbled, but she finally pulled Kaylee away.

The girl blinked, but she didn't speak. One of Katherine's nephews had gone through a sleepwalking phase when he was a preteen. It was the only comparison Katherine could make to the expression on Kaylee's face.

"Kaylee Ivers." Katherine reached up and pinched the student's ear. "Talk to me."

Kaylee's skin was cold and a little clammy. Her pupils were almost pinprick small.

Katherine heard more sirens, and shouts began to drift up from the ground below.

"Kaylee." She patted her cheek. "It's Katherine Bassi."

The woman finally blinked.

"It's Katherine Bassi, Kaylee." She pinched her ear again. "Kaylee!"

She blinked again.

Katherine was racking her brain, trying to figure out something that could snap Kaylee out of whatever trance she was in. When did Kaylee snap to attention at the lab?

She patted her cheek firmly and shouted, "Kaylee, Fred got out of his tank again! Help!"

The young woman blinked rapidly and pressed a hand to her eyes. "Oh!" She moaned audibly; then she looked down, then up. Around the roof in stark confusion. "Where am I?"

"Are you back?" Katherine heard shouting from the crowd below.

"Professor B?" Kaylee was rubbing both her temples. "What's going on?"

"Good question." Katherine was still trying to catch her breath, and the adrenaline was wearing off. "I saw you on the edge of the architecture building. You were walking toward the edge. What were you thinking?"

"What?" Kaylee spun in a circle. "None of this... I don't understand—"

"What's the last thing you remember?" Katherine sat on a marble bench under the shade cover and patted the seat next to her. "Come here. They're going to be coming up those stairs any minute. Talk to me before security gets here."

"Security?" She looked at Katherine, then over her shoulder at the ledge. "Oh my God, was I on the ledge of this building?"

Katherine nodded, still panting.

"Holy shit." The gravity of the situation finally hit her. She knelt down and sat on the roof. "Holy shit." She looked like she was going to cry. "That is like... my worst nightmare."

"What?" Katherine's lungs were starting to calm down, but her knee was going to be the size of a cantaloupe by bedtime, and her ankle felt like it was on fire. "What's the last thing you remember?"

Kaylee's face was white as a sheet. "Just being in the

office," she said. "Being in Professor Shaver's office in the behavioral science building."

"That's at least a fifteen-minute walk from here." She shook her head. "You don't remember anything after that?"

"No."

"Have you been up here before? How did you know how to get to the roof?"

It wasn't an off-limits part of campus, but it wasn't widely known outside of the architecture department either. They didn't want random freshmen throwing water balloons off the top of the building.

Even though that had totally happened.

"I, uh, I came up here once for a reception thing last year. And I actually remember thinking" —she looked toward the edge and her eyes started to water— "falling off the side of this building would totally be something my clumsy self would do. I've literally had nightmares about it."

"Really?" It couldn't be a coincidence. There was no way.

Kaylee had tears running down her face. "I'm so confused. I don't know what's happening right now. And I feel kind of sick."

Katherine pushed back the urge to ask the young woman about all her symptoms at first, but then she realized she might not have another chance. "Tell me how you're feeling. Talk to me."

"Nauseous. Thirsty. Cold, but that might be from the wind."

The breeze had turned sharp on top of the marble building, and the cold cut through Katherine's long-sleeved blouse even though the sun was shining.

"Kaylee, what were you doing this morning? Walk me through it."

"Just grading projects for Professor Shaver. Greg and I trade off helping in his Intro to Psych class, and it was my turn to grade papers. He and Greg were in class; then they got back and..." She blinked rapidly. "I don't remember much after that. They were unhappy though. There was something going on."

Katherine pressed her. "Did it have to do with the biofeedback study?"

She shook her head. "You know I can't talk about that. I can't—"

"Three students, Kaylee. And now you." Katherine felt a flood of panic in her chest. If she hadn't seen the vision of Kaylee, the girl could be dead. People would have speculated why such a seemingly happy girl had chosen suicide, and they would never know that something had been affecting her mind.

Was she losing it? Val's suggestion of a ghost haunting these students didn't seem that impossible. What could it be? Possession? Hypnosis? What the hell was making normal kids do things they'd never do in their right mind?

She wished Toni were here. She wished Megan were here. Megan would be able to soothe Kaylee, and Toni would be able to ease her panic. All Kaylee had at the moment was a reluctant seer who'd never been particularly good at understanding feelings.

"Listen," she told the girl. "I'm going to give you my phone number, my personal number, okay? I want you to call me." She heard voices on the stairs. "Will you do that? Will you call me later?"

Kaylee nodded. "Okay."

She stood and hobbled over to the girl. "They're going to want to know what happened and why you're up here." She caught Kaylee's eyes and held them. "You tell them *whatever you want*. You might have come up here for the view. You might have needed time to think about a personal problem and you had a dizzy spell. You tell them whatever you want, okay? I will follow your lead."

Kaylee nodded. "Okay."

"Professor Bassi?" A security guard shouted from the door. "Professor Katherine Bassi?"

Katherine nodded at Kaylee and squeezed her shoulder. "We're over here!"

CHAPTER 20

"She ended up telling the security officers that she'd gone up to think and had unexpected vertigo when she got too near the edge." Katherine refilled Toni's and Megan's wineglasses.

Baxter was sitting on the deck with them, but he was drinking a gin and tonic as he stared out over the ocean. "And she said she didn't remember anything?" he asked. "Nothing about how she got up there, who was with her, nothing?"

"Nothing."

Toni raised a hand. "Roofies?"

Katherine frowned. "It's possible, I suppose. I don't know much about the drug, but doesn't it incapacitate you?"

Megan nodded. "Yes. We had a whole in-service on the effects of Rohypnol about ten years ago with some alumni and all the girls active in the chapter of our sorority at school. They did a big campus-wide push to raise awareness of the effects. If someone had dosed Kaylee with Rohypnol, no way would she have been able to walk across campus and up to the roof of that building on her own."

Toni rolled her eyes. "You were in a sorority in college. Why am I not surprised?"

Megan's smile was tight. "Didn't expect you to understand."

"Let me guess, y'all raised a lot of money for charity doing bathing suit car washes?"

Megan smiled sweetly. "Don't be silly. We did car washes in cutoffs and wet T-shirts. We saved the bathing suits for all the beauty pageants we were in!"

Toni snorted. "Right."

"Like I said, I wouldn't expect you to understand." She turned to Katherine. "The sister who started the awareness drive on campus is an ER doctor in Atlanta. I can ask her if there are any new drugs she's seen in the college population that might produce the effects you saw in Kaylee."

"Yeah," Toni said. "And I'll ask my cousin at the police department if they've seen anything either."

"Pretty sure a doctor's gonna have a better take on that," Megan said under her breath.

"Pretty sure we don't need to turn down anyone's help for this since we have no fucking clue what we're doing," Toni said. "But that's just poor, uneducated me offering my useless opinion, I guess."

Katherine raised a hand between them. "Both perspectives would be great. A doctor would be very useful, and your cousin is local, Toni. He might know about things that are common around here that a doctor wouldn't."

Toni and Megan glared at each other.

Baxter leaned his arm on the wide wooden armrest of his deck chair and stared at them intently. "Interpersonal power dynamics among women are fascinating."

Toni sat back in her chair. "Yeah? I'm guessing it's not a real estrogen-fest over in the math department, huh?"

"You'd be wrong in that," Baxter said. "We're about a third female in the faculty, and the undergraduate students majoring in mathematics are nearly fifty-fifty. Varies a little from year to year, but it's quite close. I am not sure what anyone's estrogen levels are though. So I can't comment on that."

Megan cocked her head. "I'm not gonna lie, I'm surprised by that."

"That I don't know everyone's estrogen levels? I really don't think it's any of my business."

"No." Megan laughed a little. "I'm surprised that math is evenly split between women and men."

"Me too," Toni said. "I would have guessed more men."

"Admittedly, our near-equality is an aberration, and I hand much of the credit to my cochair in the department. She is a true genius and one of the most brilliant mathematicians in the state system." Baxter sipped his drink and rested his chin on his closed fist. "If you really want what the students might call a sausage fest, you'd have to look over in Katherine's department. Physics at Central Coast is almost all male."

Katherine could barely keep a straight face. After the day she'd had, laughing almost felt sacrilegious. "Did you just say my department is a sausage fest?"

He frowned. "Did I use the term correctly?"

Megan burst into laughter and Toni was watching them, shaking her head in amusement.

"You're asking me?" Katherine said. Good Lord, time with Baxter was exactly what she'd needed. He was too funny. "I think so, yes. But please don't use it again. It just feels wrong." She turned to Toni. "And yes, my department is horribly unbalanced. I gather all the female grad students under my wings so they can't escape and leave me alone to swim in a river of testosterone."

Baxter frowned. "But are you a flying fish in this scenario? You're both swimming and having wings."

She tossed a walnut at him. "I'm a duck."

"Yeah, Baxter." Toni turned to him. "She's a duck."

"Obviously," Megan said. "Bet you feel silly now."

He winked at Katherine. "Immensely."

"New rule for Wine Wednesday," she said. "No questioning of metaphors after the second bottle of wine has been opened."

"Hear, hear." Toni raised her glass.

"I swear," Megan said. "Y'all are the most adorable. Do all academics flirt like you two?"

"No, we're very special academics," Baxter said. "The kind who investigate mysterious behavioral studies and rescue grad students from sleepwalking off buildings."

"The other day, Kaylee said that Ansel Shaver and Anita Mehdi were arguing about something." Katherine looked at Baxter. "Is that your doing?"

"I may have suggested very quietly to Anita that some of the study participants were exhibiting aberrant behavior. She is firmly convinced that Ansel Shaver would never hide anything, and she was deeply involved in writing the study protocols, but she said she would take a second look."

"Does she have access to the names of the students involved?" Megan said. "Can you ask her?"

Baxter and Katherine exchanged a look. "It's quite a

violation to do that, Megan. Privacy is paramount. It's not a courtesy in academic research; it's inviolable. To ask her to hand over names—"

"For their own good though," Toni said. "To protect them."

"You won't get an argument from either of us," Katherine said. "But what Baxter is saying is that an academic would lose their career over something like that."

Baxter scooted closer to the table and reached for a slice of white cheddar and a cracker from the cheese board. "Was it the mention of Anita Mehdi that made you go looking for Kaylee today? Thank God you did; who knows what would have happened otherwise?"

Megan and Toni were watching her intently, and a feeling of inevitability began to grow in the pit of Katherine's stomach.

This. Now.

Baxter frowned, oblivious to the messages Toni and Megan were shooting at her with their eyes. Unfortunately for them, Katherine had no idea what they were trying to say.

Now. Tell him now.

"Come to think of it..." Baxter frowned. "How did you know she was on the roof? Did someone see her? It's what? Five stories? They wouldn't have known who was up there. Did she call you? Why would she call *you* though?"

Tell him. Tell him now.

She could feel the press of secrets against her skin. Tell Baxter what? About her visions? Could she tell him about her visions without revealing Toni's and Megan's powers as well?

"Katherine?" Baxter looked around the table. "What is

going on?" He waved a hand between the three of them. "This is... odd."

"I saw her." Katherine felt like a child again, offering a treasure she'd found along the beach to her indifferent father.

Look! It's a sand dollar.

There are probably thousands of sand dollars on the beach. Tell me something I don't know if you want to impress me.

But look, Father, there isn't a single crack in this one. It's perfect.

Perfection only exists in mathematics, Katherine.

"What?" Baxter was watching her. "Darling, I didn't catch that. You saw her? From the ground? Why were you on that side of campus? Were you going to see—?"

"I saw her." She spoke louder, more clearly. *Please don't break my sand dollar, my love.* "I was in my office with Keisha and Sydney." As she talked, her voice grew stronger. "I was going over my lecture notes for tomorrow and I... It feels a little like vertigo at first."

Baxter's eyes were narrowed, and he was frowning intently. "Katherine, what are you talking about?"

"Most of the visions since that day in the gym have come so quickly." She swallowed the lump in her throat and pressed on. "But I've been working to try to... stretch them. I don't know how to explain it. The first time it was just seconds. Like... a glitch in an old film reel. I saw something happen, but then when the vertigo passed, when the world came back into focus, the seconds hadn't passed. But he was right there, so I stopped him. I stopped him from shooting all those..." She let out a harsh breath. "There were so many people."

"Katherine." Toni's voice was low. "Let us—"

"At first I had no control." She rushed on, certain that if she didn't get the words out, she would lose all her courage. "It came to me in snatches. A cup of coffee I barely caught. I asked you to move your mother's vase away from the edge, so it didn't fall. But then I didn't try to fight anymore. I sat in the grey area and tried to stretch myself. Could it be longer? I tried to stay in the grey a little longer to give myself more time."

This time when she paused to take a breath, no one spoke. Everyone was watching her with wide eyes.

"I saw Kaylee in my office today. I saw her standing on the edge of the architecture building with the wind whipping her hair back, and she was crying and crying. I knew where she was." Katherine felt her heart start to race at the memory. "I knew how long it would take to get there, so I stretched and I stretched as far as I could until I couldn't keep the present away, and then I ran." She pressed a hand to her aching knee that she'd covered with a pair of loose cotton pants so Baxter wouldn't see how swollen it had become. "I ran as fast as I could because I saw what Kaylee was going to do."

Katherine's eyes locked with Baxter's, and she couldn't look away. "Just like I saw what was going to happen at the gym with Justin McCabe. Just like I knew that car accident on Highway 1 was going to happen in front of us. Just like I saw Megan's coffee spill and your mother's vase fall and break into a hundred pieces that we couldn't put back together." Her eyes were wet, and Katherine pulled the words up from her chest like she was dragging them from the waning tide.

"I'm having visions, Bax." She blinked and felt the tears

roll down her cheeks. "I'm not imagining it. I don't know why it's happening. I know how it sounds, but it's the truth."

Please. Please please please, my love...

Baxter was leaning both his elbows on the table, his eyes intent on her and his chin resting on his folded hands. "You saw Kaylee in a vision, standing on the edge of the architecture building, ready to walk off, and you ran across campus fast enough to get to her?"

Katherine laughed through her tears. "Yeah, you should see how big my knee is right now. It's like the size of a melon."

Baxter stood abruptly and walked into the house without a word.

Everything in Katherine's body felt like it collapsed in on itself. She sat back in her chair and her shoulders sank. Her chest felt like someone had punched it.

Megan grabbed her hand. "We'll tell him about us. My thing is way more visible, and he won't be able to deny—"

"Do you want me to make him more receptive to the idea?" Toni asked. "I think I can do that. I'm not saying I'd manipulate his brain or anything, but I could make him just a little less... stubborn maybe? Shit, that's probably manipulating his brain, isn't it?"

"Just let me move something," Megan said. "I'm getting pretty good, and he can't deny..."

Their voices fell away, blending into the sound of waves crashing against the stone-strewn beach. They were white noise. Part of the grey.

Please, my love...

The doors to the house swung open again, and Baxter was there, holding something wrapped in a towel. He walked over and knelt next to Katherine.

"I kept wondering why you were limping when you got home, but I didn't want to ask in front of your friends." He nudged her leg over and lifted it. "My God, Katherine, you should have iced this hours ago." He looked at Megan. "Can I borrow your chair, my dear? She really needs to elevate this."

Megan quickly scooted away. "Of course!"

Katherine's heart had started beating as soon as he opened the door. "Baxter."

He looked up. "I'm processing. Let's focus on this right now. Is your ankle hurt too?"

"Yes. I pulled it."

"Of course you did." He stood and walked back into the house, returning a moment later with another ice pack wrapped in a towel. He lifted her ankle, set it on the ice pack, and stood with his hands on his hips.

All four of them were silent for a few minutes.

Baxter looked at Toni, then at Megan. "The gym."

All three of them exchanged glances.

Baxter nodded at Toni. "You?"

"I'm empathic, I guess," Toni muttered. "I can, like, make people calm down. Or get pissed off. I'm kind of a combination of an emotional sponge and—"

"A nuclear reactor, I imagine." Baxter turned to Megan. "And you?"

Megan picked up a pistachio with her fingers and, with a flick of her wrist, floated it to hover in front of Baxter's nose. "Pistachio?"

"Well..." He swallowed hard. "How about that?"

CHAPTER 21

"*I* just want to thank you both for sticking around for my husband's low-key meltdown." Katherine peeked through the glass doors to the living room. Baxter was still pacing.

Toni asked Megan, "Hey, Katherine thought you might have contacted Justin McCabe's family. Did you?"

"I did! I was able to get in touch with them through Justin's attorney. They're being real protective right now, but they agreed to talk to me next week. He's not in jail anymore, but he is in an in-patient psychiatric facility. It was the only way a judge would let him out before the trial."

"I don't find that surprising. And he probably needs the help right now."

"His lawyer says he's devastated. So are his parents. They only agreed to talk with me because I told them that I thought he was in an altered state. I'm sure they probably think I'll be good for his defense."

"Altered state? Is that what they'd call it legally?"

"I don't know. His lawyer used that phrase; I'm just repeating it."

"Gotcha." Toni switched her focus. "Katherine?"

"Yes?" Baxter was still pacing and she was still watching. He'd made thirteen loops around the living room by her count.

Thirteen and counting.

"You know, I think Baxter's actually doing real well," Megan said. "It's a lot to take in."

"Maybe dangling a nut in front of his nose wasn't the best way to go," Toni said. "Just putting that out there."

"Why not? He's a scientist. He needed evidence."

Katherine chewed on the inside of her lip. "He's a mathematician. This was never going to be an easy adjustment for him. You might as well tell him two plus two equals five." Actually, that was probably a bad example. Nothing was as straightforward in advanced mathematics as it seemed. "Let's just give him some time."

She said that just as Baxter was marching toward the door. All three women stepped back and leaned against the deck railing, pretending they hadn't been staring at the pacing man.

Baxter pointed at Megan. "Manipulation of electromagnetic fields. Theoretical, but not out of the realm of possibility." He looked at Katherine. "You've spoken about this in the past."

"I have. And you laughed at me, but you also admitted that vestigial brain function could theoretically appear to modern humans as parapsychological phenomena."

Megan just shook her head. "None of that made sense to me. I love y'all, but you're kinda aliens sometimes."

Toni muttered, "I can't disagree with that."

Baxter pointed to Toni. "Emotions are brain chemistry influenced by complex hormonal changes that could theoretically be manipulated, even unconsciously, if a person had a hormone imbalance themselves."

Toni nodded. "Why not? Most days I'm pretty sure this is all just an early sign of menopause."

Baxter opened his mouth, frowned, then closed it. He turned to Katherine. "Precognition..."

She sighed. "Isn't possible."

"Wrong." He walked toward her and put his hands on her shoulders. "There is a researcher at Cornell who recently published a study where participants exhibited a demonstrated precognitive ability. They were able to predict when they would see a cat instead of a dog fifty-three percent of the time in a randomized study."

"Fifty-three percent?" Toni said. "That seems more like chance than—"

Megan elbowed her in the ribs. "That seems *very* significant." She spoke over Toni. "Tell us more, Baxter."

"It is significant, because what it shows is that all these traits that you're exhibiting—while they could seem magical to some—have a firm basis in demonstrable science. You have simply had a traumatic experience that spurred your minds to rapid development in these areas."

Katherine felt like Baxter was grasping at straws, but she didn't care. "You believe us."

His eyes locked with hers. "How could you think I'd doubt you?"

She blinked back tears. "I thought you'd think I had a brain tumor or something."

"A brain tumor would in no way explain a floating pistachio."

"See," Megan said. "I told you the nut thing was a good idea."

"Oh, just shut it," Toni muttered. "Let's go inside. It's freezing out here."

Katherine heard the french doors open and close, leaving her and Baxter alone on the deck. It was dark, and evening fog misted over the water.

Baxter wrapped his arms around her and pulled her close. "You've been worried about this for weeks. I knew there was something bothering you, but I thought it was residual stress from the incident at the gym."

"I've been stressed about a lot of things, but mostly I had no idea how to tell you."

"I understand that." He turned his head and pressed a long kiss to her temple. "Darling, you are my world. If you told me the sky was red, I'd simply assume that I had something wrong with my eyes for the past fifty years. I would never doubt the most honest, loving, and brilliant woman I know."

Katherine turned her face and kissed him, pressing her chilled hands against his warm cheeks. He wrapped an arm around her waist and pulled her closer, diving into the kiss, subsuming himself into the union of their mouths and breath.

She didn't know how long they stayed wrapped in each other on the deck, but her hair was damp, and the house was silent when she was able to think again.

"I think Megan and Toni left," she said.

"We should go to bed." He tapped her right hip. "And

you need to elevate that leg and your ankle. I can't believe you ran that hard."

"The other option wasn't an option."

"I know." He put his arm around her and guided her inside. "If I were a large, muscle-bound man, I'd carry you."

"Please don't throw out your back trying to do that. I can walk."

"I just want you to know that the sentiment is there even if the physical ability is not."

"So noted, Professor Pang."

THE NEXT MORNING, Katherine hobbled out to the breakfast table with a new sense of freedom, a deepened love for her husband, and two incredibly sore joints.

She sat at the table and put her legs up. "I don't know how I'm going to walk across campus today."

Baxter looked up from the electric kettle, his eyes still bleary and his hair sticking up slightly at the crown. "You need to stay off your feet today. You have to call in sick."

"Sydney could cover my lecture and I'll have to make up office hours, but I think you're right." She sighed. "It's probably for the best."

"Rumors will likely be swirling," he said. "I'll try to put them off."

"How?"

"Acting distracted and muttering a lot," he said. "That's generally a good way to keep people from talking to me."

This admission confirmed a sneaking suspicion Katherine had harbored for some time, but she let it go. "Keisha and

Sydney were with me. They saw me space out and then take off running."

He dunked a tea bag in a cup of hot water at the same time he poured boiling water into a small french press for her coffee. "Do you think they'll put two and two together with what happened with Kaylee?"

"Sydney might. She and Kaylee have worked with each other in the Fred lab."

"Maybe you need to call Kaylee this morning and work out some kind of story that makes sense."

"And tell Kaylee that I had a vision of her walking off the architecture building?"

He frowned. "I need tea for this conversation."

"I need coffee." She started to get up.

"You'd better not." Baxter's voice was a growl. "Sit. Stay. I'll get your ice and your coffee, but you need to sit."

She grabbed her phone from her robe pocket and called Sydney.

"Hey, Katherine! What's up? You kind of booked it out of the office yesterday. Everything okay?"

"I..." *Think think think!* "You know, I had a meeting with a student, and I forgot about it. Someone who'd gone to extra effort to make time for me. I felt awful about forgetting, so I ran to catch her. I'm sorry if you or Keisha were worried."

"No problem."

"Unfortunately, I overextended my knee a bit—the one that always gives me problems—and it's the size of a melon today. I need to stay off it. Can you handle the cosmology lecture today?"

"Sure! The notes on your desk?"

"Yes." Katherine went over a few points she'd been

meaning to emphasize for the freshman class while Baxter lifted her knee and her ankle to put ice on them. Then he handed her a cup of coffee, and Katherine nearly wept from gratitude.

"Thank you, Sydney. If you could just post about office hours..." She tried to think. "I'll do Friday afternoon next week. How's that?"

"I'll put it on the calendar and put a sign up."

"There were a couple of students coming to talk to me today about extensions. If they can't wait until Monday, call me and I'll do a phone conference."

"Sounds good."

"Tell everyone they can get me on my mobile today. I'll be home. I just can't walk much."

"I hope your knee feels better soon!"

"Me too. Thanks, Sydney." Katherine hung up the phone and immediately downed two large gulps of coffee. "Ahhhhhhh."

Baxter was sitting across from her, eating an oatmeal cookie with his tea. "Sydney can cover?"

"Yes."

"I'm going to call Anita Mehdi again today. And I think you should call Kaylee."

"I was thinking that, and then I realized I don't have her phone number, but I gave her mine. I'm hoping she'll call me."

"Can't you get it from someone at the Fred lab?"

"Do I want them to know I'm talking to Ansel's grad student?"

"Hmm." He took another drink of tea. "Point taken. Hopefully she'll call."

Kaylee did call, but not until the afternoon when Baxter was gone and Katherine was trying to hobble around the house and cursing whoever decided they should buy a house on a hill that had so many steps.

Her. It had been her.

Her phone rang in the bedroom just as she'd managed to get to the kitchen. She was reaching for more ice when she heard the telltale buzzing sound on her side table.

"You know…" Of all the times to have a vision, that would have actually been a convenient one. *Don't bother going to the kitchen right now, Katherine, because your phone is going to ring in two minutes.* Why couldn't she have useful visions like that instead of seeing violence?

"Hello?" She was a little breathless when she answered. And her knee felt like it was on fire.

"Professor Bassi?"

"Yes?" She didn't place the voice at first. Then it hit her. "Kaylee! I'm so glad you called. And please, after everything, please call me Katherine."

"Okay. I'm not going to lie, I'm a little freaked out."

"I completely understand that, and I want to assure you that I do not want you to violate any ethical boundaries having to do with the study. I'm working on getting the information another way so I can warn people."

Kaylee was silent for a long time. "I'm more freaked out about what happened on the roof, but thank you."

"I don't want to take advantage of you or any knowledge you might have. It's not fair when you've already—"

"Professor Shaver and Greg have been talking about

something in his office a lot lately. I can't tell you what it is, but I can tell you Professor Shaver isn't very happy about something and I think Greg is sneaky as shit."

"Okay." Katherine spoke slowly. "Have you considered filing something with the IRB?"

"I have. But... Professor Shaver is my thesis advisor."

"I understand completely," Katherine said. "Don't do anything right now, okay?"

"Okay, but I'm still kind of freaked out. How did you know I was on that roof yesterday?"

She took a long breath. "I can't tell you that. Not right now. Maybe not ever."

"Okay." Kaylee didn't question it. "However you knew, I'm really, really grateful. I wasn't lying—I'm terrified of that roof. I'm kind of afraid of heights anyway, but something about it just stuck in my head. I had visions of how easy it would be to just trip and fall off, you know? The railing isn't nearly high enough."

"I'm glad I was there." Just thinking about someone putting this bright young woman in danger made Katherine angry all over again. "Kaylee, I'm going to go now, okay? I need to get some work done. Can I save your number though?"

"Yeah, for sure. And you can text me if you want."

"Sometimes..." She deliberated on how to frame this. "I know it's sometimes tempting to put everything into text or into email. I personally like being able to check over what I say to people before I communicate with them. But for right now, let's remember that phone calls are a great way to communicate without a written record."

"Ohhh right." Her voice lowered. "I hadn't even thought about that."

"I'm just extending some old-chick, pre-texting and -email wisdom here."

Kaylee laughed. "Dude, Professor B, you're so not old."

"Katherine, remember? And I'm going to tell my husband you said that. Thank you."

They hung up, and Katherine carefully created a new contact entry for Kaylee in her phone. Then she got out a notebook and started making a map of her thoughts. There was too much going on. Too much in her head.

She really needed a large white dry-erase board in her kitchen, but since that wasn't an option, she reached for paper.

First she wrote down Justin McCabe's name on a blank piece of printer paper. Then she wrote down Sarah Jordan's name. Then Abigail Chung, and finally Kaylee Ivers.

She taped the four pages together and started writing connections. Who did they all know? How were they connected? She drew line after line. Were there more victims out there?

She'd spent two hours detailing everything she knew about the four different cases when her phone rang.

"Hello?" She was staring at the papers and answered without looking.

"Katherine?"

"Monica!" She smiled and focused her attention on the call. "How are you?"

"How are *you*? I had this feeling I should call you."

"Good instincts." Maybe Monica was more than just a

seer. "I had a vision yesterday, and I was able to keep myself in it long enough to stretch the time."

"Wow! Tell me about it, will you? How did you do it?"

Katherine explained how she'd used her senses, used the tricks Monica had taught her, to expand the vision and give herself a little longer to rescue Kaylee from the roof.

"It sounds almost like you're stretching time," Monica said. "Just a little bit. Like time passes quickly in the visions and if you can stretch it there—"

"Then I can stretch it in reality?" The idea was so mind-bending Katherine almost didn't want to contemplate it. "I don't know how to process that right now. I have too much going on."

"Your ability may still be evolving. It's hard to say what the limits of it are. Have you told Baxter anything about it yet?"

She sighed in relief. "Yes. Just last night. He took it well after he found a scientific rationalization."

"Good. If that's what it takes to ease him into the idea, go for it."

Katherine drummed her fingers on the table. "But you don't think it's science."

"I think..." Monica took a long time to speak. "I think there's a lot about life, about our spirits, about energy and the world, that we just don't understand. Call that magic. Call it science we don't understand yet. Does it really make a difference? What matters is what we do with the power we've been given."

Katherine nodded. "Agreed."

"I didn't plan on spending the second half of my life

solving problems that came to me in visions, but when you see something bad that you can prevent—"

"You have to do something."

"Yes." Monica took a long breath. "I think you, Megan, and Toni might just be getting started. Just remember to be there for each other—have each others' backs—and call us if you get into trouble. Do that and you'll be fine."

"Thanks, Monica."

"I should let you go."

Her phone beeped at her. "Is that you?"

"No," Monica said. "It sounds like you may have another call coming in. I'll say goodbye, but call me anytime, okay?"

"I will." Someone else was calling her? Usually Katherine received a grand total of three calls in an entire week. Now she'd gotten three in one day. What had become of her solitary life?

Megan's name was on the screen.

Katherine touched the button and answered. "Hello?"

"Hey! Have you eaten?"

Had she? Oops. "Uh no, I completely forgot."

"Seriously, what is wrong with you? I never forget to eat. I'm gonna pick you up and take you to lunch since you're not working today and I have a fantastic surprise."

Katherine looked at the spread of information about the case that was scribbled across her kitchen table. Then she thought about a floating pistachio and Monica's advice to have Megan's and Toni's backs. Then her stomach rumbled. "Okay, that sounds like a good idea. Maybe we can pick Toni up too?"

Megan grumbled a little. "And tear her away from the sweaty confines of her garage? We can give it a try."

CHAPTER 22

earing Toni away from the confines of her garage hadn't been as hard as Katherine imagined once Megan told her that the "surprise" she had was a reservation at Red Hill, a brand-new restaurant from a local chef that had a tiny dining room attached to a winery just off Highway 1.

Everyone in Moonstone Cove who loved food had been trying to get a reservation at Red Hill, but it was booked out months ahead. Somehow Katherine's husband, Rodney, had wrangled a coveted lunch table.

"It's just so sweet of him, you know? Rodney's been kind of... aloof lately," Megan said as they pulled away from Toni's garage. "Which I can't really blame him for. He's been working like a dog, and I've had all these... changes going on, which I haven't really told him about, of course, because I don't even know where to start." Megan steered her luxury SUV toward the highway. "Added to all that, the kids are busy with eight million things now, and I just feel like we never see each other at all."

Toni exchanged a look with Katherine. "Listen, we're

both excited to go with you," Toni said. "But are you sure you shouldn't be having lunch with Rodney since he got the reservation?"

"Can't! I guess the owner of the winery offered him a table for today, but he already had a meeting scheduled for lunch with a client in Paso Robles, so he couldn't take it, but he asked if I could use it and they promised they'd give us the red-carpet treatment."

"That's very generous," Katherine said. "I really need to meet him some time. I'd love to say thank you."

Megan glanced over to Katherine, who was sitting in the front seat. "Can you get my sunglasses out of my purse?"

Katherine looked down, but she didn't see a purse. "It's not here."

Megan frowned. "What?"

"I don't see a purse down here."

"Oh, for Pete's sake..." She looked over her shoulder. "Toni, did I put it back there?"

"I don't see it."

Megan swerved to the right and pulled over. "I must have left it on the counter. I was getting that little stool for Katherine so she could climb into the car—"

"Thank you for that, by the way. It was really thoughtful."

She shook her head. "No worries. I'm five minutes up the hill at the last turnoff." She waited for traffic to clear, flipped a U-turn, and headed back a little faster than she'd been driving before. "We might be a few minutes late, but I'm sure it'll be fine."

"No problem," Katherine said. "And Toni hasn't seen your house before."

"Toni, where do you live?"

"Kinda out in the country," she said. "But neither of you can see mine. Eventually yes, but it's a work in progress."

"Mine's one of those McMansions up in Ferraro Hills. You'll see. It's boring as hell."

"Your home is lovely," Katherine said.

"But it's so boring," Megan said. "It has no soul."

Toni laughed. "You think houses have a soul?"

"Oh definitely." She glanced at Toni in the rearview. "What made you pick your house if it's a work in progress?"

"It was cheap and I like the location."

Katherine turned. "And that's it?" She knew exactly what Megan was saying. It might not have been scientific, but Katherine adored her home's personality. And wasn't that a little like a soul?

Toni shrugged. "I don't know. I guess it felt like home even though it's a disaster. I like the trees."

"Trees are really important. Our neighborhood in Atlanta had the most magnificent oak trees." Megan steered through the carefully tended gates of Ferraro Hills and past the manicured lawns. "Look at the trees around here. Nuthin'. That's what's around here. A whole lot of nuthin'."

Toni huffed. "There used to be an oak grove here. It was pretty."

"And they tore it out? See what I mean? No soul."

Katherine spotted Megan's house at the end of a cul-de-sac. There was a sleek grey convertible in the driveway. "Is Rodney still home?"

Megan frowned as she pulled in next to the convertible. "That's weird. He's probably on his way out the door."

Katherine looked over her shoulder.

Toni's eyes were narrowed on the convertible. "That's your husband's car?"

"Yeah. Cool, right?" Megan hopped out of the car. "He got it when we moved here. I'll just run in."

Toni pushed the door open. "I'll come in with you." Her face was grim.

A curdling suspicion twisted in Katherine's stomach. Toni wasn't going in to gawk at Megan's home. She sensed something was wrong.

"I'll come too." Katherine stepped out the car, ignoring the ache in her knee and ankle. "I'd love to thank Rodney for the lunch reservation."

"Sure." Tiny lines formed between Megan's eyebrows.

Toni and Katherine flanked Megan as she walked up to the door. The minute Megan opened the door, the silence seemed to envelop Katherine. The world was cast in grey and her perception shifted. She stepped into the vision like stepping through a mirror.

Megan strode down the hallway, screaming and crying. A woman ran out, her clothes clutched to her chest and red lipstick smeared across her cheek. A glaring red handprint shone against her pale cheek.

"That bitch is crazy."

The shouting in the hallway got louder. Angry voices building and building until there was a crack and a crash. Katherine walked toward the commotion, trying to stretch the vision, trying to give her friend minutes.

"Megan, I'm calling the police!"

"You fucking bastard!"

The scream made her ears pop and her eyes cleared.

Megan was standing motionless in the entryway. She

knew something was wrong. The sudden silence that echoed in the house spoke volumes. So did the pair of women's heels in the entryway.

"Well, damn," Megan whispered, staring at the heels. "Aren't I the pretty idiot?"

In a moment of clarity, Katherine reached down and grabbed Megan's hand before she could take off down the hall. "Wait."

"I can't breathe." Megan's chest was heaving.

Toni reached for her other hand. "Megan, calm down."

"Breathe." Katherine squeezed her hand. "Look at me."

Megan turned and looked her in the eye. Katherine had never seen blue eyes so hot and so cold at the same time. "I just saw what you *don't* want to happen, so listen to me."

Toni said, "We got you, Atlanta."

"Keep your eyes on me," Katherine said. Her own heart was racing, but all she could hear over and over was the screaming and the crying. "You're going to be very calm. He doesn't get the satisfaction of making you lose control."

Megan swallowed hard, bit her lower lip, and nodded.

"Tell me quickly," Katherine whispered, "do you want this house?"

"I hate this fucking house," Megan said through gritted teeth.

"But he likes it," Toni said, "so you don't give him the house."

Katherine kept a tight grip on her hand. "You go into that room and tell them to get out of your house right now. They're expecting drama. You don't give him anything. You've been married to this man for years. You know the buttons he's going to try to push. You're going to breathe through it."

The steel entered Megan's eyes, and she took a deep breath, then nodded. "I got you." She turned to Toni, and her voice wavered for a moment. "I need... I need you to make me strong."

Toni met Megan's eyes, and all the antagonism was gone. "I can do that." She squeezed her hand hard. "You got this."

Megan took a deep breath, lifted her chin, kicked the heels to the side, and walked down the hall. Katherine and Toni waited in the entryway.

"What did you do?" Katherine said. "To Megan."

"Nothing really. Calmed her down a little when we first walked in." Toni shrugged. "She's already strong as hell."

There was a man's voice rising, but no shouts came in return. A few minutes later, a woman with long dark hair and red lipstick came walking down the hall with flaming cheeks.

"Hey there, Julia Verdino," Toni said. "Imagine meeting you at my friend's house. Does your mother know you're sleeping with a married man? Because she's going to."

"Fuck you, Toni," the woman spat out. "He said he wasn't married."

"Fuck you too. You think I'm some kind of idiot?" Toni pointed to the family portrait prominently displayed in the entryway. "Your grandmother would be ashamed of you. Get out of here, and if I hear you're talking about my friend Megan—and you know I'll fucking hear about it—you will be sorry you were ever born."

Julia grabbed her heels and didn't even put them on before she ran out the door.

Katherine was keeping her ears tuned to the back of the

house. While she heard a man's raised voice, she didn't hear Megan once lose her composure.

"You suspected something when we pulled in," Katherine said quietly.

"I noticed the car a few weeks ago, driving around town. Julia was in the passenger's seat. I swear to God, I had no idea the guy was Megan's husband or I would have told her."

"None of us had met him."

"I know, but I still feel guilty."

There hadn't been much noise from the back of the house in a few minutes. Katherine was starting to get concerned when all of a sudden, the air seemed to electrify. At once, every picture hanging on the walls around them rattled, shook, and fell to the floor.

"Uh..." Toni's eyes went wide. "He's alive, right? She wouldn't have..."

"I don't think so."

"I'm not saying I don't know where to hide a body," she muttered, "but I don't have my truck with me."

"Please don't say things like that."

Hearing a loud male voice reassured Katherine that she wasn't going to have to figure out how to deal with a supernatural murder while her knee was the size of a large grapefruit.

Katherine and Toni met the still-alive but definitely confused Rodney a few minutes later when he walked down the hallway with a duffel bag in his hand.

"Who are you?" he snarled.

Rodney Carpenter was a man who had aged well. He was classically handsome with broad shoulders and a build that said former athlete. Unlike some former athletes though, he hadn't let his body deteriorate much. His hair was grey at the temples, and his light brown eyes had wrinkles at the corners that magazines would call "distinguished" instead of "aged."

Women would call him a silver fox. Katherine wanted to punch his teeth in, and Toni looked like she wanted to do worse.

"We're Megan's friends." She forced herself to stay calm. "I'm Professor Katherine Bassi—I teach physics at Central Coast State." She turned to Toni. "I don't know why I do that. I just automatically introduce myself with my work."

"It's cool. You must be Rodney." Toni crossed her arms. "I'm Antonia Dusi."

Rodney's face paled visibly. "Dusi?"

"Yeah. One of *those* Dusis. You know us. We know everyone."

"Dusi Farms?"

"That's my brother."

"Dusi Heritage Winery?"

"That's my cousin's."

It was strange, but Katherine could almost see the "fuck" forming in a thought bubble above Rodney's head.

"And you're friends with Megan."

"We fucking *love* your wife," Toni said. "Funny, smart as a whip, and loyal as hell. Gotta love that in a person, right? She saved our lives at the gym. My parents will never forget it."

Katherine nodded. "We really admire her."

Rodney had nothing else to say. He finally started to look a little embarrassed. "I'm leaving." He looked at the family pictures, broken and lying on the ground where they'd fallen.

"California earthquakes," Toni said. "Crazy, right?"

He opened his mouth, closed it, then walked out the front door.

Katherine and Toni peered through the entryway windows and watched Rodney's convertible back out of the driveway before they rushed down the hall.

"Megan?" Katherine called. "Where are you?"

"Megan?" Toni yelled. "He's gone."

Katherine ran into the bedroom at the end of the hall, a room that was nearly as big as her entire house with picture windows looking out over the mountains and a sweep of vineyards folding over hills leading down to the coastline.

"Holy shit." Toni stopped in the doorway. "That's an amazing view."

Katherine ran to the center of the giant room. "Megan?"

She was huddled on the far side of the bed, crouched on the floor, biting the heel of her hand to stifle the sound of her cries.

"You did so good." Toni put her arms around Megan and squeezed hard. "You fucking kept your cool the entire time. He's gone, Atlanta. We got you."

Katherine drew Megan's hand away from her mouth and her cries finally broke through the calm silence of the immaculate house.

"Shhh." Katherine smoothed her hand over the bite marks that nearly broke the skin as Megan's painful cries filled the bedroom.

"I don't know what to do." Megan cried and cried. "I don't know what to do!"

Toni sat on the ground beside her. "Just do this. Just do whatever you feel like right now. It's just us."

"Why? *Why?*"

The pain in Megan's voice ripped a hole in Katherine's heart. She'd had friends who'd experienced divorce, but she'd never been there for the raw, painful ending. Not like this. She felt wholly unprepared to help. Nothing she could do *could* help.

"I'm so sorry." Katherine kept Megan's hand in hers. "I'm so sorry."

"What am I going to tell the kids?" She hiccuped. "What do I tell them?"

Toni looked at her wristwatch. "We got a few hours to figure that out. Right now, just get it all out."

Megan screamed, "I hate him so much!"

"Totally fair." Toni waved her hand. "Keep going."

Megan stood and started pacing around the room. "I moved away from all my friends! All my family! I dragged the kids out of schools they loved. I gave up my business, and he knew I was set to make more than him the next year with the way I was growing. *He knew that!* I sold the house where I brought my babies home! He knew it and *he fucking sleeps with a teenager?*"

Katherine didn't think she was a teenager, but she was definitely young.

"That girl was young enough to be his daughter!"

"I know." Toni stood. "I know her mom. I'm totally telling her about this."

"Oh God, don't." Megan looked miserable. Then her eyes got wide and maybe a little scary. "No. *Fuck* him. I didn't do anything wrong. Tell her mom. Tell your mom. Tell every damn person in this little town. I'm done putting on a happy smile for his asshole friends. I'm done pretending to be the adoring wife. Do you know how much lingerie I bought to try

223

to fix our sex life?" She put her hands on her hips. "Ha! And trust me, the problem was not with me." She marched into her walk-in closet.

Katherine leaned over to Toni. "She's even pretty when she's crying and angry."

"I know. I've never really seen that before. I thought it only happened in movies."

"I can hear you two." Megan walked out of the closet holding a massive armful of lace and straps. "I am throwing all of this away. That's the first thing I'm doing. I need all new underwear." She looked pained. "Maybe not all of... *No.* I don't want anything he's had his hands on to even touch my body. I am getting *all* new underwear."

It wasn't what Katherine would have focused on, but then she couldn't even imagine Baxter cheating on her, so she had no idea how she'd react.

"Oh God." Megan reached her hand out. "Do either of you have your phone?"

"Yes." Toni handed her a mobile. "Let me..." She unlocked it. "Here. I have a national plan, so if you need to call back east..."

Megan punched in numbers and nodded while the phone was ringing. "Hi, this is Megan Carpenter. Sorry, Megan *Alston* Carpenter, and I had a reservation for me and my friends at one and we're just not going to make that because I drove home and found my husband cheating on me."

"Oh my God, she's calling the restaurant," Toni said. "I thought she was calling her mom."

"And she's telling them about Rodney." That was definitely a level of candor that Katherine would have avoided with unsuspecting restaurant staff.

Megan continued with a wavering voice. "Well, thank you for your sentiments, Laura; I really do appreciate that. And you're absolutely right; your mother is a wise woman. I just wanted to call and let you know about the table so you're not waiting on us. There's no excuse for rudeness."

Katherine had helped friends through divorce. Sadly two of her best friends from college had gone through the heartbreak. But she had a sneaking suspicion that helping Megan *Alston* Carpenter through a divorce was going to be in an entirely different experience.

oni and Katherine were sitting on the back deck, watching the tide come in that evening. Katherine had her leg elevated and was watching the surfers bob in the fading sunlight and catch a few last waves before they retired for the night.

"I feel kind of bad leaving her alone," Katherine said.

"I feel the same way, but we don't really know her children at all. I'm sure it would be strange for them to have two random women hanging around their house while their mom explains to them that their dad is a lying cheater." Toni tapped the edge of her wineglass. "That is so fucked up."

"I don't understand men," Katherine said. "Megan is one of the most positive and socially attractive people I've ever met. Not to mention she's objectively beautiful and clearly very loyal."

"You don't understand men because you're married to Baxter, who's a male unicorn."

Katherine almost snorted wine through her nose. "Sorry, what?"

Toni smiled. "A male unicorn. Your husband is smart and cute, has a great accent, and he completely adores you. He loves his work and he's completely laid-back and confident. To most of us, he's a mythical creature. Hence, a male unicorn."

"A mythical creature? What about Henry?"

The faint hint of a blush appeared on Toni's freckled cheeks. "I don't know what you're talking about."

"Whoever was in the background on the phone the other day laughed when you called him a friend, so I'm guessing there's a lot more to that story."

Toni's smile was carefully composed. "Henry is helping me with my house, and we were fighting about how to do the floors, so that's probably why he laughed."

"If he's just a friend, why does he have a say in how you finish your floors?"

"Because he's opinionated. Can we keep talking about how awful men are? Except for Baxter the male unicorn, of course."

Katherine decided to let it drop until Megan could back her up. "I'm going to tell him you're calling him that."

"He'll probably think it's funny and charming, which is yet another thing that makes him a male unicorn." Toni smiled. "If there's one thing that Megan and I have in common, it's thinking Baxter is the bee's knees."

"The bee's knees!" Katherine laughed. "I love that saying. My grandmother used to say it."

"So did mine. I've been missing her lately, so I've been trying to use more of her grandma-isms." Toni narrowed her eyes. "The real question is, how much do we want to destroy Rodney?"

"Can you really destroy him?"

Toni snorted. "Oh yeah. Some of this shit is going to leak out no matter what. It's Moonstone Cove. The town is not that big."

"True." Katherine remembered when one of the animal science professors at Central Coast had a semipublic affair with the chair of the botany department. The university had been consumed by the drama for months, and it had eventually touched nearly every department. "I think you need to wait and talk to Megan. Let her calm down and find out what she wants. You and I need to keep trying to figure out what's going on with the students."

"Without her?"

Katherine tried to imagine her nieces and nephews finding out that one of their parents had betrayed the other. Even though they were all in their teens now, she couldn't imagine how gutted they'd be. "Her kids are going to need her. Teenagers may seem independent, but they're really children, and their world just got rocked."

"I wonder if her kids had any idea? Sometimes they're more alert to rumors than adults are."

"Either way, she's going to have a lot on her plate." Katherine looked at Toni. "But we can't lose focus. We've just started putting together what's happening with these students. Can you go get the large folded sheets of paper on the kitchen table?"

"Yeah." Toni looked relieved to focus on something else. "I'll be right back."

"And ask Baxter if he can join us please?"

"You want me to call him a unicorn?"

Katherine smiled. "Not until I can see his face when you say it."

THEY WEIGHTED the corners of the paper with a wine bottle, two wineglasses, and an abalone shell that sat in a corner of the deck.

"The clear common denominator is the study of course," Katherine started. "But Kaylee threw everything off."

"How?" Toni said.

"She wasn't a participant," Baxter said. "She was and is a graduate student. Which means that she might have participated in conducting the study, but she wasn't a subject. So if this aberrant behavior was somehow caused by the study itself, how do we explain Kaylee's episode?"

"She knew something?" Toni said. "Katherine said she'd dropped a couple of hints. Maybe whoever is behind this knew that she might expose him or her."

"That could give motive, but we still don't know how he or she is actually triggering these episodes. Why would Kaylee have been vulnerable?"

"I don't know exactly, but I think it has something to do with fear." Katherine pointed to Sarah Jordan's page. "Pinpointing fear. Sarah's greatest love and source of happiness was her horse. It could be easily imagined that something harming her horse would be a great fear." She pointed to Justin McCabe. "Justin's greatest fear was obvious. His brother had been killed in a school shooting, and his episode takes that to another level. Not only being killed in a shooting but actually causing one."

"Then there's Abigail," Baxter said.

"Do you think she was afraid of Mario?" Katherine asked. "I never sensed anything like that between them."

"She might not have been afraid of *Mario*," Toni said. "But the general fear of someone she trusted hurting her? I think any woman can relate to that."

Baxter said, "If police reports are to be believed, Abby lashed out at her own partner for no apparent reason. Random violence against or from the person she trusted the most? It's not a stretch to imagine that as her greatest fear."

"Have you been able to speak with her again?" Katherine asked.

Baxter shook his head. "As far as I know, none of her friends have heard from her. At least not the ones I know. Her family is very protective."

"Which brings us to Kaylee." Katherine put her hand on Kaylee's paper. "Same target: her greatest fear—falling over the ledge of a tall building—but one big difference. Kaylee wasn't in the study; she was helping to conduct it."

Toni leaned forward. "Okay, so explain biofeedback in more detail to me. You kind of went over it before, but I'm having a hard time picturing it. Could it be done to someone without their knowledge?"

"Absolutely not." Katherine shook her head. "Biofeed-back therapy depends on making the subject aware of their subconscious physical responses as a way of controlling them and lessening their effect. So a subject *must* be aware. They *must* be a willing participant in the therapy for it to have any effect. Added to that, there are sensors physically attached to subjects during the first phase of the treatment."

"What about, like, hypnosis?"

Baxter and Katherine exchanged a look. "Here, my dear, Katherine and I will part ways. I am a believer in effective hypnosis treatment because I saw how much it helped my brother quit smoking. Katherine, on the other hand—"

"Wait." Toni turned her attention to Katherine. "Really? I mean... really? You see actual psychic visions that predict the future, but you find hypnosis hard to believe?"

She glared at Baxter. "This is what you call throwing someone under the bus."

"But it works," Toni said. "My brother quit smoking too."

"I simply think it's debatable that hypnosis is any more effective than a placebo."

"You think hypnosis is fake?"

"No. People underestimate the placebo effect of going to see a hypnotist." She gestured to the papers on the table. "The placebo effect is very powerful. And hypnosis has nothing to do with any of this."

"But," Baxter said, "hypnosis and biofeedback do have some commonalities, and there is evidence that people can be hypnotized without their knowledge, which is not possible with biofeedback."

Katherine couldn't argue with that but... "I'm not going to say it's impossible. I'm just saying I have my doubts."

"Hypnosis could explain the amnesia too." Baxter folded his hands and frowned, staring at the scribbles across the paper. "But Katherine is also right—the common thread between all these people is the biofeedback study. And that study had nothing to do with hypnosis. It wasn't utilized in any way that we know of."

"Maybe the study was just convenient," Toni said.

Katherine turned to her. "What do you mean?"

"Maybe the study wasn't the avenue for messing with these people's minds," Toni said. "Maybe the study was just where whoever is doing this found their victims."

KATHERINE COULDN'T SLEEP that night. She lay awake, casting her mind out to the students who had participated in good faith in order to advance the treatment of a condition she suffered from herself. And in doing that, they had become potential targets for whoever was playing this twisted game.

Baxter rolled over and put an arm across her legs. "Darling, you need sleep."

She was sitting against the headboard, staring out the window at the fog-covered sea. "I don't have visions in my sleep," she said. "What if something else is about to happen? What if I can stop it?"

"You're not going to be able to stop everything." He blinked up at her. "You can't take on that responsibility."

"I feel like I have to." She gripped his hand in her own. "We've worked so hard because the legacy is so bad, Baxter. Professors, academics, we did take advantage of vulnerable people. We have caused harm in the past. So much. Tuskegee. Sims. Statesville. There is a reason we guard this process so fiercely. There's a reason we have to jump through so many hoops. And to think that someone might have used students—"

"I'm going to tell Anita about this, and if she doesn't go to the IRB, we will. But I think she'll volunteer to go. You know what kind of person she is."

"And Ansel..." As much as she personally didn't click with Ansel Shaver, she could not imagine he'd do something to deliberately put students in harm's way. "This is like a... a serial killer who's using the anonymity of an academic study to hunt for victims. Find out their greatest fear, figure out how their brain works, and then use that information against them."

"But how?" Baxter propped himself up. "That's what I can't figure out. Hypnosis can be done without a subject's knowledge, but with results like this?"

"It seems improbable."

"But not impossible," Baxter said. "Like you."

"What do you mean?"

"All your new abilities. Improbable, but clearly not impossible."

"Right." She scooted down in bed. "I should go to sleep."

"You need to. You're still healing that knee and ankle."

"I know."

"And you get very cross when you're not sleeping enough." He yawned widely. "Good night."

"Good night." She rolled over, kissed him softly, and lay on her back. "Thank you for believing in the improbable."

"You're very welcome." He reached for her hand under the covers. "Now sleep."

She tried but she failed. She kept circling around Baxter's question.

How?

Using the study to hunt for victims made sense, but for what mind game? What were they looking for? Was it about power? Advantage? Was it personal?

Isn't it always personal?

She opened her eyes. Isn't it?

Katherine closed her eyes and made a mental timeline. Sarah Jordan, Justin McCabe, Abigail Chung, Kaylee Ivers.

Sarah to Justin had been months. Justin to Abigail had been weeks. Abigail to Kaylee... days.

Whoever was playing this game, the time line had accelerated. What that meant for future victims, Katherine had no idea.

CHAPTER 24

The knock came at their door at nine o'clock the next morning. Katherine was drinking coffee and still trying to elevate her leg, so Baxter went to open it.

"Anita." She could hear the shock in his voice. "Come in."

"I'm so sorry to bother you at home, but I am just at a complete loss." A statuesque woman with braided steel-grey hair and broad shoulders walked into the entryway. She was wearing a blue-green wrap that Baxter took from her and hung on a hook near the door. "I don't know what is happening. In thirty-five years, nothing like this has ever happened to me before."

She paused when she saw Katherine at the table. "Katherine."

"Anita." Katherine smiled. "Would you like some coffee or tea?"

"I'd love some coffee with milk if you have it."

"I'll get it." Baxter motioned to the table. "Please sit down. Katherine knows about the situation, so we can speak

235

freely. She's the one who realized the connections between the incidents with Sarah Jordan and Justin McCabe."

Anita sat across from her. "Of course. You were at the gym." She glanced at her knee. "Is this injury from that?"

"No. Unrelated."

Had Kaylee told anyone about her involvement on the roof? It seemed like Anita was unaware of the incident, so Katherine kept quiet.

"Baxter approached me after his graduate student, Abigail Chung, had the violent outburst that injured her partner and herself. I was shocked and horrified of course, but also quite skeptical that anything related to the biofeed-back study we did would have had any detrimental effect on a participant. I had to check the identities of the students myself to be sure they participated, and I cannot dismiss the connection. With three different students, a coincidence is too improbable."

"That was my thinking as well." Katherine held her mug out as Baxter refilled it. "Thank you, Baxter."

"Of course." He set the carafe down and sat next to Katherine at the end of the table with his mug of tea. "I knew I could speak to you in confidence, Anita. As for reporting these—"

"As soon as I confirmed with Ansel Shaver that all three students were involved, we called Professors Bernal, Rodriguez, and Kraft. We'll be submitting our suspicions about the study to the IRB on Monday and turning over all our results for review. As Baxter requested, I've kept both of you out of the report entirely. There's no reason for them to know you're involved, in my opinion. You stumbled onto the information and came to me directly." Her eyes were anguished. "I simply don't know how anything we did in the study could have caused this violence. I'm still at such a loss."

"Can you explain it to us?" Katherine said. "I've spoken to some of the students involved about their mental state. I'm curious to hear what you have to say."

Anita glanced at Baxter, who nodded.

"The study participants were screened quite strictly. We were specifically looking for students living with anxiety who were already medicated and under the supervision of a doctor."

"Like me," Katherine said. "I was diagnosed with social anxiety years ago and I have a regular prescription. I can't say I never have a flare of something unexpected—"

"But I imagine you have various coping mechanisms."

"I do."

"I also imagine you've had to change medications over the years as your body chemistry has changed and different treatments become available."

"Yes. Tinkering happens. I think that's pretty universal."

Anita took a sip of coffee. "Baxter, this is excellent."

"I'm glad you think so; I don't touch the stuff."

"Oh no. You're a tea drinker, aren't you?"

Katherine smiled. "It's really his only fault as a husband."

Anita smiled back, and Katherine was glad to see a little of the heaviness in her eyes alleviated. "When Ansel proposed this study, he kept the focus very narrow, which I appreciate. The only thing we wanted to test was if established biofeedback therapies used for other conditions would be useful to alleviate some of that tinkering you talked about."

"So you were going to try to keep participants from building up resistance to current medications?" Baxter asked.

"I imagine you asked study participants to remain on the same pharmaceutical dosage throughout the study."

"We did."

"Did you ask about participants' greatest fears?" Katherine asked. "Was that part of the screening?"

Anita narrowed her eyes and thought carefully. "Not in that many words but... in a sense. The visualization that we designed was based on identifying the root of a patient's anxiety. So for some individuals, that might be considered their greatest fear."

"And you used the same visualization for all the students?"

"We did."

"What was it?" Baxter asked.

"It's one I've used before in my practice. Imagine that the situation you fear—a public speaking event or an argument or whatever it might be—is in front of you, just beyond a threshold in your mind. The first step is to close the door to that threshold and then take a step back from it. Take another step back. Visualize all the steps that led you back to where you are in the present. And anytime you feel an anxiety attack coming on, you take those backward steps all over again."

"...the visualization wasn't working. For some reason, instead of walking backward, I felt like someone was pushing me forward." Sarah Jordan's voice was clear in her mind. Someone had managed to take the positive visualization developed to conquer fear and turn it upside down.

Katherine asked, "And how long was the study? How many participants?"

"There were around seventy participants, almost all

drawn from the student body, but not entirely. We had twelve sessions for each participant. One session a week. So around three months. Then each participant was given a set of exercises to practice on their own and log electronically on a daily basis. We checked at one month, then six months. We were scheduled to do the third follow-up next month."

"So Sarah Jordan's incident happened soon after the first six-month check, and the next follow-up hasn't happened yet," Katherine said.

"Correct."

Baxter said, "I'm assuming any abnormal behavior or outbursts would require reporting."

"Obviously. There's quite an extensive questionnaire, and then if anything is out of the ordinary, a follow-up phone call would happen."

Baxter asked, "Who guided the biofeedback sessions? I'm assuming you had a fairly large team with that many people and that many sessions."

"Yes. We had ten graduate students who were each assigned seven individuals to meet with. So they were conducting around two hours a day of clinical work. Quite intense but overseen by all five of us in turn."

"And the biofeedback therapies were all the same?"

"They all used the same program, yes. There was a period of introduction, use of feedback sensors to measure heart rate, body temperature, and muscle tension. We paired that with awareness exercises that led to breathing regulation, relaxation techniques, and eventually guided visualization."

"And did it show promise?"

"Obviously we're still collecting data, but overall, yes."

"Negative side effects presented?" Baxter asked.

"Virtually *none*." Anita was adamant. "We didn't change any of their medications. No erratic behavior was reported. The only negative outcome was that for some participants, it simply didn't work, but we expected that result." She paused and tapped the edge of her cup. "This was not a ground-breaking study. It wasn't going to change the world."

Katherine said, "I got the feeling from Ansel that he thought there was very real publishing potential. Maybe something even directed toward the general market."

She frowned. "It's possible. I don't know that it would garner that much interest from a nonacademic publisher. Honestly, the most innovative thing about the study would probably be the app."

Katherine blinked. "What app?"

"The reporting app. That was how we required the study participants to log their exercises. Alice Kraft developed it along with one of Ansel's students."

"An app?" Something buzzed in the back of Katherine's mind. "I don't suppose you have it on your phone, do you?"

Anita shook her head. "The grad students would have all used it, I'm sure, but we didn't. I don't consider myself very technologically savvy. It was a very clever idea though. Everyone has a smartphone these days. The app was designed to prompt students at certain times of the day to do their biofeedback exercises; then they would log their results right away. The reports were automatically sent to the server, so there was no room for error or lost data."

"Fascinating," Baxter said. "Have you alerted the rest of the students in the study yet?"

"Not yet. We were going to send a message through the app to be on guard for unexpected reactions and to stop doing the prescribed biofeedback exercises immediately." She shook her head. "I want to do everything right, but I know this is going to be hard for many of the students. There were dozens of reports given to my own grad students that the biofeedback had helped immensely, especially with sleep."

"That's interesting," Katherine said. "Do you have any idea which one of Ansel's graduate students helped Alice Kraft design the app?"

"I don't."

"What would happen to that?" Baxter said. "If this hadn't happened, would the app eventually have been deleted off the participants' phones?"

"I imagine so. I'm not familiar with how that would happen. That would have been Alice's and Ansel's areas of expertise."

"Alice Kraft." Baxter tapped his chin. "She works in the computer engineering department as well as behavioral sciences, correct?"

"She does. Much of Alice's work has been related to studying cognitive reactions to technology, so she was a perfect addition to the team."

"I imagine." Katherine thought back to her conversation with Greg weeks ago. He'd mentioned working with Alice Kraft. Was he the only one?

"Anita," Baxter said. "This app you used... Who would it have technically belonged to?"

"All the data it collected would be strictly confidential, so—"

"Not the data." Katherine understood where Baxter's mind was going. "But the app itself. The design of it."

"Well, you should know from the Fred lab. Anything

designed on university time using university resources would belong to the university." She looked between them. "But does a biofeedback phone application have any particular monetary value?"

"Oh..." Baxter nodded. "I can imagine it might have some."

AN HOUR LATER, she was standing at the sink and doing breakfast dishes when Baxter walked in from a run to the grocery store. "I told you to stay off your feet."

"I need to move my knee too." She pointed to it. "Look. Not the size of a grapefruit anymore. And my ankle feels much better. We should go for a walk later."

She could see he was tempted. "Beach walk?"

"Just a little one." She rinsed the coffee carafe. "To stretch."

"Fine, but you're icing it afterward." He sat down and watched her. "I think we know the motivation now."

Katherine had been turning over possibilities in her brain. "We don't know for sure."

"Maybe not for sure, but..." Baxter cocked his head. "Think about how much people spend on meditation classes, wellness apps, that sort of thing. If a smart graduate student figured out how to create at-home biofeedback technology and pair that with an app that uses proven cognitive therapy techniques from PhDs in behavioral science?"

"You're saying it's a grad student? Why not the professor who designed it?"

"The grad students were the admins."

"The professor was the designer."

Baxter shrugged. "Six of one, half dozen of the other, Professor Bassi. Either way, a mobile phone app could be far more profitable than a book deal."

"And easier to pull off," Katherine said. "Provided no one caught on to how you created it in the first place."

"If the study is never published, then the only ones who'd really know about it would be the professors and grad students involved," Baxter said. "The graduate students are all looking after their doctoral opportunities. And listen to Anita—she didn't even know you could make serious money with an app. The majority of our colleagues probably fall in the same category unless they're in technology."

Sarah Jordan and Tucker.

Justin McCabe.

Abby Chung and her partner, Mario.

Kaylee Ivers.

"Can you imagine, Baxter? All these bizarre and tragic events for the most boring motivation possible. Money."

"It's a classic for a reason," he said. "We need to figure out who designed the biofeedback app and what exactly was on that thing."

"We need to find out more than that," Katherine said. "According to Anita, the app was the main vehicle for communication with study participants."

"Correct."

"I want to know if everyone got the same version." She finished and turned to reach for the towel and dry her hands. "This didn't happen to all seventy students. It happened to Sarah, Justin, Abby, and Kaylee. Did they all get the same app? Did they all get the same messages and prompts?"

"That's a good question. Do you think you could get Sarah's phone? Or Justin's? Maybe we can look at the history."

"Maybe not the phone itself, but possibly a record of the messages on it."

"I had another thought while I was at the grocery store," Baxter said. "Everyone affected by this is largely out of commission. Sarah left school. Justin and Abby are either in jail or in the hospital. Everyone except Kaylee."

"Whatever he tried to do to Kaylee failed," Katherine said. "You think she's still in danger."

"I don't think there's any reason to think that whatever made her a target has changed. She probably knows something but isn't aware that it's dangerous. She may not realize it, but whatever it is, she's still a threat to whoever is behind this."

Katherine sat down and picked up her phone. She tapped on Kaylee's name and waited for the phone to pick up.

It rang. And rang. And rang.

"Hi! This is Kaylee. I'm not available right now, but please leave a message and your number so I can call you back."

CHAPTER 25

*B*axter and Katherine flew down the highway. It was Saturday, and the traffic around the university was a fraction of the usual bustle. Katherine was on the phone with Britt at the Fred lab.

"Is there anyone working today? I'm sorry to bug you, I know you were going to take this weekend off, but I couldn't get ahold of Job."

"Yeah, no problem. He should be there with a couple of his kids."

"You mean grad students?"

"They're all infants to me." He cleared his throat. "Speaking of grad students—"

"Is Kaylee Ivers one of the students working today?"

"Kaylee? Don't think so. Shaver brought some other kid in last week to help out. Can't remember the name. He said Kaylee was going to be busy with a new project he had going at the BS office."

"Right." She put a hand over the phone. "Head to the social science quad."

"Right."

She spoke to Britt again. "Thanks."

"Is everything all right?"

"I think so, but I need to speak to her, and she's not answering her phone."

"Huh." He said something to someone on the other end of the phone. "Does this have anything to do with why she was on top of the architecture building the other day?"

"You heard about that?"

"Katherine, everyone heard about that. And about you tearing across campus and joining her. Is she doing okay? She's a great kid."

"She is. And I think she's fine. I can't say anything more than that right now."

"Okay." He fell silent. "Well, if she needs any help—"

"I'll let you know." They'd arrived at the faculty lot nearest the social science complex. "I need to go, Britt. I'll talk to you on Monday."

"See ya."

The School of Social Sciences occupied three squat, midcentury buildings at the end of a tree-lined cul-de-sac on the north end of the university.

"Do you know which building behavioral sciences is in?"

"Yes." Baxter strode across the lawn. "I consulted with Anita, remember?"

"Right." They walked up the steps, and Katherine followed Baxter as he led them to the right.

At the far end of the building was an office with DEPARTMENT OF BEHAVIORAL SCIENCES written on a glass door. The office behind it was dark and obviously not staffed on weekends, but there was the relic of a computer lab right across from it, and there were lights on there.

Baxter stuck his head in the door and barked at the three students parked in the corner. "Kaylee Ivers. Is she here?"

The students looked up with wide eyes. "Uh..." One of them stammered. "W-we're not in this department. We just use this old lab for... stuff. On weekends."

Katherine didn't even want to guess. She nudged Baxter to the side. "Have you seen any older students come in this way? The one we're looking for is short and thin. She's white and has really long brown hair. Very cheerful."

"Oh." The girl in the group piped up. "I saw her. Yeah, she came in with two other people. One of them was a professor, I think. They went up the stairs."

"Thank you."

Baxter couldn't resist. "What *are* you doing in here?" None of the desktop computers were on. Backpacks spilled notebooks and folders onto the worktables and three laptops were open, but all three students were also on their phones.

The girl stared at Baxter with wide eyes. "Political hacktivism."

"Right, carry on." He pulled Katherine away from the lab and toward the stairs. "The elevator is broken in this building right now."

"Wait, did they say activism or hacktivism?"

"Not sure. We should go find Kaylee."

"But—"

"Kaylee." He pushed her ahead of him on the stairs. "Priorities. Can you climb with your knee?"

"Yes. I'm okay." She stopped at the second floor landing

and poked her head into the hallway. She heard nothing, not even papers shuffling. "Third floor."

They walked up to the third floor, which was the top of the building, and opened the door. The landing was in the exact center of the hallway, but there were only voices coming from the right.

"This way." Katherine walked toward the voices, two of which she recognized, Kaylee and a deeper male voice that sounded familiar. She had her suspicions, which were confirmed when she saw Greg Hammond sitting across the table from Kaylee and a professor that Katherine recognized as Alice Kraft, one of the newest tenured professors in the computer science department.

Alice Kraft had very distinctive red hair, and she was young enough to be frequently mistaken for a student. All three were on laptops, and Kaylee had a clipboard and a printout next to her.

When she heard them at the door, Kaylee looked up. "Katherine?"

"Kaylee." Katherine was breathing a little hard from climbing the stairs. "Hi."

Greg and Alice Kraft were staring at them.

Professor Kraft frowned. "Professor Pang?"

"Professor Kraft, how are you? Have you met my wife, Katherine Bassi?"

"I haven't. Physics, correct?"

"Biophysics, yes. I work at the Neuroengineering and Marine Sciences lab with Kaylee."

"How interesting." She frowned before she glanced at Greg and Kaylee. "Is there something we can help you with?"

Katherine and Baxter exchanged a look.

"I needed to speak to Kaylee, and she wasn't answering her phone."

"Yes, we turned all our devices off because we're working on confidential study files," Alice Kraft said. "I don't want to offend you, but we're quite busy and this is something that has to be done quickly, which is why we're working on a *Saturday*." She was clearly annoyed that they'd been interrupted.

"If I could borrow Kaylee for a brief moment, I'd appreciate it," Katherine said. "It shouldn't take long."

Her mind flashed back to her brief conversation with Greg at the student center.

"You're a busy young man. Psychology and technology?"

"I want to focus on how data from wearable devices could potentially transform how mental health professionals evaluate patients."

"That's very interesting."

"Yeah. I mean... Everyone lies, right? But our bodies don't."

Greg Hammond. Greg and Alice Kraft? Could Greg have been the student who helped her design the app? Katherine and Baxter guided Kaylee down the hall and into a small alcove near the stairwell.

"Do you have your phone on you?" Katherine asked.

Kaylee glanced at Baxter.

"Professor Pang knows about what happened on the roof," Katherine said. "He knows about what happened with Abby and Justin and Sarah. You can speak freely."

"I don't have my phone." Her voice was a near-whisper. "Professor Kraft's, like, super strict about putting it away when we're working. It's in my backpack."

"As soon as you can take it out, you need to go on and delete the reporting app for the study."

Kaylee frowned. "The reporting app?"

"We think it could be the key that links all the strange incidents. All the grad students and the study participants had the app, right?"

"Yeah. Uh, we got notifications pushed through depending on our role. The study participants got their visualization prompts and reminders to log. Grad students just got reminders, messages from the professors, stuff like that."

"Who designed it?" Baxter asked. "Was it Alice?"

Kaylee nodded. "Professor Kraft and Greg. And Greg was the admin on the system."

Katherine didn't want to alarm Kaylee, but she didn't want to ignore possible danger either. "It's possible that something they put on the app—maybe unintentionally—has triggered these episodes."

Kaylee laughed a little. "I mean... that seems a little far-fetched. It's just an app. And it's not even a fancy one. It's kind of clunky, to be honest, but it gets the job done."

"Just..." She clasped her hands in front of her. "For me. Please. The study is off, so please just delete it. To be safe."

Kaylee frowned. "The study is off?"

Baxter nodded. "I can't tell you details, but please delete the app."

"Okay." Kaylee shrugged. "I mean, it's not like it'll delete any important data so—"

"Wait." Katherine had a realization. "Yes, you will."

"Will what?"

"Delete important data. We need to look at it before you delete it."

Baxter frowned. "Darling—"

"There could be information on it." She looked at Kaylee. "Have you cleared your notifications lately?"

"I don't think so. I usually get them and I just open my phone and they go away."

"The roof happened Thursday and today is Saturday." Katherine frowned. "Really? It's only been two days?"

"Katherine, focus."

"Right. Unless you've cleared your notifications, we should be able to see them, which would show us if anything was sent to you before you went onto the rooftop. I also want to check it for spyware and make sure there's nothing on there that could be monitoring you. It's possible that someone has gained access to your phone via the app."

Kaylee's eyes widened. "Okay, I promise I'll keep my phone off until I finish here. And then—"

"Meet me at the North Beach Coffee Company as soon as you're done here. What time?"

She shrugged. "Maybe around three? I'll text you when—"

"No," Baxter said. "Don't text. Don't turn on your phone at all until Katherine can look at it. Don't turn it on, and don't tell Greg or Professor Kraft what we talked about here."

"Tell them I needed to talk to you about something at the Fred lab," Katherine said. "They know they can't butt into that."

Kaylee nodded. "Okay. I'll try to get away by three."

"Just be careful," Katherine said. "Don't do anything suspicious. I'll wait for you there."

Iᴛ ᴡᴀꜱ ɴᴇᴀʀʟʏ four by the time Kaylee arrived at the North Beach Coffee Company, and Katherine and Toni were on their second coffee. The fog had rolled in early, so the beach was nearly deserted except for a clutch of surfers bobbing off the point.

"Hey." Kaylee sat at the table in the corner that looked over the ocean. "You're Katherine's friend! I can't remember your name though." She held her hand out to Toni. "I'm Kaylee."

"No worries. I'm Toni." Toni took her hand and held it slightly longer than she normally would. "You're worried about something. Don't be. Katherine's the smartest person I know."

Kaylee's eyes were round. "Do I look worried?"

Katherine jumped in. "Toni usually has a really good sense about people. How did the rest of the day with Greg and Professor Kraft go?"

"Greg was, like, super curious what we were talking about. He kept trying to bring it up. Professor Kraft was curious too, but you know her. She's strictly business all the time."

"Do you have your phone?"

"I do." She reached in her back and grabbed a phone in an aquamarine case. "I haven't turned it on, not even when Professor Kraft and Greg got theirs out. It was kind of weird."

"How so?"

"So we finish and we're packing up, and they both get their phones out to, like, check their messages and stuff. I didn't, and Professor Kraft noticed. She told me, 'Kaylee, you can check your phone now.' But I didn't. I told her I was almost out of battery and needed to charge it."

"Good thinking."

"Greg noticed too. He looked... weird." She took a deep breath. "Katherine, if I think about who could have manipulated things in the study—"

"You think Greg has something to do with it," Toni said. "And you're afraid of him."

Kaylee blushed a little. "I mean, I wouldn't say I'm afraid."

"He intimidates you, and you don't know why." Toni thought. "He pushes your buttons. Makes you react to stuff you normally wouldn't."

"Yes." Kaylee was clearly annoyed. "Every stinking time I'm with that guy, I find myself doubting myself. Like... questioning my methods, second-guessing the answer to something. It's so annoying! I'm not like that with anyone else. But there's just something about that guy that always gets to me."

"Interesting." Toni narrowed her eyes. "Has he always been that way?"

"I only started working with him on this study with Professor Shaver, but I know he's kind of a loner. No one likes working with him."

"Except Alice Kraft," Katherine added. "Greg mentioned that she's been working with him on his thesis project as well. Did she pick him to administer the app?"

"Yes. I just thought it made sense because, according to Greg, they were already working on something together." Kaylee rolled her eyes. "All the guys in the program were like... jealous or something. I don't know."

"Why?"

Kaylee looked to the side. "Well, it's Professor Kraft. They get like that."

"Why?" Katherine thought about the willowy redheaded professor who was often mistaken for a student. Alice Kraft generally wore casual clothing, jeans or leggings, T-shirts, and a jacket as a nod to professionalism. Katherine had admired her jackets more than once.

"All the guys talk about how hot she is."

"Really?" Katherine turned to Toni. "There was a website for a while that rated professors by their looks. I think those who were deemed the most attractive were given a chili pepper as a rating. Because chilies are hot."

"Yeah, I got that." Toni rolled her eyes. "I'm so sorry I didn't listen to my mom and go to college. Imagine all the really deep, important stuff I missed."

Kaylee said, "They don't rate them with chili peppers anymore but... I mean, they still rate their hotness."

"Of course they do."

Katherine held out her hand. "Let me see your phone." She brought out her laptop and opened it. "I'm going to clone it so I can see the data completely."

"What?" Kaylee nearly squealed.

She held up a hand. "Purely to get the information we're looking for and to make sure you're not carrying any spyware. I'll grab the data from the reporting app; then you can watch me delete everything else, okay?"

"Okay, I guess."

Toni took a drink of her coffee. "Do you think Greg and this professor had something going on?"

Kaylee cocked her head. "I mean... I try to stay away from gossip because so much of it is stupid and—at least in my department—totally about creating drama. I don't have time for that. But yeah, there were rumors about Greg and Professor Kraft."

"What kind of rumors?"

"Just that he kind of pursued her. And they kind of have a thing. But nobody says anything because it's not like what happened with Professor Boehner or anything."

Toni looked at Katherine. "What happened with Professor Boehner? Other than having a really shitty name."

"A name he totally deserves," Kaylee said. "So gross."

Katherine said, "Albert Boehner was fired last year for trading sexual favors for grades with undergraduates. It had been going on for years and people mostly looked the other way."

"Gross." Toni turned to Kaylee. "But Professor Kraft and Greg, no one saw it the same way?"

"I mean, he was pretty clearly going after her. And you could tell he was proud of himself."

"Still highly inappropriate," Katherine said. "She *will* be fired if she is or was having an affair with a student, but... I don't think the affair is her biggest problem." She turned her computer screen toward Kaylee. "You received two notifications from the app on Thursday, one fifteen minutes before you walked on that roof, and one ten minutes later. Do you remember them?"

"No." Her eyes were the size of saucers. "I don't remember anything about that at all."

CHAPTER 26

"*H*ave you been able to determine what the notifications led to?" Anita Mehdi was on the speakerphone in Katherine and Baxter's dining room.

Katherine had been granted permission by Kaylee to fill Anita Mehdi in on her experience with the app since her phone was the only proof they had that someone was using the reporting app to manipulate students.

"No. I am not an app designer, but the size of the app was way too big for what it was supposed to do, even if Kaylee got a version intended for grad students. Plus there were data mining programs integrated into it."

"So the app was spying on the students and gathering data it shouldn't?"

"Yes. But whatever message or task it directed Kaylee toward on Thursday, I can't tell you." Katherine rubbed her temple. "I clicked on the notifications again, but they just led to the app's home screen."

"So someone is covering their tracks," Baxter said. "Trying to hide what they did to Kaylee."

"What kind of data was it gathering? Like... social security numbers?"

Baxter continued. "Nothing that simple. It gathered all sorts of things about students. Locations of where they were, their internet search history, their personal financial information, all of it."

"Well, where did it go? I haven't seen any data like that."

"I imagine it went to a different server than the one dealing with the biofeedback study."

This was all getting to be so sordid. Students committing violent acts, an app that looked like it was solely created to spy on users, an affair between a professor and a student.

"Everyone who has the app needs to delete it," Katherine said. "But that would also destroy evidence, so I don't know what to do."

"They're probably already deleting it. I spoke to Alice about it this morning."

Katherine covered her face and tried not to scream. Baxter put a hand on her shoulder and said, "I'm afraid that wasn't a good idea, Anita. See, Alice Kraft is the one who designed the app. Which means she may be the one gathering data on the students, which is in violation of the IRB guidelines, which means that she has a vested interest in making sure any evidence of that disappears."

"What?" Anita sighed. "Well, I just don't know what to do at this point. Nothing seems right."

"No." Katherine opened her eyes. "No. You did the right thing. The safety of the students is the most important thing. We have to make sure none of them can be influenced in this way again."

"What should we do now?"

Baxter said, "Why don't we meet at school? I'll help you put together a report for the IRB to submit Monday."

Katherine rose. "While you do that, I'm going to contact Justin and Abby's families and see if they still have their phones. And I'll try to contact Detective Bisset and tell him what we know so far about the app and the study."

Baxter said, "Tell him we can email him a copy of the report tomorrow. The university will have to work with the police on this. I don't know what crimes have been committed, but I imagine there is more than one. Plus they may have a forensic computing team that can take a look at the program that was on Kaylee's phone. They might have run into something like this before."

"THANK YOU FOR DRIVING." Katherine glanced at Megan from the corner of her eye.

"No problem. I don't think Justin's parents or lawyer would talk to you without me anyway."

It was Sunday morning, and Megan's face was pale. The armor of makeup and accessories she normally donned was absent, and she was wearing a tracksuit. It was color-coordinated with her shoes and nail polish though, so Katherine had no doubt her vibrant friend was still there.

"How are you doing?"

"Well," she began, "neither me nor any of my three children have heard from the cheating bastard in three days. I have transferred fifty percent of all our accounts into a separate one in my name only, so that's taken care of for a little while."

"Do you have savings?"

"I have all my business accounts that were always my own, which he hated, but I am so grateful to have that now."

"Good." Katherine's heart ached more than a little.

They were driving down to Santa Maria because that's where the McCabe family made their home. Megan had offered to drive when Katherine told her she wanted to look at Justin McCabe's phone if it was available. Megan called the lawyer and arranged a meeting with Justin's parents, who would hand over his phone.

"So you don't think your marriage with Rodney is salvable?"

Megan took a deep breath before she spoke again. "This isn't the first time, Katherine. When the kids were little, Rodney had an affair. I found out, kicked him out, he groveled, we did counseling and managed to put things back together. I thought it was a one-off. He claimed it was. Now I'm wondering just how much a fool I was."

"You're not a fool. Don't say that."

"Doesn't matter either way. I told him years ago if he *ever* did that to me and the kids again, he was gone. So I'm done. I uprooted my entire life to support him and he does this to me? That's not a slipup. We started living completely separate lives once we moved out here, and I'm starting to think that was his intention."

"How are the kids?"

"Upset, Adam and Cami especially. Trina remembers the first time, so she gets it. I don't even think she's that surprised."

"And how are you?"

"Hell, Katherine, I don't know. My mama flew in yesterday, which is good and bad. My kids are glommed onto her and she's cooking up a storm, which is how all good Southern women deal with family upheaval. British people have tea; we have my mother's chicken pot pie."

"That sounds delicious."

"It is. And the house smells amazing all the time. Of course, my mother immediately started criticizing my lack of seasonal decorating, which is just... *so* on brand."

"Seasonal decorating?"

"Seasonal. Decorating." Megan's eyes turned steely as she watched the road. "Let's begin in January, keeping in mind there's probably gonna be some holdover from Christmas still hanging around. Nothing too churchy, but anything generally wintery—snowflakes, snowmen, stuff like that—you're still good."

"Okay..." Why did Katherine feel like a storm was approaching?

"For February, you're gonna want to liven that up with some hearts and flowers. Maybe a red wreath of some kind for Valentine's Day of course. It's not a church holiday, but everyone likes red hearts, and how else you gonna remind your man that he's gotta get those flowers ordered? March is Saint Patrick's Day, but depending on timing, you might just be skipping ahead to Easter. Now, you can't skimp on Easter."

Katherine's head was already spinning, and they weren't even halfway through the year. "What if you don't celebrate Easter?"

"Secular holiday now, Katherine, you're out of luck. That's right, lots of church stuff for the Baptists. Crosses and angels and whatnot, but don't forget the eggs and bunnies too. You *will* be expected to host a combination brunch and egg hunt, and you will be judged on how well your children have kept those Easter whites clean."

"Oh my God."

As she spoke, Megan's voice became ever so slightly more manic. "We're not even halfway there, but take a breath. Put your feet up for a hot minute because you have a brief respite in May before you go all out for Independence Day. Now, if you do a good enough job integrating your Fourth of July stuff into general summer seasonality, that should last you until the end of August. But once September hits, you're looking at harvest festival madness, my friend."

"I am so afraid of where this is going."

"We're talking decorative corn and enough pumpkins to sink a battleship, Professor Bassi. And pumpkin-spice candles through your entire damn house—don't argue, it's the law."

"Should I mention that it's seventy degrees here on the coast? And sunny?"

"Doesn't matter because this is *Seasonal... Decorating.*" She emphasized each word like a single sentence. "You're gonna throw a few cutesy bats and ghosts over that harvest glory to get ready for Halloween, but as soon as that ship leaves the harbor, the real marathon begins. You're gonna have to transition the harvest glory into a suitable bridge through Thanksgiving—go ahead and add some turkeys to all those pumpkins—but get ready because as soon as bowl-game kickoffs happens, it's the Super Bowl of seasonal decorating. The Olympics and the World Cup all rolled into one."

"Christmas?"

"Bet your booty, Bassi. We're talking yard displays, house displays, roof displays, lights, trees, poinsettias, and enough gold-painted crap to make it look like Midas went on a bender in your living room."

Katherine was speechless. Slightly horrified. But mostly speechless.

"Now, I haven't done *any* of that nonsense since we moved out here because my kids are teenagers and they don't really care. Plus all the friends I would decorate with—the only part that made it a little bit fun—are back in Atlanta. But if my mother is staying through Easter like she's threatening—"

"Easter? Do you *want* her to stay through Easter?"

Megan's eyes were wide. "She has her own room in that mansion. It doesn't much matter whether I want her there or not. She's there."

Katherine faced forward. "Well... obviously she loves you and she wants to take care of you. That's really wonderful when you think about it."

Megan had pulled up to a light and was staring at her. "I'm making you help me," she said softly. "Just for saying that."

"Making me help you with what?"

"The decorating. All of it."

Katherine considered that, along with her complete lack of life experience with seasonal decorating. She had to admit she was slightly curious. "Do I get chicken pot pie?"

Megan pursed her lips. "That could probably be arranged."

She shrugged. "Then I can help with some decorating."

Megan patted her hand before they pulled away from the light. "Oh, you sweet, innocent child."

"Just think, now that you have telekinesis, decorating a roof display is going to be so much easier."

"Okay... that is a good point."

CHAPTER 27

*J*ustin McCabe's lawyer was a man with weary eyes and a guarded expression. "Ms. Carpenter—"

"Alston Carpenter." Megan had freshened up in the car and held her hand out confidently. "And this is Professor Katherine Bassi from Central Coast State."

"You were also there at the fitness center on that day."

"Yes."

Megan continued, "We're not here to do anything but help Justin."

"You understand my skepticism obviously." He looked around the empty room. They were the only three there. "I hope you understand. Mr. and Mrs. McCabe decided at the last minute that they didn't want to be here, but they did tell me that I could meet with you on their behalf."

"Think of us as allies," Katherine said.

"You're the woman who tackled Justin at the gym."

"Yes. But please know that I believe if he had been aware of his actions, Justin would never have committed a crime."

Katherine would never forget the confusion and sorrow in that boy's face. "I am confident there's another explanation."

"Okay." The weary eyes turned suspicious. "I understand you want Justin's phone?"

"Yes." Katherine pulled out her laptop. "I want to clone it. We think there might be a connection between Justin and three other students who have all committed random acts of violence in the past six months due to an app that they downloaded as part of a research study."

"Megan gave me a quick rundown on the phone. I'm not sure how much you'll discover on it. According to the Moonstone Cove Police Department, it's a brick."

"What do you mean it's a brick?"

"They think it was water damage, but they don't know how it basically drowned when it was in his pocket." The lawyer pulled out a black smartphone in a Ziploc bag. "They even sent it home with us when he was released into psychiatric custody. They took the SIM card and told us the rest of it was completely useless."

Katherine held out her hand. "Well, I guess we'll see."

THEY DROVE AWAY DISAPPOINTED.

"Yep," Katherine said. "Completely useless."

"Are there, like, computer science experts that might be able to do something with it? A programmer? My seventeen-year-old daughter? I'm just saying, she's constantly attached to hers, so maybe she has a way of absorbing information by digital osmosis."

Constantly attached...

The vision came to her quickly. There was a man walking out onto a porch, limping a little and holding a hand flat to his abdomen as if he'd just had surgery. He sat and stared at the corral in front of his house. She could hear a flag flapping in the distance.

"Katherine?"

Her ears popped. "Megan, do you need to get home right away?"

"Why?"

"I just saw someone we need to talk to. Mario might be the key."

"Mario?"

She put her phone to her ear. "Abby's boyfriend. He might not have been part of the study, but he was living with someone who was."

Megan's eyes lit up. "Great idea!"

"Hello?"

"Baxter!" Thank goodness he'd picked up. "I have a favor I need to ask."

AFTER MORE THAN a little cajoling on Baxter's part, Mario agreed to speak with them at his parents' home in Nipomo. They drove through acres of farmland and horse ranches before they found the simple white ranch house beneath a grove of cottonwood trees. It overlooked a white-railed horse corral.

Sitting on the porch was a tall, long-legged young man with bronze skin and curly dark hair. He sat up and waved as they approached.

"Please don't get up!" Katherine shouted as they approached. "Please. I know you're still recovering."

He waved and sat back down, holding his abdomen. "Thanks, Katherine."

"It's good to see you." She smiled. "Even under these circumstances. This is my friend Megan."

"Nice to meet you." He nodded toward the door. "My mom said if you want anything to drink, just knock and she'll bring you whatever. Sorry, she's watching my nieces and nephews today, so she's gotta stay with them."

"Maybe it's better that she doesn't come out, because I wanted to ask about Abby."

The pain was evident in Mario's eyes. "Baxter said you'd want to talk about her."

"First off, I need to know, did you have any inclination that—"

"Nothing." His voice broke a little and he cleared his throat. "There was nothing. I've gone over everything in my head so many times, but there's just... nothing." He breathed out the last word. "You know Abby. She was... sunshine." Mario looked heartbroken. "I was the pessimist in the relationship, you know? She was always upbeat. I used to tease her if she got mad because..." The corner of his mouth turned up. "I'm not gonna lie, it was so cute it made me laugh. She hated that."

"She hated it?"

"Not like that." His eyes turned inward. "We were good, Abby and me. It was good."

Whoever had sabotaged these students belonged in jail. For a very, very long time.

"Mario," she started, "I know you've talked to the police

about it, but can you tell me what Abby's demeanor was that day? Had she been drinking? Did she appear to be under the influence of anything?"

"She had a beer with lunch. Just one. So nothing like that. She never took drugs, just her prescription or allergy medicine sometimes."

"And later?" she asked. "When it happened?"

He cleared his throat. "If I had to describe the way she was when it happened... It was like she was possessed. Her eyes were open, but there was nothing behind them." He kept his voice low. "Don't mention that to anyone because I honestly think my mother and father believe that she was actually possessed. They haven't said that—they don't want to look superstitious—but nothing else makes sense."

"What if I told you we think we know what might have happened and it had nothing to do with Abby's feelings for you? It didn't have anything to do with Abby at all."

He frowned. "What? Really?"

Katherine took a deep breath. "Abby was part of a study last year, right? The one about anxiety?"

He shook his head. "The police tried to get me to blame this shit on her meds, but I am telling you, that girl never abused her medication. She never had a weird reaction in all the time I knew her. No sleepwalking or altered states. Nothing like that. Like, how many people do you know on Xanax and shit? That was all she took. Fucking Xanax. Or... I don't know, the generic of that one, I think. She'd been on it a long time."

"But the study she did wasn't related to her medication, right? It was related to biofeedback."

"Yeah." He nodded. "She talked to me about it before.

Said there were no side effects. It was kind of like a meditation thing."

"Biofeedback involves a laboratory component where Abby would have been hooked up to sensors to make her aware of her body's reaction to stressors. Then, combined with that, there are visualizations that she would have done after the in-person treatments, and then she would report back on her independent exercises. That was part of the study."

"Yeah. That sounds right."

Megan piped up. "Do you remember her checking her phone a lot?"

Mario frowned. "I mean... no more than usual. Everyone checks their phone, right?"

"Did she have different reminder tones or alarms for the reporting app for the study?"

He nodded slowly. "Yeah. I've never thought about it before, but if I think back, yes. Her regular text tone was like... a lightsaber noise."

"Oh, I remember that!" Katherine grinned. "She showed me how to get it once, but then I thought it would feel like copying her if I got it, so I didn't."

Mario smiled a little. "I remember that dinner. Yeah, but for the app, it was some kind of chiming noise. Kind of like wind chimes."

"And do you remember her getting those regularly?"

"Oh yeah. I used to tease her about it." He shook his head. "I teased her that her boyfriend was calling. Not that she ever cheated on me, but she liked the meditation part of the study so much I called it her boyfriend because whoever narrated that part was a dude."

"So there was a guided visualization part of the app with someone narrating?"

"Yeah. She'd usually just go in another room twice a day when it chimed, but every now and then she'd get the notification at an odd hour and she'd do it then. Or if she was stressed about something."

"What about that day?" Katherine asked. "Did you hear the chimes then?"

"On the day she attacked me?" He frowned. "Yeah. I told the police even. I heard that notification once, and then again like five minutes later. I thought maybe she was ignoring it even though she was in the bedroom. But then maybe fifteen minutes later, she comes out of the bedroom, goes to the kitchen, takes the trash out to the corner, comes back, and..." Mario clammed up. "You know the rest."

It mirrored the timeline of Kaylee's notifications too. One notification and then another five minutes later, then an erratic outburst fifteen minutes after that.

"Thank you, Mario." Katherine rose. "For what it's worth, I know Abby loves you, and I think there's a logical explanation for all this."

CHAPTER 28

"Could a guided meditation really do all that?" Megan asked as they were driving back to Moonstone Cove. "Could it make you do something that completely out of character?"

"It seems like a stretch, but you have people who have willingly allowed this program access to their brain. Mario said the voice was male," Katherine muttered. "Greg Hammond. He helped write the app. He was the administrator. It had to be him."

"Why though?"

Isn't it always personal?

"Sarah Jordan's incident was months before any of the others." Katherine pulled out her phone and called Sarah.

The phone picked up after three rings and a man answered. "Jordan Ranch."

"I'd like to speak to Sarah Jordan please. Tell her it's Professor Katherine Bassi from Central Coast State."

"She's out of the house right now. Probably be back in an hour or two. Can I take a message?"

271

"I have a question for her. If you could have her call me back as soon as she's able, I would appreciate it." Katherine told the man her number and hoped Sarah would call her back. "What if it was all an experiment for him too? What if Greg targeted Sarah for some reason, trying to use her participation in the study to manipulate her?"

"And it worked, so he tried it on other people? Why?"

"I don't know that part yet." Katherine picked up her phone again. "We need to call Detective Bisset." She dialed the number of the Moonstone Cove Police Department and put the phone on speaker. "Detective Bisset please."

"One moment."

After a few minutes, a male voice came over the line. "This is Drew Bisset."

"Detective Bisset, this is Katherine Bassi again. Before you hang up, I want to tell you that we've discovered a link between all four students who've had violent incidents in the past few months."

"Did you say four?"

"I told you about Sarah Jordan weeks ago."

He was silent for a moment. "You're saying they're connected?"

"Obviously. This most recent incident was averted; there was a student who was on top of a building at the university last week and something bad was going to happen. Her name is Kaylee Ivers. You can ask campus security about it if you wish. I was there."

"You were there?"

"It was another odd coincidence, but I know this girl from one of my laboratories and she is the last person who would—"

"Professor Bassi, I appreciate you trying to help, and I know you care deeply about the school, but—"

"They were all part of a study, Detective." She pressed forward when he fell silent. "Sarah, Justin, Abby, and Kaylee. They were connected to a seemingly harmless biofeedback study that utilized an app on their smartphones. Tell me something—was Abby's smartphone damaged like Justin's was?"

He was silent for a long time. "How did you know his phone was damaged?"

"I have my sources. Was Abby's phone damaged?"

He huffed out a breath. "She dropped it in the sink in the kitchen before she attacked her boyfriend. Water damage."

"That's convenient. There was an app on her phone to help her with the visualizations she'd been practicing for the study. She received two notifications from the app prior to her violent outburst. Her boyfriend told you about them, about the wind chime noise, but I imagine you didn't realize the significance."

"Professor Bassi, are you saying that a meditation app caused these people to commit violence? Isn't it usually the opposite of that?"

Katherine took a deep breath. "This study carefully pinpointed deep-seated sources of an individual's anxiety or fear, and then someone exploited that fear through guided visualizations that caused the students to react in the opposite way they normally would." She pressed her eyes shut. "Think of it as a form of very intense hypnosis."

"You know, my brother used that to quit smoking, but I don't see him going off and trying to stab someone after a session."

Katherine covered the phone with her hand and said, "Did everyone's brother quit smoking via hypnosis?"

"No," Megan said. "But I had a cousin—"

"Seriously?" She uncovered the phone and continued speaking to Detective Bisset. "Instead of calming them down, the visualizations played on their fears, eventually causing them to lash out, probably as a form of self-defense. Then, like hypnosis, they forgot what they'd done."

"And you think a phone app can do all that?"

"Detective Bisset, if you can think of another explanation for normal kids to be committing violent acts like this, I'd love to know it."

He sighed. "Who made the app?"

"Two people, a graduate student who helped run the study, Greg Hammond, and one of the professors, Alice Kraft."

Detective Bisset was silent.

"You know one of those names."

"Give me your phone number, Professor Bassi." Drew Bisset's voice was grim. "If I have any other questions, I'm going to call you."

"Are you going to look into Greg and Alice Kraft? While you're at it, can you get a warrant or something to search the server at the behavioral science building? I think they were also using the app to data-mine the students without their permission and—"

"Your number, Professor Bassi. Please."

She gave him the information, and he hung up the phone. "He knew one of the names."

"My money is on Greg." Megan shrugged. "Don't know why; just feeling kinda anti-man right now."

"That's understandable. I'm leaning toward him because he's the app administrator. So if there were special messages pushed out to only a few students, he had to know about it. But I'm not sure that Alice Kraft wasn't involved too. She's the one who wrote the app. She has far more experience in computer programming. It's her specialty. So there's no way Greg could have included all the extra data mining without her knowing about it."

"I may have to stop hanging out with you so much," Megan said. "My brain hurts."

"Coffee?"

"Is it too early for wine?"

Katherine smiled. "Let's go by North Beach Coffee and get a drink. Maybe take a walk. We'll both feel better and we can clear our heads."

ONE HOT CAFFE latte and an iced macchiato later and Katherine and Megan were walking along the boardwalk that bordered North Beach Drive and listening to the sound of waves as the sun glinted on the water in the distance.

The ocean was at low tide, and outcroppings of tide pools and mussel-festooned rocks littered their corner of the cove. Seagulls squawked overhead, and plovers ran across the kelp-strewn beach.

"I'm starting to love it here," Megan said. "There's been about a dozen times since Friday where I've thought, 'That's it. I'm packing up and moving back to Atlanta.'"

"I wouldn't blame you. When bad things happen, it's

understandable to seek familiarity. I would miss you, but I'd completely understand."

"But then I'd be pulling the kids out of their new schools, which they like. And taking them away from their father. He wouldn't fight me, but... I don't know. I don't want them to be lying, cheating assholes like him, but I also don't want them to not have a father, you know?"

"I get what you're saying." She took a drink of coffee. "But don't idealize all fatherhood. I would probably be a healthier person if my father hadn't been a part of my life. My parents never divorced, but he was largely absent and when he was there, he was critical."

Megan shook her head. "That just boggles my mind. Why on earth would any parent poison a relationship with their kid like that? I know Rodney. He's gonna regret all this as soon as he realizes what he's lost, but I'm done. Fool me once, shame on you. Fool me twice, shame on me."

"No shame." Katherine felt a little awkward, but she reached over and gave Megan a one-armed hug. "You trusted someone who was supposed to love you. There's no shame in that."

"I'm done with him," Megan said. "But I also don't want to cut him off from his kids if he decides to make amends."

"So you're staying?"

"For now? Yeah." Megan looked out over the ocean. "I'm selling that house though. As soon as it's mine."

"Maybe you can get him to buy you out of that one and you can find a fixer-upper somewhere else that you can really make your own. Probably won't have that view though."

Megan smiled. "I can live without the view now that I have your back porch."

"You're welcome."

"I'm gonna have to start working again though. For sure."

"I don't know why you weren't before." Katherine turned to look at the rows of multimillion-dollar homes in the neighborhood they were walking through. "All these people have gobs of money and probably half your taste. Think about how many weddings you see on the beach and at the point every weekend. It'll take some time, but it sounds like you were really good at your job. You should definitely start another business here."

"Alston Event Planning." She sipped her macchiato and nodded slowly. "I like the sound of it. My daddy'd be proud." She made a face. "He never really liked Rodney all that much. Put up with him for my sake."

Katherine didn't have anything to say to that. Her father didn't have an opinion about Baxter when they'd gotten married, other than to say that she'd never reach her potential as a physicist if she was a wife and mother.

"It'll be good to be working again," Megan said. "I think it'll keep me—"

The sound of a car screeching on the street behind them caused both Katherine and Megan to turn. People shouted as a grey sedan jumped the curb and roared along the boardwalk, chewing up the old boards that protected the dunes.

"Is that car—?"

Megan grabbed her arm. "Run!"

They dashed across the street, only to have the car tearing up the boardwalk turn again and head for them.

"It's trying to run us down!" Megan screamed.

"What is happening right now?"

ELIZABETH HUNTER

"Run back and forth," Megan shouted. "Maybe it'll bust a tire!"

They ran back toward the boardwalk and jumped across the old railroad ties that bordered the walkway. The car turned to follow them and revved the engine as it careened in their direction.

"Tree!" Katherine pointed to a large and tangled cypress that arched over the boardwalk. "We can cut though there and run down the dunes!"

"Go!" Megan pushed her toward the overhanging limbs.

The sound of the engine was deafening. Katherine could hear onlookers screaming in the background, and a siren wailed nearby.

Katherine ran across the boardwalk and under the cypress tree, but she twisted her ankle on a jutting root and fell to the dirt.

"Megan!" Katherine was helpless on the ground.

Megan spotted her, turned and faced the car, and stood between the oncoming vehicle and Katherine. She held up both hands and, as the sedan approached, seemed to throw it into the twisted trunk of the cypress where it impacted with an anticlimactic crunch and a series of loud pops.

She ran to Katherine. "So glad I've been practicing."

"Did you just throw an entire car into a tree?"

"I more redirected it, but I was real pissed off. It's a lot easier to use the psychic stuff when I'm angry." She helped Katherine off the ground. "Maybe I owe Rodney a thank-you after all."

"Are you okay?" Her ankle was so painful she'd forgotten to ask about Megan.

"I'm fine! Got my heart pumping, that's for sure." Her

278

cheeks were flushed, and her hair was flying around in the breeze. "Dropped my coffee though. Asshole." She scowled at the busted sedan.

A small crowd had gathered around the driver's side, and more people were running toward them. Dozens of bystanders were on the phone and at least three people had their phones up, recording the incident.

"Are you okay?" A man ran over. "I think that car was trying to run you two down."

"Katherine?"

She spotted one of her neighbors waved a limp hand. "Hi, Ron."

"My God, are you okay?" He held her other arm as Megan helped her to a bench. "That man was headed straight for you. I was walking Trudie and saw the whole thing."

Ron's golden doodle, Trudie, was wagging her tail with such vigor Katherine couldn't resist the comfort of petting her fluffy blond head. "I really want a dog. I'm just going to get a dog and bring it home, and Bax will have to manage."

"I think that's a good idea."

Sirens were wailing on the highway.

Katherine gripped Megan's arm. "Did you see who it was? Who's the driver? Let me see." She was betting it was another unsuspecting student from Central Coast State. She saw an ambulance racing up North Beach Drive. It was already near the coffee shop. "Megan, help me over there."

"I think he's out cold," Ron said. "He's stuck in the car, and all the air bags deployed."

Megan and Ron helped her hobble over to see who was behind the wheel.

"Back up!" Ron yelled as they tried to get through the crowd. "Leave him alone. The EMTs are almost here. Back up."

Trudie offered a few helpful barks in solidarity.

The crowd parted, and Katherine saw the man who'd been trying to run them down.

"Oh my God." She didn't think she could be any more shocked than she already was that day, but life was unexpected. "Megan, I know him."

"Is he one of your students?"

"One of your students tried to kill you?" Ron was horrified. "That's insane."

"He's not one of *my* students." She turned to Megan. "*That's* Greg Hammond."

CHAPTER 29

*D*etective Drew Bisset watched the EMTs load Greg Hammond in the back of an ambulance. "So that's the guy who developed the app?"

"With one of the professors, yes." Katherine was parked on a bench.

Ron had called Baxter, who'd already left work and was on his way. Megan was standing next to her, calling Toni as Detective Bisset and Katherine spoke.

Katherine shifted her ankle, which was already swelling. "Tell me where you heard his name."

"I can't do that."

"Is it part of an ongoing investigation?"

"That's possible." He frowned. "You know, I took this job because I figured that detective work in a little college town was bound to be pretty boring. I'd be able to coach my girls' soccer team. Make dinner for my wife every now and then. Things like that."

Katherine looked up and down the block. The crowds

were now denser on North Beach Drive than she'd ever seen them. "Do you want me to apologize or something?"

He sighed and stuck his hands in his pockets. "Maybe just explain all this to me like I'm a freshman at your college who's majoring in physics instead of philosophy."

She squinted. "*Did* you major in philosophy?"

"I did."

"And you became a police detective?"

"I guess I read too much Hobbes."

"The tiger?"

Detective Bisset couldn't stop the smile. "The philosopher. The tiger's pretty good too."

"Agreed." She scooted over and he sat next to her. "The principle of biofeedback is that you learn your body's reaction to things in order to manage your stress responses. That part, the awareness, is done in a lab under the direction of a professional or, in this case, graduate students in psychology and behavioral sciences who were supervised by professors."

"And Greg Hammond was one of those students."

"Yes. He worked directly with Ansel Shaver, the lead on the study."

"But you mentioned another name too. Alice Kraft."

"Alice Kraft is another professor participating in the study. Her background is in computer science. She and Greg developed the app that sent notifications to the students who were affected by all this."

"Only them?"

Katherine shook her head. "I don't know. I'm not privy to that information. But when I realized that this study was the tie that bound these cases together, I spoke to my husband, who spoke to Anita Mehta, another of the psychologists who was part of the study. Anita and her colleagues are now in the process of contacting all the study participants to delete the app off their phone before reporting all this to the review board at the university."

"If there was something rotten in that app, why would Greg have used it?"

"What do you mean?"

Detective Bisset drew a clear plastic bag from his pocket. "Greg appears to have been under the same influence that Justin and Abby were."

"What makes you think that?"

He handed her the bag. "Phone. Waterlogged, just like the others."

Katherine stared at the phone in confusion.

But...?

How...?

"There must be some mistake. He was the administrator. It was a male voice reading the visualization exercises. Mario told us."

"Maybe this Professor Kraft is the one we need to be looking at," Detective Bisset said. "Maybe Greg got caught in the middle of something."

She rubbed her eyes and suddenly realized how exhausted she was. The sun was starting to creep behind the horizon. Katherine stood and braced herself on the back of the bench. "I need to go home."

"Professor Bassi—"

"No." She held up a hand. "I need to go. If you want another round of questions, you can follow me..."

She didn't make it to the end of her thought before a vision hit her like a brick between the eyes.

The interior of the ambulance was grey, like a black-and-white movie. One EMT sat on a bench beside the patient, shouting at the other, who was driving.

"*You planning on going to that movie with Kim?*"

"*Not sure.*"

"*I'm telling you man, she's into you. She picks a romantic kind of movie, she's into you.*"

Katherine didn't know who or what she was seeing in the vision, but she resisted the urge to pull away.

"*It's not a romance, man.*"

"*It's got a romance in it, right?*"

"*I mean, there's a hot girl, but I don't think it's a romance.*"

She felt the pull of consciousness, like the tug of a wave pulling sand from beneath her feet. She nearly fell off-balance, but she remained in the vision, knowing that there was more.

"*Just because there's, like, a love interest in an action movie, that doesn't make it a romance. By your definition, Die Hard is a romance then.*"

A subtle whisper of sound started in the background, like a radio left on in another room.

"*Die Hard was superromantic! He was fighting for his wife, man.*"

The sound grew and grew until the whisper was one long murmur of nonsense filling the truck.

"*You are such an idiot.*"

A hand shot up and grabbed the EMT by the throat, choking him.

"*Hey, Ernie?*"

The EMT flailed. He banged the flat of his hand on the wall of the van, and the ambulance lurched to the side.

"Holy shit, Ernie!"

Katherine snapped back into reality with a gasp. Her ears gave the telltale pop of awareness and she grabbed for Detective Bisset's hand. "Send an officer after that ambulance."

"What?"

"Send an officer after that ambulance, he's going to get away!"

KATHERINE STOOD next to the crashed ambulance. Both doors were hanging open, and two EMTs were rubbing their heads and pacing by the side of the road.

"Katherine?" Megan touched her shoulder. "I followed Detective Bisset's car. I hope you don't mind."

"No, that's fine." She'd practically forced Drew Bisset into his car and didn't even ask if she could join him as she gave directions to where she knew the ambulance carrying Greg Hammond probably was.

By the time they got to the junction of Valley Road and Highway 1, the man was already gone and a highway patrol cruiser was at the scene.

"How did you know this was going to happen?" Drew Bisset marched over and he was glaring. "How did you—"

"I often see connections other people don't," Katherine said calmly. "That's what makes me so effective in my research. That's what happened this time."

Where would he go? What was this about? Was it... an

alibi? An accident? *I can't be the bad guy because see? It happened to me too.* What was his next move?

"Has anyone called Alice Kraft?" Katherine tried to change the subject. She didn't need Drew Bisset asking a bunch of questions about her visions.

"Why would we call her?" Megan asked.

"If Greg wasn't the one who sent the strange notifications, then it was Alice Kraft. So either she's behind all this, or Greg could see her as a threat and a loose end to tie up. He's already tried to kill us today."

Drew pulled out his phone and punched in a number. "Jackie, get me the number for Professor Alice Kraft."

No one was lingering at Alice Craft's neat bungalow near the edge of the village. Drew Bisset parked on the quiet street, and he didn't object when Megan and Katherine pulled in behind him. In fact, he looked at Katherine first.

"When I talked to her on the phone, she seemed calm. No signs of anyone influencing her; no sign of Greg Hammond in the neighborhood. She didn't want to come to the station, but I'm not sure it's safe for her to stay here."

Katherine looked at Megan, then at Detective Bisset. "You may be overestimating my influence with Professor Kraft. We both work at the university, but I don't really know her."

"But you speak professor." Drew unconsciously patted the gun strapped to his abdomen as he walked toward the house. "Maybe you can convince her to hang out at the precinct, at least until we bring Hammond in."

"I can try."

Megan was looking up and down the road. "I love this neighborhood."

"It's cute, right?" Katherine nodded. "Walking distance to the village from here and an easy bike ride to the beach. You can take the Ferraro Ranch path."

"Nice."

"If you're done talking about real estate...?" Drew motioned to the gate.

"Oh right."

Megan and Katherine walked through the white picket fence and across the flagstone-paved garden. The house was simple and well kept, but there was an element of soulless-ness that Katherine sensed, as if it was empty even though she could see movement though the front windows.

Before they could ring the bell, Alice Kraft opened the door.

Out of her professional wardrobe, there was something forcefully sensual about Alice Kraft. Her hair fell around her shoulders in soft waves, and her eyes were wide but hardly innocent. She wore lounge clothes, as Katherine often did when she finished work for the day, but Alice Kraft's clothes clung to her body.

Detective Bisset paused, blinking. Katherine didn't blame him.

"You must be Detective Bisset." Professor Kraft frowned at Katherine. "Professor Bassi, why are you here? Are you limping again?"

"Yes. Greg Hammond just tried to run me over. I tripped trying to get away."

Megan snorted.

"I..." Alice Kraft was briefly at a loss for words. "The police said there'd been some kind of threat against me. Did you say Greg tried to run you over?"

Detective Bisset stepped in front of them. "Professor Kraft, can you tell me about the computer program that you and Greg Hammond developed?"

Alice Kraft looked at Katherine, who didn't look away even for a second. Finally she turned back to Detective Bisset. "Since I've been informed that the study is being self-reported to the university review board, I suppose I can answer your questions."

"That's very kind." Katherine didn't have to read people well to know that Drew Bisset was annoyed by Professor Kraft's attitude.

"We often sign very strict nondisclosure agreements," Katherine said. "To protect privacy."

"This is a police investigation," Detective Bisset said. "I don't care about your nondisclosure agreements."

Alice Kraft cocked her head. "And university IRBs don't generally care about your criminal investigations. What is this about?"

Oh, Detective Bisset really didn't like that answer. The corner of his mouth turned up. "Sarah Jordan was part of your study last year. She had a psychotic episode a few months ago. Killed her horse."

She raised a single sculpted eyebrow. "How awful."

"Greg Hammond once had a romantic relationship with Sarah Jordan—did you know that when he was assigned to be her supervising grad student in the study?"

"It would have made no difference to him. Greg understands professionalism. We try to keep things as anonymous as possible, but in a school as small as Central Coast, some students knowing each other is inevitable."

"So it's pure coincidence that the day Sarah Jordan killed her horse, Greg Hammond was seen at the stables?"

Whoa, what? Katherine and Megan exchanged a wide-eyed stare.

Alice Kraft shrugged. "You'd have to ask Greg about that."

"What's your relationship with Greg, Professor Kraft?"

She took a deep breath and considered. "Let's see, I worked with him on this study of course, and I've advised him in a limited capacity during his thesis development. He's preparing a doctoral thesis on the use of so-called smart devices in neuropsychology."

Drew took out his phone. "Like smartphones?"

"Wearables more than devices, but that's the general idea. Developing the app for the study helped him clarify some of his own work. It was an overall positive interaction."

"Nothing personal?"

She shook her head. "I'm sure there are rumors—there always are about young, attractive professors when they advise students—but none of them are true. I was his professor and advisor only."

She was too smooth, too practiced. She'd been expecting this series of questions and didn't hesitate with a single answer. Her entire demeanor was superior. Condescending even.

"What about the data mining?" Katherine said out of the blue.

Her eyes shifted. "Sorry, what?"

Hmmm.

"Data mining in the app." Katherine stepped forward. "You said you oversaw the app development. There's a lot in that program that patients wouldn't be expecting. Location tracking. Access to health data."

"I don't know anything about that."

Detective Bisset said, "But I thought you designed the app. You said you did. Are you saying that Greg Hammond snuck all that programming in without your knowing?"

She raised another eyebrow. "You'd have to ask him."

"And I don't suppose you know where he is?"

She shook her head. "Sorry. I really have no idea."

Her eyes said it all.

And I really don't care.

Detective Bisset took another step closer. "Let me be frank, Professor Kraft. I think you're full of shit. I think you and Greg knew exactly what that app did. Or at least you thought you did. I looked you up. I thought it was interesting that about five months ago, right after the incident with Sarah Jordan, you formed a limited liability corporation called Pacific Tranquility and trademarked the name STIL in all caps for use in a computer application. At least that's what the trademark application states." He held up his phone. "An app. You were planning to put out a smartphone app."

Alice Kraft's composure hadn't cracked. "I'm a computer scientist. Is it so hard to believe that I might develop an app on my own?"

"But you weren't on your own," Katherine said. "You had plans to take the biofeedback app from the study—after you'd tested it on students and worked all the kinks out—and sell it as your own."

Megan said, "Everyone wants to cash in on that sweet

California wellness lifestyle, right?"

Alice Kraft narrowed her eyes at Megan. "I'm sorry. Who are you?"

"Don't be sorry, hon! I'm Megan. And I'm the one who's been cleaning up the messes you've been leaving around Moonstone Cove. I stopped two of your experiments from killing people so far. Now would you be a peach and fill me on how many more are out there?" She smiled sweetly. "I'm a planner."

She tried to step back in the house. "You're all very misguided, and you can speak to my attorney."

"What was the plan?" Detective Bisset asked. "Were you always going to sabotage the results for the others so they couldn't publish? Sweep everything under the rug so you could launch your little company with no questions asked?"

She said nothing.

"Did Greg get in the way?" Detective Bisset asked her. "You didn't have the control you thought you did, did you? He went... a little off script."

Alice Kraft shut the door in their faces, but Katherine had seen enough. Detective Bisset had hit every nail on the head.

"She really created an LLC?" Megan asked as they walked to the car. "Doesn't she know those are public record?"

"Who was going to look?" Detective Bisset asked. "That's the thing. I think she's dirty, but she's not an idiot. Creating this much chaos attracts the wrong kind of attention. No..." He opened his car door. "I think Greg saw an opportunity to get even with a girl he resented. And after that, it was all his game."

CHAPTER 30

Drew Bisset sat on the back deck at Katherine and Baxter's house, drinking a cup of Earl Grey that Baxter had brewed for him. After the two men had bonded over the vulgarity of the coffee drinkers they were forced to spend time with professionally, they joined Katherine, Megan, and Toni on the porch. Megan already had their notes spread out on the table.

"I called my wife," Drew said. "Told her I'm working late tonight."

"Sorry about that," Megan said. "I know you have children."

"No worries. Happy to say it doesn't happen too often around here."

"Is there any word on Greg Hammond?" Toni was examining their notes.

"Not so far. I parked a car outside Alice Kraft's house and a couple of plainclothes men in the neighborhood to keep an eye out. If he tries to go there, we should spot him."

Katherine watched Drew study their notes. "How long

have you known about Sarah Jordan's connection to Greg Hammond?"

"Months." He looked up. "I caught that case months ago and something about it always bugged me. The girl had no memory of the events. Vet said the horse had been euthanized, but there was no way of knowing who did it. People were in and out of that stable all day. Sarah claimed she doesn't remember anything before being in that pen with the animal and finding him dead."

Toni shook her head. "That's so messed up."

"Agreed. Everyone I talked to said the girl adored that horse. Best friends. I've never been a horse person, but I get the feeling that she was highly attached to the animal. I don't think there's any way she'd hurt it if she was in her right mind."

"I grew up around ranchers," Toni said. "Horses are damn smart, and if they're attached to a human, they're very devoted."

"My initial thought was that someone had killed the animal to get back at Sarah. It made the most sense since she was so wrecked about Tucker. A couple of Sarah's friends mentioned Greg Hammond, so I checked it out. Sarah and Greg had only gone out a few times. She didn't think he was right for her, broke things off. He didn't agree, made a nuisance of himself for a while, but eventually backed off. According to her, months passed and she never saw him. Then Tucker happened."

"You said Greg was at the stables that day?"

"A man matching his description was seen, and Greg didn't have a good alibi. Said he was home studying. But other than that? It wasn't enough to really determine anything solid. Nothing close to real evidence. The woman who saw him couldn't be certain. I had to let it drop." Drew turned to Katherine. "But then you mentioned her name after Justin McCabe nearly attacked that gym."

"It was Kaylee who mentioned Sarah's name to me," Katherine said. "I spoke to her, and she told me about the study, but I couldn't tell you any more details than that without risking my professional reputation."

Drew frowned. "So people really take the confidentiality of those student studies that seriously?"

"Without question," Baxter interjected. "Breaking confidentiality in an academic study like that could ruin a career."

"Seriously?" Drew nodded. "Well then, props to you, Professor Bassi. Didn't realize you were sticking your neck out so far on that one."

"I just wish I could have told you more," she said. "I feel like we have all the pieces of this puzzle except the last."

"Greg Hammond." Drew pointed at the board. "If you're right, he manipulated Sarah Jordan with this app to get revenge. But then there's a big gap here." He pointed at Justin's page. "What made him go after Justin and Abby?"

Megan said, "Maybe he found out about Professor Kraft's plans for the app. Maybe she told him, maybe she slipped. Maybe they decided to tank the study altogether so they could make money off the app."

"One student having an episode wouldn't be enough to throw out a whole study," Baxter said. "Not in my opinion. But four or five?" He nodded. "I believe that would do it."

"But murder? Mass shootings?" Detective Bisset shook his head. "I don't know if Greg Hammond was behind all that. I think Alice Kraft could be the mastermind on this one."

"Because she's a professor?" Toni asked.

"Because she's cold." Detective Bisset looked up at Toni. "Something about her? All I get is ice."

Katherine noticed that Megan was mulling over something in her head and absently floating a handful of sea glass she'd taken to carrying in her pocket.

Katherine kicked her leg under the table.

"Ow!" The glass fell into her palm. Megan glared at Katherine. "What was that for?"

Katherine looked at the sea glass and raised an eyebrow.

Megan made a small O with her mouth and shoved the handful of glass and pebbles in her pocket. "Right."

Drew looked up. "I miss something?"

"We all did." Katherine nodded solemnly. "We really need to find Greg Hammond."

Two days later, Greg was still in the wind. The university was abuzz with news about the behavioral science experiment, but no one could seem to satisfactorily assign blame. The professors who'd led the study had come forward voluntarily after a series of unexpected and tragic incidents with students, and no obvious wrongdoing had been identified.

Baxter folded a newspaper and placed it on the table at the university student center. "Very unsatisfying for all the gossips."

"I imagine." Katherine picked at her lackluster chicken salad. "You know, we have a culinary program here."

"I know we do. And we live in one of the most agricultur-ally rich regions in the state. The fact that you can't get a decent lunch here is appalling." He smiled at her. "I can't complain about the company though." He reached down and brought her ankle up to rest on his knee. "How's it feeling today?"

"Better. I think it's given up trying to be an old-lady ankle and has realized it's going to have to toughen up."

Baxter's eyes lit up. "Is that how it works? I'll have to tell my shoulder."

"You should. You could get back to murdering John on the racquetball court."

"Alas, I think our days of racquetball murder are well behind us." His smile fell. "Has Detective Bisset made any progress finding Greg?"

She shook her head.

"That man tried to kill you and Megan, and the police don't have any kind of protection assigned to you."

"Drew thinks that Greg won't come after me again. He's focused on Alice Kraft. He thinks she's the mastermind."

"And you?"

"I think Greg staged the wild scene and tried to run me over to make himself look less guilty. I don't know who the mastermind is."

"So he's still a threat."

"I'll be very careful, okay? And I'll stay off public side-walks as much as possible."

Baxter grumbled, but he didn't say anything more.

Katherine poked his side with her toe. "I'm getting a medium-sized fluffy dog. I don't expect you to clean up after it or walk it or anything. It will be my responsibility."

He narrowed his eyes. "It can't sleep in our bed."

"That's fine. We can close the door. It can sleep in the kitchen."

"Nothing that lifts its leg."

"I'll look for a girl."

He wasn't smiling, but he wasn't frowning. "Fine."

Katherine grinned. "I'll start looking at rescues this week."

"That seems like the most ethical decision."

"You're going to love it."

"It's an animal living in our house. Much of human civilization has progressed specifically so we no longer have to live with animals in our houses."

"I don't know if that's actually true."

"Nevertheless." He patted her ankle, and she put it down so he could stand up. "You shall have your dog, and I'm sure I will learn to live with it."

"I'll find one that doesn't shed."

"Excellent." He bent down and gave her a kiss. "I have an evening lecture tonight. Toni and Megan will be at the house by the time you get home, correct?"

"Yes. I won't be at the house by myself."

"Good."

"Will John be dropping you off later?"

"Yes, which means he'll want to get a drink before we make it home. I could be late."

"No problem. Have fun." She raised her briefcase. "And I have much grading to do. Enjoy your lecture."

"Always, my darling." He hooked a messenger bag over his shoulder and turned to go.

"Professor Pang."

He turned with a half smile on his face. "Professor Bassi."

"I love you more than *Star Wars*."

He put a hand over his heart and pretended to swoon. A smile lit up his face as he walked away.

Katherine had been fortunate to find a parking spot near the student center, so she walked to her car instead of calling the student security patrol in the little golf carts. Her department chair told her to make use of them since her ankle was hurt again, but she felt silly asking for help. She made it back to her car just as two-o'clock classes let out, which meant she sat in traffic for nearly twenty minutes just trying to make it out of the parking lot. At three thirty, she was heading home.

Megan called her on the way. "Hey, I'm running a little late. Maybe just wait in the parking lot at the coffee shop, okay?"

"I'm sure Toni will be there. No worries."

"Are you sure? Baxter was really set on you not being alone."

"I'll be fine. See you soon."

Katherine started to get excited about the dog. She already knew what rescue organization she wanted to adopt from. They specialized in poodles and poodle mixes. She wanted medium-sized. She wanted fluffy and smart. She didn't much care if she got a puppy; she thought a grown dog would probably be better suited to her and Baxter. Maybe something two or three years old.

She pulled into the driveway and got her phone out, looking at profiles of the animals as she walked toward the house. She unlocked the door and walked inside, kicking the door closed as she set her bag on the table.

Her vision went black and white, time slowed down, and her senses went haywire. She felt the rope around her neck—

Katherine spun and threw her phone at Greg Hammond's face, startling him as he reached for her with both hands.

"Bitch!" He sputtered and grabbed at her arm. "Get back here!"

She ran through the kitchen and down the short steps leading to the living room, heading for the back doors that led to the deck. Her vision had given her only seconds to react, but if she could make it out the back doors and scream for help—

Katherine's neck jerked back, pain ripped along her scalp, and she fell hard. He'd yanked on her braid and dragged her back. Thankfully she had enough padding that she didn't feel anything break, but her whole body was jolted.

"You think you can get away that easy?" he muttered. "Old bitch. Think you can ruin everything I've done. Think you're so much smarter than me?"

Greg dragged her back to the kitchen by her braid, and Katherine couldn't stop the cry that left her lips.

He chuckled. "You have no idea. This is going to be fun."

"No?" She gasped, but she kept speaking. "Tell me about your brilliance, Mr. Hammond. Please. I'm sure I'll be so impressed." She made her voice as patronizing as she could while she was in so much pain.

Toni, where are you?

"You wouldn't understand." Greg shoved her into a corner by the sink. He stood over her with his hands on his hips and looked around, the rope still resting in his left hand. "Nice house. I noticed it in one of Abby's Facebook pictures last year. She was such a bitch to me. Thought she was so much smarter. Her and her stupid boyfriend."

"You knew Abby?"

"I made sure the random students assigned to me weren't too random." He poked her knee with his booted foot. "By the time they were finished in the lab, they all thought I was best friends with them again."

"So you were... what?" She rubbed the back of her neck and looked for ways to escape. Greg had cornered her in their L-shaped kitchen and was blocking the exit. "You were just getting back at women who wouldn't go out with you? What about Kaylee? Justin?"

"Justin was just a challenge." Greg grinned. "I wanted to see if he'd do it. Kill all those people. He was so self-righteous about it, you know? And he had a thing for Sarah. He pretended he didn't, but he totally did."

"How did you do it?" She struggled to sit up, making herself look more injured than she was. "Was it hypnosis? Deep meditation? What?"

Greg ignored her and looked up. "Love the construction on this place. These open rafters are perfect."

Katherine touched her scalp, searching for blood. "Perfect for what?"

"Poor, lonely Professor Bassi." He threw one end of the rope over a rafter. "Never see her walking with anyone but her husband. Never see her with friends. Stuck in her little office, talking to herself or eavesdropping on students. Kind of pathetic, right?" He jumped a little to grab the end of the rope and pull it down. "Isn't it strange how she keeps getting injured? Now she's talking to the police, looking for attention."

Katherine narrowed her eyes when she saw him tying a noose. "You actually think you're going to make people believe that I killed myself? You're not as smart as you think you are, Mr. Hammond."

"I'm not going to make people believe anything." He finished the noose and crouched down next to her. "I'm going to talk to you and make you do it." The corner of his mouth turned up, and he put his palm on her cheek. *"Relax."*

His voice had an odd timbre, and Katherine felt the press of something in her head.

"Relax." He repeated himself, and this time the pressure was stronger.

Still, she could think—she could *feel*—past it.

"Oh!" The final puzzle piece clicked into place. "That's it. That's how you made it happen. You're like Toni."

Greg frowned. "What?"

"You're like us."

CHAPTER 31

*O*f course. It never made sense that they were the only ones with psychic abilities.

After all, there were the three psychics in Glimmer Lake. Katherine had done her research and found that police departments and intelligence agencies often quietly used people with psychic and remote-viewing abilities behind the scenes.

"Well, it never made sense that the only psychics we knew of would be *good*." Katherine straightened her back. "I imagine if you surveyed the prison population in any meaningful way, you'd find a range of psychic abilities among the more skilled criminals."

Greg was still crouched in front of her, but his mouth was hanging open. "What the fuck are you talking about?" he snarled.

"You." She pressed her back against the kitchen cabinets. Her whole body ached, but she refused to let him see it. "You're an empath like my friend Toni. You can influence others' emotions. That's how you were able to make them do things they wouldn't normally do."

He glared at her. "You're delusional."

"No, I'm not. They were already susceptible to suggestion because of the visualization exercises. They already trusted you because you'd worked to regain their trust in the lab. You said so yourself. No doubt there was some remote hypnosis you were using via the app. But you had to have some contact with them as well." She frowned. "How did you do it?"

Greg slapped her hard across the cheek. "Shut up."

"Yes, yes, yes." She nodded. "Of course you couldn't be entirely remote. You need some contact. You were at the stables before Sarah killed her horse. You just made her forget. You were at the locker room in the gym when Justin went to cool down. I bet you're even on surveillance footage if we look."

"Shut up!" He raised his hand and struck her again. "You're a fucking loony. No one is going to believe you."

"You think they're going to believe that I *killed* myself?" Her eyes watered, but she didn't stop talking. "Don't be ridiculous, Mr. Hammond. You're not as smart as you think you are. Does Alice Kraft know about your empathy? I bet she doesn't. I bet you used it on her. Or rather, you tried. She has several markers of sociopathy, so you might not have been able to manipulate her. I bet you think you've outsmarted her. I imagine you even believe you have the upper hand in that relationship."

"I do."

"You don't. Of *course* you don't." She let the pity seep into her voice even as she could feel her left eye swelling.

"Boys like you don't get the upper hand with women like Alice Kraft. She sees through you, exactly like Sarah and Abby and Kaylee did. She's using you, Mr. Hammond. If you were more rational, you'd see that."

"You crazy old bitch." He laughed. "I think I'm putting you out of your misery after all."

If she could keep him distracted long enough, Toni or Megan would come.

"You saw all of us? Like, in your vision?"

"You were holding a gun on someone. You looked... intent."

And if Katherine was guessing correctly, Toni was coming with a gun.

"So tell me, Mr. Hammond, what are you going to do now?" Katherine's eyes teared up from the pain in her face, but she refused to look away from Greg or act scared. "I'm resisting your empathic suggestions, probably because I'm also psychic."

He rocked back on his heels. "You're what?"

"Isn't it obvious? I've been one step ahead of you over half the time. I have *visions*. You haven't figured that out yet?" She leaned forward. "That's how I stopped Justin at the gym. That's how I knew what you were trying to do to Kaylee, so I stopped that too. I saw it, Greg."

Could she bluff? Was that possible? She could try.

Katherine closed her eyes and took a deep breath before she opened them again. "I can see what's going to happen to you too."

She had no idea what was going to happen, but Greg was still back on his heels, staring at her with wide eyes.

"It doesn't end well." She kept her voice a pained whisper. "Turn yourself in. That's the only way to avoid—"

Someone rapped hard on the door. "Katherine, it's me!"

Greg turned his head, and Katherine lifted her foot and kicked out hard, right into Greg Hammond's groin, with as much force as she could gather.

He fell back shouting. "Fuck!"

"Katherine?" Toni pounded on the door and rattled the knob, but Greg must have locked it.

"He's here!" she shouted. "He's trying to—"

"Fucking bitch!" Greg managed to scramble to his feet and started kicking Katherine. "You ruined it!"

"Leave her alone!" Toni pounded on the door; then it fell silent.

Katherine curled up and covered her head. Getting kicked by Greg Hammond was a little like falling down a rocky hill on a trail run. She focused on protecting her vital parts, curling into a ball while she tried to roll away.

His feet landed on her thighs and her hips. That was fine —those were two large muscle groups that could take the damage.

She heard glass breaking, and a second later, Toni's voice rang through the house.

"It's loaded, and you wouldn't be the first, asshole."

The kicks stopped. Katherine felt her vision go wobbly, but not because of precognition. She was just going to pass out. That was okay. Megan's voice was in the background now too. She heard sirens in the distance.

Poor, lonely Professor Bassi....

She wasn't alone; she had Baxter, she was getting a dog,

and even better, she had the two best friends a forty-seven-year-old newly psychic professor could hope for.

She smelled Megan's perfume as soft hands stroked her back. "We're here, hon. I already called 911. The police are on the way."

"Good." She relaxed a little bit and reached for Megan's hand. "I'm getting a dog."

"Good. Maybe a real big one."

"I don't need a big one. Look at Toni. Clearly, little things can be very dangerous."

Megan sniffed. "Uh-huh."

"Are you crying? Why are you crying? He's like us, Megan. He can use people's emotions like Toni. Is that why you're crying?"

Megan smoothed her hair back from her forehead, still sniffing, and Katherine's vision started to go dark.

"Katherine?"

Sorry.

Her vision swam, and everything went black.

KATHERINE LOOKED at her reflection in the tiny mirror. "Good Lord, no wonder you were crying. I look like death."

She had a black eye and several cuts near her ear where Greg Hammond's boots had managed to land. The entire backside of her body was bruised and aching. She handed the little mirror back to Megan and lay back on the hospital bed. "Nope, that's not comfortable either."

Toni had her feet propped on the side of Katherine's bed. "Have you tried your side?"

"I do lie that way, but I have to keep moving or everything hurts."

"Please tell me they're at least giving you the good drugs," Megan said.

"Oh yeah." Katherine's head was swimming. "I'm flying high."

"Good."

She moved her neck to look toward the door. That hurt too. "Is Bax out there?"

"I saw him talking with Detective Bisset when I came in," Megan said. "Before he comes back, you said Greg was an empath like Toni?"

"Maybe not exactly the same. I've never seen Toni try to mind-meld like Greg tried with me."

"But he couldn't do it, huh?" Toni nodded. "Good."

"I think he could with the others though." Katherine looked at Toni. "Think about it. If he already had them in a suggestible state with the visualization program on the app, then all he'd need was a little contact, a little push, and he'd be able to influence them."

"Sarah Jordan?" Megan asked.

"Drew said that someone matching Greg's description was seen at the stables," Toni said. "And the others..."

"Justin said he went to the men's bathroom at the gym. It was the last thing he remembered. Greg could have been there."

"That would explain how he got a gun too," Toni said. "Greg could have brought it with him and given it to Justin."

Megan said, "And Mario said Abby took the trash out. Right before she attacked him, she'd taken the trash out." She frowned. "Justin and Sarah both said they remembered doing their visualizations and feeling like someone was pushing them toward their fear. Do you think that was Greg?"

"I don't know how he'd do it," Toni said, "but that makes sense. Push them when they're vulnerable and plant suggestions. Then make them forget they ever saw you."

"Tell them to dump their phones in water to destroy the evidence," Katherine said. "We wouldn't have even known about the connection with the app if I hadn't saved Kaylee on that roof."

"Wonder why he targeted her," Toni said.

"He targeted Sarah Jordan because she rejected him and Justin because Sarah admired him. I get the feeling Greg also wanted Abby and she didn't reciprocate. It's not a stretch to think that Kaylee might have rejected him or disrespected him in some way she might not have even realized. He was pretty delusional."

"What matters is that Detective Bisset seems to think that Greg and Alice Kraft are responsible for all this," Megan said. "Which means that both Justin's and Abby's defense lawyers will be able to use that in their defense."

"Hopefully they won't even press charges." Katherine was exhausted. "Hey, you guys?"

"What do you need?" Toni sat up straight. "You want a nurse? My cousin Leah works here."

"Why am I not surprised?" Megan asked.

"I'm tired," Katherine said. "I'm going to fall asleep pretty soon. Can you guys stay with me until Baxter gets back?"

Megan and Toni exchanged a look.

"You got it," Toni said. "We're not going anywhere."

"My mama's already decorating my house for Easter."

Megan walked over to get a chair. "You couldn't get rid of me if you tried."

"Thanks," Katherine murmured. "You guys... the best."

THEY RELEASED Katherine from the hospital the next morning. She had two cracked ribs and a fractured radius, but they couldn't do anything about the ribs and her arm was already in a cast. She had two stitches by her ear that her hair would cover up when it grew back in, and lots and lots of bruises.

"I'm never going to complain about having a large butt again." Katherine winced when Baxter helped her out of the car. "If I had more padding on my back, I might not be so sore."

"I've never complained about it," Baxter said. "And I concur."

He wasn't as keen to make jokes about the situation as she was. He was more concerned about her going back to the house where she'd been attacked.

They paused at the front steps.

"Are you sure you're okay being back here?" he asked.

"Bax, it's our home." She put her hand on his cheek and pulled him down for a kiss. "We have a million wonderful memories here, and one bad one. I'll be fine."

"I've already contacted a security company," he said. "No one will be able to break in again."

"Did you talk to the insurance about the back doors?" She frowned. "Does homeowners' insurance cover damage from your friend breaking in to stop a home invasion?"

"I don't need to because Toni already had a cousin come

over and replace the doors yesterday. I told her I was more than happy that she broke the doors since she rescued you from a madman, but she insisted." Baxter helped her up the stairs and unlocked the front door. "Apparently the builders need to stain them to match the rest of the house, but she said the repair was finished."

Katherine walked into her beautiful cozy home, and nothing had changed. It was still her cozy refuge, paneled in teak with sweeping views of the stormy grey ocean and the rocky point in the middle of Moonstone Cove. The new french doors blended seamlessly with the existing picture windows. There was not a single thing out of place.

Her copper pans shone on the wall of the kitchen. The furniture had been straightened and the floors showed not a trace of blood. Throughout the house, bunches of flowers were visible and the faint scent of linen and green grass drifted over the sharp smell of lemon oil cleaner.

"Did Megan and her mom come over to clean after Toni's cousin fixed the doors?"

Baxter smiled. "Yes, how did you know?"

"Seasonal decorating." She smiled and felt her soul relax. "Apparently it's the law."

EPILOGUE

"*W*ait, Archie!" Katherine called to her five-month-old golden doodle, who looked over his shoulder, pausing before he said hello to the children on the beach.

His tail was wagging furiously, but she saw the children's mother hesitate.

"I'm so sorry!" She ran over, her right knee still aching a little. "I'm supposed to have him on a leash, but we live right over there and sometimes he jumps off the deck if he gets excited. He's very friendly."

"Can I pet him?" the little girl asked.

"You can if your mother says it's okay. Sit, Archie."

Archimedes Bassi-Pang—conveniently referred to as Archie unless he was being naughty—plopped his furry backside on his pebbled stretch of North Beach and quivered in excitement as the little girl held out her hand. Soon her little brother was bravely petting Archie too.

The dog was in heaven.

"He's so fluffy!" The little girl giggled. "What's his name?"

"Archie. And he's still learning the dog rules." Katherine clipped his leash on since it was the middle of the day.

Most mornings, Katherine took Archie out for a walk at sunrise. He chased the gulls, dragged ropes of kelp up and down the beach, and got treats from the local surfers, who had all adopted him as their mascot. But it was Saturday and the beach was filled with visitors, so she'd kept Archie on the deck.

Two weeks after the attack on Katherine, their neighbor Ron was extolling the virtues of Trudie's skills as a watchdog. Three calls later, Baxter had discovered a lone three-month-old male golden doodle whose prospective owners had been forced to move cross-country and couldn't take on a new dog. Four hours after that, Baxter had a pile of blond fluff in the front seat of their car.

"He's male, so he'll have to be neutered." Baxter plopped the dog on Katherine's lap. "But he's large enough to guard you, and the breeder said he won't shed."

Katherine had fallen in love at first sight. Archie was a lovable, wiggly dog who was larger than she expected, but he was already house-trained, so she wasn't going to complain.

Baxter had lasted exactly two nights before the dog was sleeping in their room. Within a month, Archie had her previously indifferent husband completely in his thrall.

"He's so cute." The little boy's face was glowing. "He really likes me."

Archie loved everyone from the mail carrier to the grumpiest old man on their block, but Katherine wasn't going to say that. "You must be very special. He's a good judge of character."

"Kids, we have to go." The mom gathered her little ones and headed toward the stairs leading back to North Beach Drive. "Thanks," she said to Katherine. "We can't have a dog at our apartment. Guys, say bye to Archie."

They all waved. "Bye!"

The little girl yelled, "Thank you for letting us pet you!"

Archie watched them leave, whining a little. Then he looked up at Katherine and whined more.

"No. You can't go off leash while there are people around," she said. "You know that."

He sighed deeply.

"I know. It's very unfair. We'll go to Aunt Toni's house, and you can chase rabbits later."

He woofed a little, probably from hearing Toni's name.

Toni had finished her house enough that she'd invited Megan's family, Baxter, and Katherine over three weeks before. Her little house was an old Spanish-style cottage in the middle of a vineyard. It came with two acres of land, a few fruit trees, and lots of privacy. It had been an old foreman's cottage for one of her uncles, but she'd bought it and fixed it up for herself. It was tiny, but it had a lot of incredible scenery and a huge barn she could use for her car collection.

And rabbits. Archie loved the rabbits.

They walked back to the deck, and Katherine saw a familiar face waiting with Baxter at the table under the umbrella.

"Detective Bisset." She climbed the stairs. "This is Archie."

Drew Bisset's grin was wide and his hands reached out.

"Archie, my man. Look at you. I'll tell you like I told your owner, you can call me Drew, not Detective Bisset." He looked up. "So you took my advice, huh?"

"No." Katherine pointed at Baxter. "He's the one who surprised me."

Drew reached over and held out his fist for Baxter to bump knuckles. "Baxter, that's a good-looking dog there."

"The most intelligent dog I have ever met," Baxter said. "Truly. They often use this breed for service animals because they're so bright."

"Really?"

"Yes." Since adopting Archie, Baxter had become an expert on the breed. As he extolled Archie's virtues, Katherine got herself a cup of coffee. She was fairly sure Drew hadn't come to the house to meet their dog.

"...so he's protective but not aggressive." Baxter finished the recitation of Archie's merits, his hand scratching the sainted dog's ears.

"You know, in my line of work, I see people get all these big dogs for protection. Unfortunately, a lot of those people don't have any idea how to train a large, dominant kind of dog." Drew stretched his legs out. "I tell people, the most protective dog you'll ever have is a good, well-behaved family dog that's devoted to its people. Can't do better than that."

Baxter might have adopted Archie for Katherine's protection, but she had a hard time imagining him attacking anyone.

"So is there news?" Baxter asked. "About Abby?"

"The DA has decided not to press charges against Abby Chung," Drew said. "Considering everything that's come to light about Greg Hammond, Alice Kraft, and their plans, they decided that the psychiatric facility where she's been staying should guide the case, and the doctors there have cleared her and told the DA that she is not a danger and the incident was isolated."

"So basically the same outcome as Justin's case."

"Yes." Drew nodded. "Thankfully. Now, the charges against Hammond and Kraft keep piling up, so I can't tell you that you won't have to testify in those cases."

"They would be two separate trials?"

Drew shrugged. "I don't think Kraft will go to trial. She's got a real smart lawyer from San Francisco who's already working the angles."

Baxter asked, "Is she still claiming that Greg did everything on his own?"

"She's admitted to the affair with Hammond and claims that they planned to basically steal the app after she screwed with the data to make the study unpublishable. But she says Hammond is the only one who used the app to hypnotize the students."

The police had settled on the theory that Hammond had hypnotized students via remote voice recordings, and Katherine just hoped that they had an expert witness who could back that up.

"For me though?" Drew shook his head. "I'm not buying that she had no idea about what Hammond was doing at all."

"Why not?"

"Because she formed that LLC right after Sarah's horse died."

Baxter nodded. "You think Greg told her."

"I think he had to. It might have gone further than he intended. I don't know. But she was the only one other than him who really understood what that app was capable of doing. I think he told the woman he thought was his girl-friend, and she realized it was the perfect pretense to sabo-tage the study, which would leave them free and clear to steal the app when the study went to hell."

"And the other students?"

"I don't think she planned that part," Drew said. "Too much attention. I have a feeling Greg started going a little overboard. Or maybe he wanted to frame Kraft and take everything for himself. Either way, he doesn't escape jail time. With his attack on Katherine? No way in hell. Kraft? Maybe."

"She's finished in academia," Baxter said. "After the scandal with the study and admitting to an affair with a grad-uate student, she'll never work at a reputable university again."

"There's always Silicon Valley," Katherine said. "They don't care much about morals there. Just money."

Drew shrugged. "Sounds like a good fit then."

Katherine knit her fingers through Baxter's, and Archie took the opportunity to stick his furry head underneath their joined hands.

"Wherever they go from here," Katherine said, "at least they'll be leaving Moonstone Cove."

Drew raised his mug of tea. "Good riddance."

"Don't worry, Detective." Baxter rubbed Archie's ears. "I foresee Moonstone Cove returning to normal very, very soon."

"Do you?" Katherine reached for the pile of sea glass on the edge of the table and let the smooth weight of the stones grow warm in her palm. "I don't know." She watched the ocean rise and fall in the morning sunlight. "These days I think normal is a little harder to define."

Thank you for reading *Runaway Fate*!
Continue reading for a preview of the next Moonstone Cove novel,
FATE ACTUALLY.
Now available for preorder!

FIRST LOOK: FATE ACTUALLY

Antonia Dusi slicked a clay face mask over her olive-toned skin and set the timer for five minutes.

Five minutes.

She leaned on the edge of the counter and glanced to her right, drumming her fingers on the edge.

Four minutes, fifty seconds.

What was she supposed to do with four minutes and fifty seconds? Toni hated sitting still. She hated wasting time. She had too much going on in her life to waste time. It was Wednesday morning, she had a dozen things to do at her garage that day, and her dad was supposed to be coming in; she wanted to get her butt going out the door.

Four minutes, thirty seconds.

Drip.

Drip.

Drip.

The rhythmic pat of a water drop at the bottom of her sink snagged her attention. She cocked her head and put her finger to the faucet. It was one of those little jobs she hadn't quite gotten around to doing since she bought the old cottage at the bottom of the hill.

It was probably just a washer. She could fix that in five minutes.

She glanced at the counter and the numbers ticking by. Okay, four minutes, fifteen seconds.

Toni opened the bathroom door and walked through her bedroom and toward the kitchen where she kept her toolbox under the sink. Eventually, she'd keep the toolbox in the laundry room, but since the laundry room was torn up while she refinished the cabinets in there, she kept her tools in the kitchen.

Just as she grabbed her toolbox, she felt her phone buzzing in her pocket.

She slid it to answer. "Morning, Dad."

"Toni, you're not at the garage."

He was early. Of all the days.

"I'm just running a little late. I'll be there soon."

"There's like three guys just sitting around in the bay."

She looked at the clock on her phone. "It's five til eight. They're not on until eight."

Bobby Dusi huffed and muttered something about "his day."

She walked the toolbox back to the bathroom. "Dad, I'm sure Glenn has them all scheduled. It's a busy day, and he knows what's going on."

"Is this Glenn's garage, or yours?"

It's mine, you old coot! "Dad, do I go to the club and tell you how to play bocce ball?"

"You act like I didn't run this place for forty years."

"You act like I haven't run it for the past fifteen." She

could feel her temper start to rise. So much for that careful meditation she'd been practicing every morning since she'd been struck with unexpected psychic powers earlier in the year.

The traumatic near-shooting that had triggered her empathy was a fading memory, but the unexpected wash of emotional energy still took her by surprise most days.

If she was happy, she could make other people ecstatic. If she was pissed, she could start a fight. Not to mention the emotional sponge she'd become. Most days, she hardly knew whose feelings were swimming through her body.

Her two new friends, Katherine Bassi and Megan Carpenter, were dealing with changes too. Katherine was still having flash visions she couldn't control and Megan had become telekinetic. Megan seemed to be most devoted to understanding their new situation and she'd been the one to suggest meditation for Toni.

Meditation worked. Until your seventy-five year old dad went and blew your zen to hell.

"Dad, I don't have time for this." Shut it down. Shut it down. "Listen, I'm not sleeping in. I have a leak in the bathroom I'm fixing."

"A leak?" Her father calmed down. "Ah, I know how that is. Take care of it and I'll see you here. It's a good old house, but we all know how old houses can be."

"I know."

"I helped build that house, you know, so I know how solid it is. But everything needs maintenance."

"I know, Dad."

"You need any help?"

"I got it." She reached under the sink to turn off the water lines. "If you can help Glenn out this morning, I can take care of this. But really, don't worry about it, because Glenn's got everyone scheduled for the day." Her foreman had been working with her for ten years. Glenn could likely run the entire garage on his own, but then what would she do for fun?

"Okay, honey, I love you. Mom made us lunch today."

Her stomach rumbled, then gurgled, despite the tea she'd sipped that morning. "That sounds great. I'll see you later."

She hung up the phone and glanced at the counter. Two minutes.

Okay, so she'd fill a couple more minutes than five. She'd just gotten her channel lock pliers around the faucet when her phone rang again.

"Seriously?" She hit the button and put it on voice mail. "What now?"

"Toni?" It was Glenn. "Did you know your old man is here?"

"Yes, I'm sorry. I didn't know he was coming in today. I have a leak in the bathroom I have to fix. I'll only be a few minutes late." She heard the timer go off and quickly hit the button before she continued. "Just uh..." She glanced down and blinked. "Just keep my dad occupied for a while until I get there, okay?"

"All right." Glenn cleared his throat. "I might have him help the new kid at the parts counter. I really don't want him trying to change tires again."

"I know, I know." She swept everything on the counter to the side so she had room for the faucet parts. "Bobby tends to forget he's not thirty-five." Her dad may have been retired, but he wasn't very good at taking it easy.

"I'll take care of things here."

"Sounds good." She stared at the glossy edge of water forming at the lip of the faucet.

Drip.

"Okay, I'll see you when you get in."

"Thanks, Glenn. You're the best."

Drip.

Toni blinked and grabbed a red rag before she started taking the faucet apart.

Drop.

She had the faucet head in her hand when her phone rang again.

"Seriously?" She grumbled. She glanced at the screen.

Henry.

Nope. Not today, Satan's better looking brother.

No, that wasn't fair. Henry wasn't Satan or even in Satan's extended family. He was good, so ridiculously good that she didn't know how to handle him that morning.

"Go to voicemail," she muttered. "Take a hint."

She pried the old washer out of the faucet and set the cracked rubber on the counter. "Out with the old, in with the new."

It was kind of her motto for everything these days. When she'd bought the house she knew it needed work; that was why she got it for such a low price. The old stone cottage was at the base of the hill that marked the boundary of her cousin Nico's winery and his nearest neighbor Fairfield Wines. She was ten minutes from Moonstone Cove, fifteen minutes from the beach, and smack in the heart of Central California wine country in a seventy year old cottage surrounded by a stand of oaks.

It was heaven, leaky faucets and all.

She was putting the new washer in when her mother's name flashed on her phone's screen.

Toni groaned. "How? How do you all know the exact worst time to call?"

No matter. She hit the green button because if she didn't, she'd regret it later. "Hey, Mom."

"Toni, your dad says a pipe burst in the bathroom. Did you call Nathan?"

Oh for Pete's sake... "It's a leaky faucet; I don't need to call Nathan."

"He's your cousin; he wouldn't charge you for going out there."

"I'm good. I've already got it fixed." She tossed the red rag on the counter and reached under the sink to turn on the water.

"I knew that house was just going to be a money pit, Antonia. A *money* pit."

The house had been the old foreman's place on the Dusi family winery, but no one had lived in it for nearly twenty years. It was taken over by spiders and mice, had a family of rabbits living in the back bedroom, and generations of cats running wild in the old red barn. But the house was solid.

"My house is not a money pit." In fact, she'd insisted on a very thorough inspection by someone she was *not* related to before she agreed on the price. "It's just maintenance stuff. Already done." She tossed the washer in the trash and glanced at the clock on the counter. Ten minutes. Not bad at all. "I better say goodbye. I gotta feed Shelby and head into work."

Other than her overfed grey shorthair, Toni lived alone

and she liked it that way. The cottage was her haven. She'd scooted the bunnies out the door, called the Humane society for most of the cats, and adopted one gnarly looking tomcat to keep the barn free of mice and gophers.

She'd had the old man neutered and he still hadn't forgiven her. Enzo ran from her every time she got close. He was the fastest cat she'd ever seen, hence the name.

Her own house cat, Shelby, had barely left her sunny perch in the living room window since she'd moved in the year before. She watched the birds flitting outside, but knew that Toni would never let her out.

Enzo might have evolved to evade coyotes, but Shelby would be dinner.

"I made you and your dad lunch," Rose Dusi said quickly. "And we're having Sunday dinner at Frank's place and Luna and the kids are coming down too."

"Sounds good. I'll be there." She ran some hot water and wiped the cracked clay mask off her skin, which looked fresh and glowing. "Have a good day, Mom."

"You too, baby, I'll see you later, be nice to your dad."

"When am I not nice to dad?" Leave it to her mom to throw that in at the end.

"Oh, you know what I mean. Love you." Her mother blew kisses and hung up the phone.

"No." Toni spoke into the empty bathroom. "I have no idea what you mean."

She'd fixed the sink, but in the back of her mind, she could still hear it dripping.

Toni was getting in her car when her phone rung again. "Why do I know so many people?" she yelled into the barn. "Hello?"

"Oh. Bad time?" It was her friend Katherine. "I was just calling to remind you about Wine Wednesday. It's tonight."

"Thank God," she breathed out. "I'll be there."

"Bad day? It's not even nine o'clock."

"Isn't it?" Everything that morning was moving fast. The ocean fog had even burned off for the day, leaving the grass covered hills glowing gold in the sunlight. "I think everyone and their uncle decided to call me this morning specifically, just to fuck with me."

"Well, make it through the day and you can tell us all about it tonight. Have you been meditating?"

"Yes?"

"That sounded like a question."

"That's because I am, but I'm not sure it's helping. That is, it would help if I could magically make my entire family disappear and not talk to me ever, but I don't think that's really an option."

"Seeing as you're related to half the town, making your family disappear seems like it could lead to disaster and a fairly significant economic downturn."

"Thanks, professor."

"You're welcome. Come at six. We have wine and food."

In the six month since they'd met, Katherine and Megan had become the closest Toni had ever had to "girlfriends." She'd always been the girl who played with the boys. As an adult, she was close to her mother, her sister, and her myriad female cousins. But girlfriends? Not much. She hadn't had time to cultivate friendships until fate had basically forced her into it. Now? She couldn't imagine life without Wine Wednesday, Katherine's adorable husband, and snarking at Megan, who gave as good as she got.

Toni's life was full.

So very full.

Too full?

Her phone rang again and she nearly cried. She looked at the screen and only picked up because it was her cousin Nico, who hardly ever called, even though he was her closest neighbor.

"Yo." She started her vintage Mustang and backed out of the barn.

"Toni, please tell me you're not under a car right now."

"No, in fact, I haven't even left for town. What's up?"

"Thank God." He let out a breath. "Can you come up to the house? We're supposed to start picking the pinot today, the harvest crew is all here, and the tractor won't start. I'm panicking."

"I'm not a diesel mechanic, Nico."

"I know I know I know, but I need to know if it's a quick fix or if I need to call a neighbor to try to wrangle a favor."

"I'll come." She pulled out of her driveway and turned left, taking the gravel road up to Nico's house at the top of the hill. "You owe me two bottles of wine."

"If you get it started, you can have a case."

"Seriously?" She smiled for the first time that morning. "Awesome."

People always thought she could grab as much wine as she wanted since her cousin owned the farm, the winery, and the whole operation. Unfortunately, she was one of dozens of cousins. If everyone got free wine, Dusi Heritage Winery would go out of business. She had to pay, just like everyone else, unless she could trade favors for wine.

When she pulled behind the barn, she could see dozens of workers hanging out along the edge of the field. Though all the wine grapes were cut by hand, the tractor pulled the bins through the rows. No tractor meant way more walking, a much slower harvest, and very pissed off employees.

"What's up?"

Nico was standing next to the small tractor with a grimace on his face, looking completely stressed out. "I have no idea. Henry and Danny are in Paso Robles to pick up some valves and on they're on the way back now, but everyone is waiting. I don't have time for this. It was working fine yesterday."

Oh good. Henry was gone.

Nico gestured to the trailer stacked with empty crates. "And we've got to get the rest of the pinot today or I'm fucked. The temperatures are going to spike tomorrow."

"Hey." She tried to use her superpowers for good by putting her hand on Nico's forearm and giving it a little squeeze. "Relax. I'm sure it's fixable."

Nico immediately chilled out. Toni could feel his stress leave him and soak into her. It didn't do much for the upset stomach she'd been battling all morning, but there was considerably less tension floating around her.

"Thank you for coming up," he said. "You know I wouldn't call if it wasn't an emergency."

"Okay, keys out?" She walked over and stepped up on the running board. As soon as she flipped up the seat, she spotted the problem. "If you knew a fraction as much about engines as you do about grape vines, you'd be able to figure it out. Someone cut the line on your primary safety switch."

"The what? Someone messed with a switch?" Nico craned his head. "How do you know?"

She pointed to the cut wires. "I mean, it's pretty obvious. They put that in there so if the driver falls off the rig, the engine shuts off. Without a working safety switch there, the engine could be perfect and the tractor still won't start. I don't know of any way to bypass it."

Nico's face turned red. "Could it be an accident?"

"I mean..." She shrugged. "It looks cut to me. The wires are pretty clean. You're gonna need to get someone out here to rewire it if Danny can't do it." Henry was Nico's wine-maker, but Danny Barba was his foreman on the farm and kept all the equipment working. "I'm gonna say at least a couple hours."

"Shit!" Nico slammed his hand on the top of the tractor and Toni heard something fall from the tractor with a thunk.

She hopped down and stared at what had fallen in the grass.

"Oh my God." She covered her mouth with the back of her hand. The queasy stomach roared up with a vengeance. Toni ran for the edge of the field and puked into the grass.

"Toni?" Nico ran to her, but she shook her head and waved him back. "What the hell?"

"Finger." She cleared her throat and tried not to wretch again. "Nico, look."

"What are you...? Oh *fuck*."

That was two fucks in one day. Yep, her Aunt Marta was going to be hearing about that one.

But then again, what else were you supposed to say when a bloody human finger fell out of your broken tractor?

———

Preorder Fate Actually for release on December 15, 2020 and sign up for the Elizabeth Hunter Newsletter for more information about books, sales, and new releases.

ABOUT THE AUTHOR

ELIZABETH HUNTER is a *USA Today* and international best-selling author of romance, contemporary fantasy, and paranormal mystery. Based in Central California, she travels extensively to write fantasy fiction exploring world mythologies, history, and the universal bonds of love, friendship, and family. She has published over thirty works of fiction and sold over a million books worldwide. She is the author of the Glimmer Lake series, Love Stories on 7th and Main, the Elemental Legacy series, the Irin Chronicles, the Cambio Springs Mysteries, and other works of fiction.

ElizabethHunterWrites.com

ALSO BY ELIZABETH HUNTER

Glimmer Lake

Suddenly Psychic

Semi-Psychic Life

Psychic Dreams

Moonstone Cove

Runaway Fate

Fate Actually (December 2020)

Fate Interrupted (Spring 2021)

The Cambio Springs Series

Long Ride Home

Shifting Dreams

Five Mornings

Desert Bound

Waking Hearts

Dust Born

(newsletter serial)

The Elemental Mysteries

A Hidden Fire

This Same Earth

The Irin Chronicles

The Scribe

The Singer

The Secret

The Staff and the Blade

The Silent

The Storm

The Seeker

Linx & Bogie Mysteries

A Ghost in the Glamour

A Bogie in the Boat

Contemporary Romance

The Genius and the Muse

7th and Main

INK

HOOKED

GRIT

CPSIA information can be obtained
at www.ICGtesting.com
Printed in the USA
BVHW031308250121
598685BV00011B/66